DECOMPOSITION BOOK

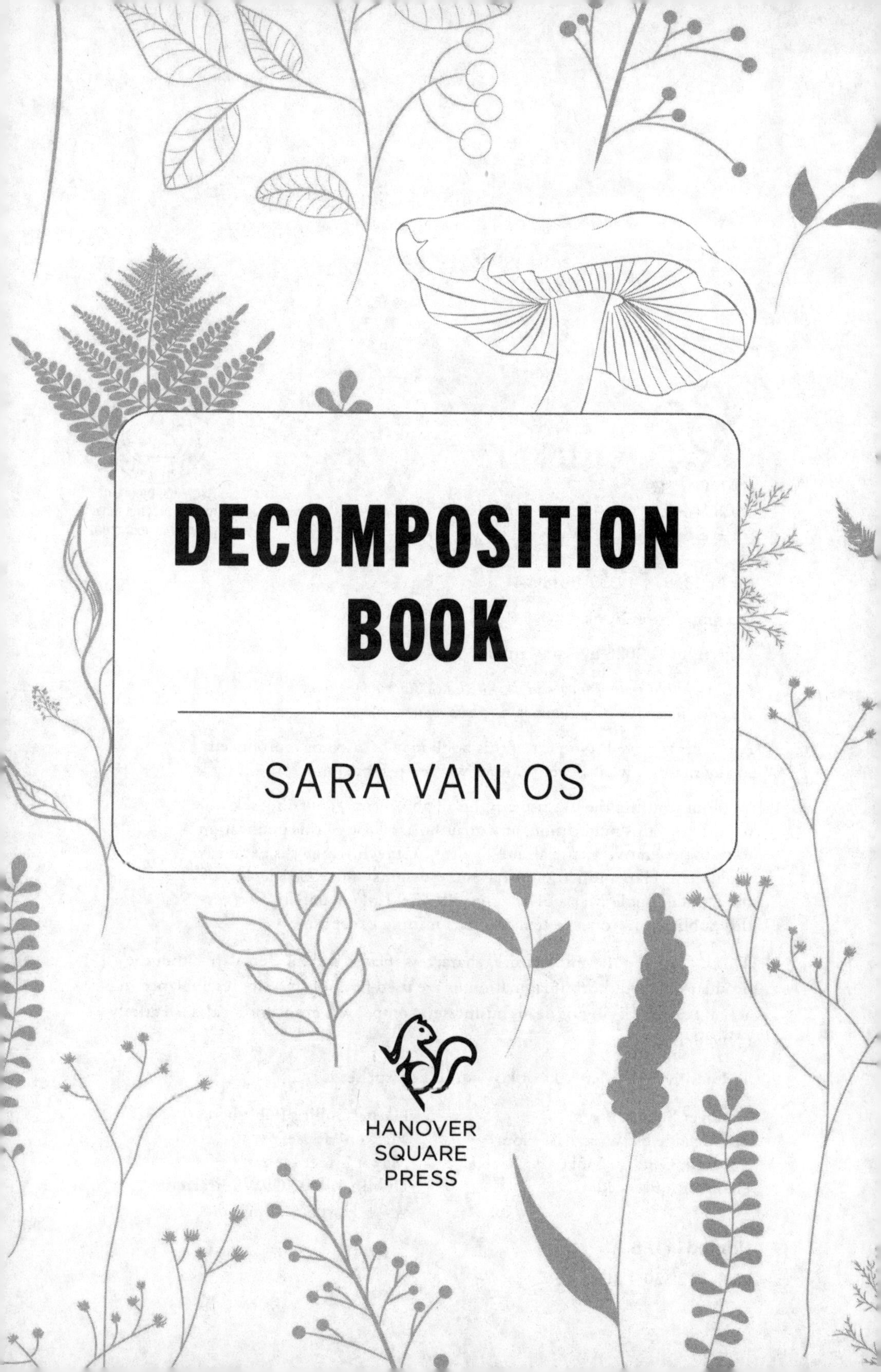

DECOMPOSITION BOOK

SARA VAN OS

HANOVER SQUARE PRESS

ISBN-13: 978-1-335-00189-4

Decomposition Book

Mushroom illustration (pages iii, 35) by hatch/stock.adobe.com.
All other illustrations by Iuliia/stock.adobe.com.

Hanover Square Press
22 Adelaide St. West, 41st Floor
Toronto, Ontario M5H 4E3, Canada
HanoverSqPress.com

HarperCollins Publishers
Macken House, 39/40
Mayor Street Upper,
Dublin 1, D01 C9W8, Ireland
www.HarperCollins.com

Printed in U.S.A.

26 27 28 29 30 LBC 5 4 3 2 1

For Elizabeth,
I love you the most.

PART ONE

Autolysis: The process of self-digestion, which begins immediately after death.

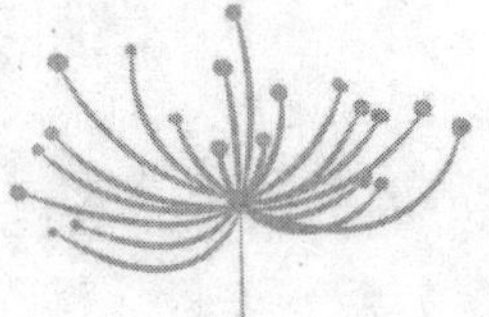

AVA

Hello. My name is Ava Addison Brown. If you're reading this, I'm either safe or dead. Either way is fine by me—I just want there to be a record of me somewhere. There were three of us before and now there's not, and the only one who knows what happened is me. Maybe that's how it will always be and that's fine, but I feel a responsibility. Plus, do I have anything better to do right now? No. All I ever do is sit in the stupid cave and cry. At least now I can get artistic about it: write a memoir, get my teardrops on some paper, make it a whole aesthetic. And if I live, I can publish it, get it made into a limited series on Netflix, have some money for once. That would be nice. I've never been able to turn my trauma into a paycheck before.

I fantasize about that a lot, staring at my crumbling ceiling—not about Netflix, but about comfort, about becoming someone beloved and brave. It's different to picture it now than it was in college and grad school, when I thought of being beloved as having my name on a dressing room door at the Met, of opening night galas and beautiful strangers chucking flowers over orchestra pits. It's all different now, what I want. It's so much less about being beloved and so much more about simply feeling safe. For one thing, while I've been out here, I've already been beloved. Not on the stage, but in the dirt. And in the end, the love I got wasn't shiny. It was gross and scary and hungry and better than anything I'll ever have again, even cleaned up, fed, and rich.

Like I said, there were three of us.

On September 3, 2022, I went on a hike in the Adirondacks with my coworkers Megan Isabella Steele and Chad Johnathan Bottswell. We made some stupid choices and we got really, really lost. It's currently January of 2023. If you want to know the whole story of what happened, keep reading. I hope you will. I lived to entertain after all! Fair warning though: it's going to be very sad and pretty gross. But hey, that's life.

~AA Brown

SAVANNAH

ON DAY TWENTY-SEVEN of isolation, I make blueberry pancakes for dinner. Michelle and I used to do breakfast-for-dinner all the time. To her, it was mostly an excuse to have bottomless mimosas in the middle of the night on a Tuesday, but I was in it for the pancakes and the mountain of bacon. The bacon was my job, but, being a first-generation Californian whose family are all from the middle of nowhere, Kansas, Michelle had a Midwestern knack for pancakes. Never from a box, and she knew all the measurements by heart.

I remember sitting on a stool at the poor excuse for a dining table in our outrageously expensive dorm, watching her. The wood, once shiny and tan, had been graying since the '70s. It was on its way to the color of pencil lead and had settled into a swamp green in spots. Someone had written Chloe luvs Fucknuts along one corner. I traced it with my left thumb while I sipped my pomegranate mimosa. I wondered what the guy did to deserve the nickname Fucknuts from Chloe's friends.

Michelle pulled her shiny blond hair off her back and held it up in a ponytail while her other hand ladled another perfect circle of batter onto the skillet, where it pooled with a soft sizzle. She repeated the motion twice more and then stepped back, pulling a hair tie off her right wrist with her teeth and twisting her ponytail into a messy bun.

Dots of sweat dappled her thin blue shirt where it clung to her shoulder blades. Michelle hated visibly sweating, so I didn't point it out, but I thought she looked perfect.

I can't hear what she was saying now. When I peer into the memory, all I can see is the liquid in her champagne flute lapping up against her lips, peach colored and glossy with too much apricot lip oil. Then she laughs and turns back to the stove to flip the pancakes, fast enough to make her bun wobble and cause the prosecco bubbles to kiss the rim of the glass, so very close to spilling over the edge but not quite . . .

The smell of burning takes me away from the image of her and back to my own charred hockey puck of a pancake.

"Shit," I say to no one, nudging the failure out of the pan and into the sink with a spatula.

The phone rings, and I answer from my watch.

"Yeah, Mom?"

"I'm just calling to see how you're doing. You didn't call me yesterday."

"I'm not going to call you every day, Mom. I'm almost twenty-two."

"Well, it's different when you're taking a—what are we calling it again? A mental health vacation from school?" She chews hard on the word *vacation* and guilt pools in my stomach like too much acid. "The deal was that your father and I would leave you alone as long as you called to check in every day. Has he called you at all, by the way?"

I close my eyes and rub the space between them with a finger, prepping for some comment about how my dad never did put any effort into raising me. I breathe in. I breathe out. I try to open my lungs like two parachutes for more oxygen, but can't. I can never get enough air these days. My rib cage constricts like a bra that's too tight. I wonder if I'm becoming hypoxic, slowly, without even knowing it. DIY carbon monoxide poisoning. "No, he hasn't called."

"Of course he hasn't," my mom quips. "It's always been my job. I don't know how he just lives his life and doesn't feel the need to know if his only daughter is still breathing all alone in the woods. Typical. At least *I care* about your health and well-being. Who arranged your little stay at the lake house for a semester even though we're not even supposed to be using it until the divorce is finalized? Me. I talked to the lawyers and made all the calls, and I'm the one sending you money. Me. You know who isn't doing shit? Your fucking father, that's who. Or should I say sperm donor? Because that's—"

"Mom."

"Okay okay, sorry. I just don't understand why you insist on having him in your life, that's all."

"Mom, please. Can we just not?"

I can't deal with my dad right now. I'm already hypoxic.

"Fine, fine." She sighs and flips her voice into artificial cheeriness. "So, what are you doing?"

"Making pancakes."

"Isn't it a little late? You aren't sleeping all day anymore, are you? You're supposed to be keeping a schedule."

"I am keeping a schedule. It's breakfast-for-dinner. Michelle and I used to do it all the time."

"Ah."

I smirk. She doesn't know how to respond when I bring up Michelle. I pick up my glass, but it's empty, and so is the bottle sitting on the granite countertop. I bend and grab a new one from the stocked wine fridge. My mom asks what kind of pancakes I'm making, and I say blueberry as I ease the corkscrew down. I hold the bottle against the counter with one hand and pull with the other. The cork comes out with a satisfying pop.

"What was that?" my mom asks. "You're not drinking on those pills, are you?"

"No," I say, muting my phone so she can't hear the *glug glug* of the liquid sloshing into the glass as I pour. I count the seconds in *glug*s, trying to pour fast. I worry that if I stay muted too long, she'll get suspicious, and then I'll confess because I always do, and she'll make me come home, or, God forbid, she'll fly here. One *glug*, two *glug*s, three *glug*s . . . I unmute and take a long, slow sip, swooshing it in my mouth and savoring it. I don't like that wine smells like vinegar, but somehow I've gotten used to the taste. "It was Zelda. She's playing with a rubber ball."

Zelda Fitzgerald II, my scruffy gray emotional support kitten, squints up at me from the couch, her sleep disturbed by the mention of her name. I make a silent promise to give her extra treats tonight in exchange for blaming my drinking problem on her.

"Aw, how is Miss Zelda?"

"She's good. Cute. Um, I have to go. I keep burning these pancakes and I'm almost out of batter, so I have to focus."

"Okay, honey, but make sure you call me tomorrow. I just want to make sure you're okay."

"I'm fine and I will call you."

"Promise?"

"Promise. Okay, I'm hanging up. I love you!"

"I love you, too!"

She's halfway through the word *goodbye* when I kill the call with my thumb. I relax, feeling my shoulders drop, and lift my glass to my lips. It's already empty again somehow. I'll have to fix that.

AVA

We were lost about a day before we knew it, and for that day everything was pretty good. We spent it following a stream, thinking that as long as we stayed near the water, we wouldn't have a problem getting back to the trail. All of us were experienced outdoors people after all, with so many hours of Naked and Afraid *watched between us that we were basically survivalists in our minds. Hubris. Every high school English class had warned me about it, and I hadn't listened.*

What happened was around 9 am, about a mile into our wilderness adventure, Chad suggested we turn our backs on the trail and head downstream toward a pair of waterfalls. One of his buddies swore they were just a few miles away. All we had to do was take a left off the trail and follow the stream until it expanded. I remember wavering on the edge of the decision as many a Discovery Channel documentary flashed before my eyes, ones about hikers wandering off the beaten path and soon finding themselves in need of rescue.

I started to bring up said documentaries and said I wasn't sure leaving the trail was such a good idea, but Chad insisted we weren't just wandering into nowhere. His friend was positive about the location of the falls, and we'd regret it so much if we didn't go. Brian—that was Chad's friend—told him it was one of the most beautiful places he'd ever seen and that there were even caves and stuff to explore. I wavered. I do love a good cave. Well, I did *love a good cave.*

Chad said, "Look, worst-case scenario it's a little farther than we thought. That's no problem. We're camping anyway. If we don't have time to turn back and make it to our original site by dark, then we just set up camp by the falls, sleep in a beautiful location, and have even less of a walk back to the car in the morning."

I opened my mouth to argue but then Megan, the least experienced and most beautiful among us, piped up with "I mean, it's a straight stream, right? Following a line of water doesn't sound much more complicated than following a hiking trail. And I do want to see those waterfalls! It's supposed to get into the 90s today—we can reward ourselves for the hike by going swimming!" She flashed a devious grin at us, a few freckles getting eaten by her dimples. I couldn't say no to her. I caved. Chad cheered. We stepped off the trail.

~AA Brown

SAVANNAH

I TAKE MY plate of slightly charred pancakes to the couch and turn on Food Network. I'm hoping that somehow watching other people make and eat delicious food will trick my mouth into believing these pancakes are the height of luxury. I prod one with my fork. It's not round, but the shape is kind of fun, like Mickey Mouse, if Mickey Mouse were a slightly crispier critter and had lost part of his ear to a glue trap.

I swirl my wine in the glass and watch the legs slouch down the sides like little ghosts. I sip it, then slice into my pancakes. A blueberry pops, and whitish liquid runs out. As I chew, it dawns on me that blueberries and pimples look the same inside. A design flaw. I check my watch. It's 10:37. I chew the inside of my lip until the syrup on my tongue starts to taste like I'm licking it off a penny. I worry about scars forming on the insides of my cheeks. I worry that the next person to kiss me will notice them and pull away, knowing for a fact that they could never love a cheek chewer. I think of Michelle. I wonder if she knew I was a cheek chewer. I wonder if that was why. I chew my cheek some more.

This part of the night is tricky, because there's nothing to serve as a buffer between me and my brain, and my brain is the worst. I can't believe I let the public school system trick me into thinking brains are good.

I have to keep my routine, which I'm sure my therapist explained to me while I stared at the wall and skimmed her speech for the magic words "referral to a psychiatrist." I don't want yoga; I want drugs. Not Zoloft, which made my brain feel damp and limp, like an unbuttered noodle. I want the good kind of drugs, the kind we used to give housewives who were one inconvenient sniffle away from a lobotomy, but Hils—that's my therapist—thinks that I should first try my coping strategies. I only get one good drug a day, and it's the one that turns my thoughts off so I can sleep. I am not supposed to mix it with alcohol. I am not allowed to have it until midnight. Until then, I'm supposed to practice self-regulation. I refill my wineglass. Namaste.

I finish my pancakes and polish off the wine and check my watch again: 10:50. Damn, Bobby Flay hasn't even won yet and here I was thinking I'd achieved the kind of mastery of night that would make Hils proud. I stare at my watch until the minute hand clicks into its next spot. It absolutely crawls there, like someone shot out its legs. Maybe the watch is just broken and it is midnight already. I check my phone: 10:50. Fuck. I check Instagram to see if Michelle still has me blocked. She does. I check all of our friends' socials to see if any of them are with Michelle. I just want to see if she looks sad, if a forehead crease of regret has made its way into her skincare routine, if she ever loved me at all. I check my watch again. It's 10:51. I stare away another minute that takes eight years. I have to look away before I die of dread. I hate nighttime. I hate it.

I take a deep breath that goes ragged in the middle and focus on the TV, my millionth hour of Food Network this month. A sad win for routine. Bobby Flay pulls out crispy rice again. The judges eat it up, literally. He wins, again. The crowd boos, because nobody watches this show and roots for Bobby Flay. 11:00 p.m.

Chopped comes on next. I should probably change it, because Michelle and I used to watch this together, but thinking about watching something else just makes me sad. Part of me wants to sit in my memories of her; they're familiar in the way loneliness isn't yet. I wish she had died, because that way I'd have an excuse to be like this, but then I feel guilty about wishing she had died and I worry that maybe by thinking about it, I've manifested it into existence. I think about all the ways Michelle could be dying right now. A fentanyl-laced party drug, a sinkhole in the middle of the street—or maybe falling scaffolding, her skull cracked open and leaking, little chunks of brain on the pavement like gray flecks of old cottage cheese. I google her to make sure she's still alive. I'm not sure why I care; she doesn't care if I'm still alive. I check all of my ex-friends' socials again, looking for some shade of performative grief. Nothing has changed in the last ten minutes, but it could just be too soon to tell. Michelle could be in the middle of her last heartbeat right now.

My palms are sweaty and I wipe them off on the couch. I try to shake the image of Michelle's brain bits out of my head, but I can't. I tell myself that I'm okay, that it's not real. None of this works. I reach for the wine. When I pick the glass back up, I notice I've left a humid handprint on one side. I chug it with my eyes closed so I don't have to see the mark and get a new glass from the kitchen, leaving the old one in the sink, inspecting the new one for watermarks before filling it fresh. I'm weird about glasses being clean and clear. It's not really even a cleanliness thing. It's more that I'm worried the marks on the glasses are going to stick to my throat or the sides of my stomach. I'm worried they'll taste chunky and rotten, that the rot will spread and climb the walls of my throat like a fungus, that it will be all I can taste forever. I probably wouldn't have drunk from this one at all if I wasn't already feeling the wine. Hils says I should be drinking out of the marked glasses, even if there might be a rot that spreads like a fungus. The itch to switch the glasses out is a compulsion, Hils says, and I'm not supposed to be doing the compulsions, but I feel like I deserve this solitary harmless one after everything, so I let myself switch the glasses as a little treat.

But I want the record to show that I did drink out of the marked glass first, even if it was with my eyes closed, even if I already can't stop thinking about my rotting throat, even if I can almost taste it. That should count for something.

I get back to the couch just in time for the introductions. The first chef is this white hipster-looking guy. He's wearing a beanie even though he's entering a kitchen full of stoves and fully preheated ovens and studio lighting. Asshole. He's totally going to sweat in the food. I hate it when they sweat in the food. I keep my eyes fixed on the screen, but I'm not really looking. I'm half in my head, watching Michelle drape her legs over my lap.

Rapist, she says, and I laugh.

The second chef comes out. He's short and heavily tatted. He immediately launches into a speech about how his parents wanted him to become an engineer, but he dropped out of Harvard his junior year to take a kitchen job. He thinks winning would prove to his parents that he made the right decision.

Michelle leans over so her mouth is up against my left ear. She's drunk and loose. *Daddy issues,* she whispers, giggling. Her breath makes the dangling star earrings she got me for my nineteenth birthday swing. Combined with her laugh, it reminds me of a wind chime. She rests her head on my shoulder.

The third chef is a woman. She's tall and skinny. Her hair is green and cropped short. She has a cheap-looking black nose ring. Michelle shrieks and claps her hands. The sound is so sharp I jump and wine drips onto my nightgown. It matches Michelle's, only mine is white because she likes white on me. Hers is red. I like the red better, but she was so excited about the white for me when I picked it out. I frown at the stain, thinking about how if I had gotten the red, the wine wouldn't even show.

There she is! Ladies and gentlemen, the obligatory Chopped *dyke! We're rooting for her. Oh no, what happened to your nightgown? It was so perfect and pretty a minute ago.* Her French-tipped fingernail drags across my breast, tracing the stain. *It's okay, you're still so pretty.* She throws her arms around me and kisses my neck playfully, then withdraws, settling cross-legged next to me like it was nothing. We've missed the last chef. It's some guy. There's a lump in my throat. It's a scream, but it feels like a stone. I swallow and force it to scrape its way back down. I turn off the TV so I can stop seeing her. 11:11. Make a wish.

I pace in silence for a bit, then do the dishes just so I have something to do with my hands. At least all the glasses are clean. 11:25.

I check everyone's socials again to make sure Michelle is not dead. She's not. I think of new and exciting ways she could be dying right now. I retreat to the bathroom, where I wash my face like Rachel Hollis told my mom she should. 11:29.

I put on a sheet mask, open YouTube, and zone out while a fifteen-year-old who looks my age shows me how to do a cut crease. In my head, Michelle chokes on a watermelon Jolly Rancher. Her last breath tastes like sugar. 11:59.

I can hear her laughing at me for thinking too much about things that aren't real and then I can't get her laugh out of my head. I can't breathe with the scream in my throat. I'm already hypoxic. I start to pick at the scabs on the tops of my feet from last night when I scratched off all the skin. As I draw out a few drops of blood, enjoying the small distraction of pain, my phone starts buzzing and beeping. Midnight, finally. I made it. I jump up and run to the kitchen counter where the bottle of Ambien is sitting and shake a ten-milligram pill into my palm. I pick up my wineglass, ready to down it, but stop.

My mom said not to mix pills with alcohol, so instead I grab a LaCroix from the fridge and take it with that. There.

I leave the LaCroix to get warm on the counter.

AVA

We never did find those waterfalls. We found some *waterfalls, but that wasn't until weeks later and by that point neither of us could know for sure whether or not they were The Falls. It doesn't matter. What does matter is that on the first day, all we found was more of the same stream.*

For two hours, I trailed a few feet behind Chad and Megan, pushed out by Chad's competitive masculinity. I didn't mind. I felt much worse for Megan. She was the one who had to smile and nod while he went on and on about different equipment he had in his bag, putting extra emphasis on a pair of hunting knives and an honest-to-god flintstone.

"Do you have some sort of distrust in lighters? Or does flint just work better?" Megan asked.

The muscles in Chad's back tightened as he stood a little taller, pushing his shoulder blades together to puff out his chest. It was like he was trying to hulk up. "Well," he said, "you can never be too careful. What if your lighter ran out of fluid or you lost it? Then what would we do for fire? Rub two sticks together? Nah. This way we're set no matter what."

I was glad to be behind them so no one could see me rolling my eyes. I said something like "Don't flintstones run out too though?"

He whipped around to shoot me a sharp glare. "Yeah, after weeks of use. I doubt we're going to have any problems after one night."

"Right." I pushed harder. "So by that logic, shouldn't a lighter be fine too? For one night?"

Megan buried her face in her elbow, trying to disguise her laugh as a sneeze. Chad's disproportionally tiny white ears went red. I felt a Grinch-like smirk spreading across my face. He stopped walking and turned his whole body around to face me. I leaned against a tree and crossed my arms.

"Look," he said. "I have a couple lighters too. I just thought it would be cool to be like cavemen for the night, go back to our primitive roots."

I did look. I looked at the vein tightening on his temple like an angry worm. I savored his rage like a piece of hard candy. "Ah, yes," I fired back, "we'll roast primitive s'mores and eat primitive hot dogs that we hunted from the grocery store. True cavepeople."

This time Megan didn't put mouth to elbow in time and her laugh bounced off the trees. It wasn't a pretty laugh. It was like the honk of a surprised goose. I loved it.

Chad grabbed a leaf from a branch and started ripping it to shreds.

I decided to take pity on him. "Dude, relax. I'm just fucking with you. I know it's good to have multiple forms of fire. I brought matches and lighters myself. Let's just keep moving. We'll have to stop for lunch soon and I'd rather be overlooking a waterfall than not."

He mumbled something that sounded like agreement and turned to go.

Megan jumped in to save us both. "Actually, it's almost two. I think we should stop for lunch now and then we can eat dinner at the falls."

Chad and I looked at each other and brokered a truce consisting of some eye contact and a tense nod from each of us. An alliance practiced by lesbians and straight men for centuries: we yield to the woman we are both after.

"Yeah, lunch sounds great," I said.

"Starving," Chad agreed.

I almost have to stop writing here because the thought of that lunch just kills me. At the time, it was nothing special: three cans of Coke that were almost warm because Chad didn't push them to the bottom of the cooler, Subway sandwiches that we'd stopped to pick up on the drive, potato chips, chocolate chip cookies in little white paper bags. My sandwich was just turkey, cucumbers, and tomatoes. I stacked it with chips for a little crunch and Megan made fun of me until I made her try it and she agreed that it was "actually pretty good." Actually pretty good. *God, I'd give the little that's left of my right titty for a Subway sandwich right now. At the time, "actually pretty good" seemed too generous for what that sandwich was. Not anymore. Now that distant memory of overripe tomato juice making my bread slightly too soggy feels holy. That sandwich deserves its own cult. Do you think if I make it back they'll let me be the new Jared? I promise I will be MUCH less creepy.*

Anyway, back to the getting-lost part. After lunch, we kept moving in the same direction. We chatted on and off the whole time, but I don't remember what we talked about. I go over that first day a lot. I mean A LOT. I spend whole nights cursing myself to replay the day over and over again, picking apart all possible roads I could have taken that would not have led to this.

What I remember about that day surprises me, because for such a fateful fucking day, I really don't remember much. I remember, in grave detail, the conversation that led to us going on the waterfall goose chase. And then I remember snippets of watching Megan suffer while Chad talked at her, me trying to figure out if she was even gay as I followed along. No nose ring, no constellation ear piercing, no visible tattoos. Long hair, her natural color as far as I knew, usually light makeup, and on her hands, always medium-length almond acrylics with a white French tip. I'd only worked with her for six months, and I was too chicken to ask in the office. I wanted to figure it out on this camping trip, our first big outing together outside of short lunches at the Sweetgreen downstairs and a few office happy hours, and maybe shoot my shot. So that was a good chunk of time, and then there's this really big splotch of my memory that's dedicated to the taste of lunch, and then everything was just pleasant for a while until Megan pointed out the time.

She didn't say anything at first, just stopped walking when we reached the first big break in the trees after a few hours. Megan had this impeccable instinct for timing. She always knew when to stop and think. Chad and I would have walked until it got dark and then regretted it. Even before lunch, Megan had sensed that something was wrong and we needed to reassess, but she'd let Chad and his days and days of survival tools lull her into a false sense of security. The hours I watched her smile and listen, she had been secretly worrying that we'd gone astray. Because of that instinct, she was paying attention to things like the time, our collective energy reserves, the environment we were in, etc.

"It's six," she said, hands on her hips, feet planted.

"It's six?" Chad repeated, checking his watch.

"It's six," I confirmed, having gotten eyes on my phone screen first.

Chad frowned at his phone and said, "There's no service so I can't look it up, but it really can't be too much farther."

"Exactly," Megan added. "We don't have service. We don't know where we are. It's six. We can't guess, because if the sun goes down before we can camp, it's really going to suck."

"She's right," I said. I'd already put my bag down while Megan was talking.

"Are you guys sure you don't want to go for like thirty more minutes? We can set a timer," Chad suggested, clearly realizing how stupid he looked now that we'd walked all day looking for his waterfalls that didn't exist.

Megan shook her head. "I really think it's best that we just put up the tent and make some food and relax." Then she put on a big smile, one I later learned took a lot of effort because it was at that moment Megan knew we weren't leaving the woods anytime soon. She added, "We'll see the falls tomorrow on the hike back and it'll be so much nicer when we have the sun. We aren't going to be swimming tonight anyway."

Chad nodded but didn't say anything else.

I broke the silence by offering to help Megan clear a spot for a tent or to help Chad put it up. Chad insisted on doing the tent by himself, so I got to work building us a fire pit and fire in the spot Megan had designated. Chad managed to get the tent up alone and I was relieved for him. His ego needed a win. Megan unpacked all of our sleeping bags and rolled a joint to pass around before dinner. Chad distributed cans of Pabst Blue Ribbon from a six-pack in the cooler. I skewered hot dogs and roasted them over the fire and popped open a family-sized bag of nacho cheese Doritos. We ate, we drank, we smoked. We let the food, booze, and weed ease the tensions of the day. We had a storybook-perfect last night of normalcy. Even Megan managed to relax a little and allow herself some hope that the situation wasn't what it seemed.

Spoiler alert: it was much worse than it seemed. Now excuse me while I go pine for Doritos and drugs. Be so grateful you still have Doritos and drugs.

~AA Brown

SAVANNAH

SOMETHING IS POKING me in the back and I'm cold as fuck. This information on its own is not concerning enough to get me to peel open my probably hungover little eyeballs. I roll off the pokey thing and reach for my comforter, but I come away with a handful of dirt instead. That *is* enough information to cause me to pry open my definitely hungover little eyeballs. It does not help that I find myself squinting into the cold, cruel light of dawn.

"What the fuck?" I say to myself, sitting up with a groan. No way I'm actually lying in the woods in my nightgown. This is it. This is the day I have to check myself into rehab.

I stand up and turn to make my walk of shame home, glad that I at least recognize this spot as a place I used to play when I was little, and then I stop so hard I wobble—because I'm looking at a corpse. I'm looking at an actual true-crime-documentary-in-the-woods human woman's most likely murdered body.

For all the times when I was a kid binge-watching *Investigation Discovery* with my mom, all the times when I knew for *sure* what I would do if I murdered someone or found a body or any of those shows' scenarios, for all of my intricate and foolproof plans and backup plans that I knew I'd definitely carry out with the cool-headedness of a trained assassin, I do not react as planned or backup planned. Instead I stare at her like Donald Trump stared at that solar eclipse: I blink twice, dry heave, turn ninety degrees to the left, and absolutely haul ass out of there.

I'M DODGING TREES, because my contact lenses are dried out from sleeping in them, so I can't see. I'm trying to wipe that weird goop—the stuff that oozes out and glues your eyes together while you sleep—off my eyelashes when I think I see someone brush against my right side, like a cat trying to get my attention, but when I look, there's no one. I skid to a stop, squinting into the trees, trying to figure out where I am. I have to blink several times to verify that I'm still alone. Sometimes I swear I can see the version of Michelle that lives inside my head and exists to taunt me. She's so good at being almost real.

Damn, Savage, Michelle says. *You finally did it.*

"What?" I'm not supposed to talk to her. It's a compulsion. And it only makes her worse. I don't look at her, though—that's gotta count for something.

Finally found a body! Michelle says with a smile.

Fuck, I looked. It's okay. I just won't say anything else to her. She isn't real. She isn't real. I look around. I can't see the edge of the trees from here. That means I'm going the wrong way. Okay. Backward. I turn and start to walk back toward the body, trying not to think of it as "toward the body."

Don't you remember? That summer of sixth grade when your mom was really big on the true crime documentaries and you got all obsessed with death. You wanted to find a body so you could see what it was like to be dead. So we looked. We climbed that big, brushy hill in front of your old house and started looking behind trees and under bushes, hoping at the very least we'd find someone's severed arm or something.

Michelle continues on, pulling the memory up from deep in my mind like she's pulling a loose thread from a sweater. She projects it up on the inner wall of my brain for me to see. It's true. We did look. I don't know why; I just found being dead fascinating and I didn't love its certainty. I thought seeing it would help me prepare for the thing that was coming for me, too.

I stare hard at the ground to stop myself from unraveling. I need to focus on getting back. I know where the clearing with the body is relative to my house. I used to take a lot of walks out here when I was younger, and that clearing is the only real break in the trees I've ever found. The rest of the forest is super dense, so I used to stop at that clearing and chill. I found the spot to be peaceful, probably why I went there last night in the first place. My stomach tightens as I get close. I'm nervous. I remind myself that I'm not going back to gawk at the body; I'm only trying to get home.

So? How was it? The more I try to ignore her, the louder Michelle speaks. *Are you fascinated? Is that why your heart's beating faster right now—because you're excited to go back and poke her with a stick? I can hear it from here.*

I stop walking and close my eyes, hoping that when I open them, she'll be gone. I try to breathe slower and regulate my heart rate. I count my heartbeats. Too many of them, too fast. I push on my sternum with my palm to try to make it stop. I worry my heart will burst and then there will be two corpses out here. Behind my eyelids is an image of myself poking the body in the stomach with a stick. I push too hard and it pops and something green and sludgy oozes out. I shake my head back and forth, hoping to clear the image like an Etch A Sketch. The me in my head pushes the stick even deeper and twists. I open my eyes, panting, and there's Michelle again, laughing at me.

Jesus, you're sick. Always have been, though, clearly.

I drop my hand to my side and start walking again, faster, fists balled, denting my palms with my nails. It starts to look brighter up ahead, where the trees open up. I slow down until I've stopped. The tree just in front of me is the tree that she's behind. When I inch to the right and look down, I can see half her hand, peeking out from the end of a raggedy sleeve, fingers curled into a stiff cup. It still looks so much like a living hand, but there's something uncanny about it that gives me the ick. But I can't look away; I don't breathe. This is what I will become. A statue of flesh. An almost person.

How do you think she died? Michelle asks, snapping me out of it so abruptly that I jump with a squeak—I'm almost glad the woman on the ground isn't alive to hear it.

I force my cement feet forward, straight past the body, refusing to turn around and look back at her, trying to stay ahead of Michelle, but Michelle moves alongside me with ease. The body doesn't bother her. Meanwhile, I can't shake the feeling that it's staring at me.

I mean, Michelle continues, *it's not like people just drop dead around here. How'd she even get here, anyway? You don't have neighbors. The nearest house is, what? A mile away? Two?*

"She could be homeless," I mutter, and then scold myself for answering. I count my breaths in sets of two. I take two steps for every breath. I just need to get home.

Michelle huffs. *Homeless? Around here? Babe, that's like being homeless in the Hamptons. It's not really done.*

One, two. One, two. She's not real. She's not real.

She was probably murdered. That's the only way a corpse ever really ends up in the woods. And if she was murdered, you know what that means?

I do not want to know what that means, but Michelle tells me anyway.

That means either some crazed killer decided to dump the body here in the middle of the night even though he would have had to drive right up your driveway and past your house to get here, and then drag her through the woods and dump her against that tree even though he for sure knows you live here and will likely find his kill OR—she pauses for dramatic effect—*you killed her.*

I skid to a stop. "Me?"

Her smile spreads wide, lips sealed shut. Her blue eyes are sharp, like glass when it cracks. I squeeze my eyes shut as tight as they'll go, trying to crush her with the darkness so she'll go away, but it doesn't work. *Who else?* she asks. *As far as we know, you're the only one who knows where that clearing is by memory. Another killer would have had to root around for that spot, all while dodging trees in the dark and carrying a dead-weight corpse. Not likely. But you used to go there all the time when you were sad, didn't you? Look at you, navigating us back to the house with ease as we speak.*

"I didn't . . ." I didn't. Did I? No. I wouldn't have.

Are you sure about that? I always knew you were ruthless. That's why I call you Savage.

"I didn't." I'm not supposed to be talking to Michelle.

Again, are you sure? What's the other explanation? Someone else murdered her and knows about that spot and was able to find it in the dark and also didn't care about the fact that your house is on this property? Who dumps a body on someone else's property? Who else knows about that spot? You didn't even tell me about it when we were friends. No, it's just you. You're a murderer.

"I'm not."

Then give me another explanation.

"Maybe she just died."

Where did she come from?

"I don't know."

Why'd you kill her?

"I didn't."

How do you know?

We reach the end of the trees. The sun's so bright that it hurts as it reaches toward me through the last gasp of woods. The guilt in my stomach gurgles. Every time I blink, I see myself luring a reanimated version of the body into my kitchen in the middle of the night, sliding the biggest of my mom's Rachael Ray–brand knives into the space between her ribs.

I guess you really wanted to see a dead body, didn't you? Maybe the urge has just been growing inside you all these years and you couldn't take it anymore.

It's getting hard to count in twos. My heartbeats are so close together that they're slamming into each other. Almost there. Almost free of the trees.

What did you do, Savannah? She laughs and then she's gone and I'm alone in my brain again.

I squint into the sun, leaving Michelle and her big laugh behind me in the trees. I reach into the crevices of my mind the whole walk across the lawn, trying to remember anything about last night, but the last thing I see is myself popping that pill. I swallow the acid taste rising in my throat. Michelle's right. I can't remember. I don't know what I did.

I'M NOT EVEN off the doormat before I start pulling out my phone to call my mom, but I stop with my finger hovering over her name in my recent-call list. I want to call her, because who else do you call in this situation? It's either her or the spouse I don't have. I'd hit up my best friend, but I'm fresh out of those, too.

But if I called her, what would I even say? *Hi, Mom, funny story. I may have lied last night and mixed the pills and the wine, and I might have, possibly, sleepwalked into the night, murdered a stranger, and then dragged her body into the woods. Please do not tell your divorce lawyer or the cops.*

The grand number of things my mom could or would do with this information to accidentally get me arrested and imprisoned flashes before my eyes. So instead of calling anyone, I completely freak out and cry while rocking back and forth on my couch until the guilt makes my stomach hurt and I have to move the pity party to the bathroom and rock back and forth on the toilet instead. I mutter over and over to myself that I don't really know whether or not I killed anyone. I tell myself I need to relax. I don't know for sure; I can't know for sure. But how *would* anyone else be able to find that spot in the dark? Did I see any tire tracks where this hypothetical other killer drove the body past the house? No. And believe me, I looked!

When I finally leave the bathroom and end up in the kitchen, I go to the sink and splash cold water on my puffy face, hoping it'll wake my brain up so I can start spiraling about a solution to all of this. I brace my hands on either side of the gray-and-white marbled granite lining the basin and look up.

My mom had a window installed above the sink so she could look out at the scenery while she washed the dishes—the scenery being the woods with the corpse. The body must be a pretty straight shot from here: about a half mile forward and I'd be looking right at her again. And yet, from here everything looks fine, beautiful even. The sky is clear. The trees are patchy with mostly dead leaves. The birds are chirping. The sun is shining. The tank is clean. And I'm a fucking murderer.

I wonder if this is how I got the idea to take her there; I wonder if I was standing here, drugged out of my conscience, washing the blood from my hands when I thought to stash her in my clearing in the woods.

God, I can't be a murderer. I'm not even twenty-two yet. Not that that's totally relevant, but I feel like you should at least be old enough to be off your parents' health insurance to be a whole murderer. I guess I'm just special.

The muscles in my upper arms start twitching, so I pry my fingers loose. I shake the blood back into my hands and look out at the woods. My eyes threaten to well up with tears again, so I shut them tight like a baby's swaddle. I turn around with my eyes closed to avoid the window. When I open them, I see the kitchen island and my phone, sitting right where I left it. I stare at it, chewing my lip. Then I pick it up, put it down, pick it up, and drop it from a respectable distance like I'm frying it and I don't want the oil to splash up and burn me. I pick it up again and check my recent calls to make sure I didn't accidentally call anyone in the night and tell them about this, but the last call is still just my mom from when I was making pancakes, way before the murdering. I check my search history. I check my social media. Nothing. I chew off the edge of my thumbnail while googling "dispensary near me." The nearest one is in Massachusetts. Fair, I guess I deserve to be sober today. What was it that Kourtney said when Kim lost her earring in the sea? "Kim, there's people who are corpses in the fucking woods"?

I allow myself five more minutes to rage like an absolute toddler in the kitchen, during which I yell at the birds chirping around outside just for having a good day. How dare they? Then I turn off my phone, cross to the living room, and shove it between the couch cushions. It needs to be off-limits and it can't leave this house, because what if I take it out to the woods with me and then the police track where I've been and they see me going out there and then they know to check her neck for my fingerprints?

I get to work inspecting both the house and the yard for any evidence I should be trying to destroy. I'm thorough and look for about two hours, but there's nothing. It's all just the detritus of a sad college girl, same as it was yesterday, same as it was the day before. This lack of evidence should comfort me, but it doesn't, because all it means is that I'm going to have to look elsewhere for my answers. I have to go back to the body, but first I have to check that my phone is off and in the couch cushions. I know I put it there, but what if the couch cushions pressed against the button and turned the phone back on? I go back to the couch and pull the phone out. It's still off. I put it back in the cushions.

I take a deep breath and head upstairs to change. Like Michelle said, the closest neighbors are miles away, but I still decide to dress like I'm just going on a walk. I pull on black leggings, a forest-green tank top, and a black windbreaker. I dump out the contents of the backpack I use for school and fill it with a water bottle and a couple of pairs of surgical latex gloves. I also tie my hair up in the tightest ballerina bun of its life, never mind the fact that I was literally rolling around in the dirt by the corpse for an unknowable period of time. I head back downstairs. On my way past the couch, I check again that my phone is off. Hils wouldn't like it, but I have to be *sure*.

The Nike walking shoes I haven't used since last summer are waiting for me on a wooden rack by the back door, next to my dad's abandoned New Balances. I'm not surprised he left them. He sprinted away from my mom so fast, he couldn't have done it without upgrading to running shoes. As I tie my laces with shaky hands, Zelda looks up from munching at her automatic feeder. Her gray kitten gaze asks where I'm going at 10:00 a.m. of all times, when within the hour I'm supposed to be available to her for coffee-time pets while we scroll through my TikTok FYP.

"I'm trying not to go to jail, okay?"

In response, Zelda just yawns and returns her face to her food. I sigh, tell her I'll be back, and step into the sun. It's a beautiful day, March 3, and already a sunny sixty degrees. I guess global warming has its perks.

The trees close in on me and I crunch forward on a path of rotten leaves and broken branches. A bit of white catches my eye, a piece of my nightgown must have caught on a tree branch and torn. I stop walking, put on my gloves, and remove the evidence of my presence from the branch, pocketing the fabric.

As I get closer, I find myself sniffing the air like a cadaver dog, involuntarily looking for the smell of death. Of course there's nothing to smell but damp earth—she hasn't had time to decompose and it's not hot out—but the smell of a dead body has been so hyped up that I'm bracing for it. The clearing opens and there she is, looking less scary when not a surprise.

She looks dead, but not as dead as she could look. There are no big bloody wounds, no rot or bugs. Her eyes aren't open and staring at nothing. Her mouth doesn't gape. She really does look like she could be sleeping. I was there in the hospital when they pulled the plug on my grandfather after he had an aneurysm. His face was contorted and his skin was waxy and thin, more like a Halloween mask than a man. The only sign of life was the sound of his breathing, which was rough, like getting a big piece of plastic stuck in a vacuum cleaner. It was clear he was dead hours before he actually was, whereas she looks more like an automated doll that sat down and ran out of batteries.

The closer I get, the weirder it is. She looks like she's been living off the grid for a while. I can still hope she was homeless and ended up here by chance, maybe? But she's wearing a pair of diamond stud earrings that I'm 99 percent sure are real by their complete lack of tarnish; even though everything else on her is wrecked, the gold shines against her grimy gray earlobes. Her hair is short, black, tangled, and very dirty. The cut is uneven and shaggy, falling past her ears in the longest places. It reminds me of when Michelle used the quarantine to grow out her pixie cut. She looked like this after a few months and hated it. She wore a hat along with her surgical mask every time she left the house, even to drive. I told her it made her look like she was on her way to rob a bank. She said that was fine as long as nobody recognized her, but she swapped out the beanie for a sky-blue bucket hat and added big Prada shades so the look would "give Coachella" more than criminal.

I kneel beside the body, still holding on to a shred of hope that maybe she's just stiff because being homeless hurts your back. As I reach for her neck to check for a pulse, I make a silent promise to a God I don't even believe in that if she's alive, I'll help the shit out of her. She can live with me in the lake house until she's less homeless for all I care, just please, please . . .

Nope. I know the second I feel the cold hard flesh of her neck that she's gone. Still, I reach for the frayed sleeve of her jacket and roll it up to double-check. As I push aside a thin gold chain bracelet to press my fingers to her pulse point, I notice a tattoo just above my hand. It's a dagger, running vertically with her veins, the words *vissi d'arte* engraved on the blade in typewriter font. It's cool, honestly. I don't know what the words mean or why she chose them, but it clearly wasn't done in a cheap street shop or in jail. And then there's the gold bracelet. Never mind me, what the fuck happened to this woman before I got to her? Maybe I really didn't kill her after all. I try not to let the flood of hope please me too much; it seems disrespectful to celebrate in front of her.

I spend the next several minutes poking around at the body, holding my breath, trying to find a cause of death and coming up empty. I bite my cheeks to keep from smiling and push my nails into my palms to keep from pumping my fists, because I really don't think I did this. I'm thanking a God that I am now considering believing in and making a plan to go home and call the cops to report this when I see something else. Tucked behind the tree she's leaning against is a green JanSport backpack. I don't pick it up right away, but when I consider that I'm wearing gloves and am allegedly not a murderer, and also that I really want to know what's inside, I pick it up and shake it off. I turn around and walk into the trees a few paces. It'd be rude to snoop through her stuff in front of her.

I hang the bag on a chest-height branch and open it up. I'm disappointed by the normalness of the contents at first, although, what did I expect? The main pouch contains two mostly empty reusable water bottles—one pink Stanley Cup and one Hydro Flask in lavender; a sheathed hunting knife; three dead iPhones and a charger; some loose pens; a stained blue T-shirt; a plastic Subway bag with a faded logo that has some beef jerky in it; a wallet, fat with a wad of cash and credit cards; and a notebook. Okay, definitely not homeless.

I take out the notebook. It's a composition book that has seen much better days. The white spots on the cover are grayed out, and some of the pages are wavy and bloated with water damage. Someone has added a large and angry-looking *DE* at the beginning of the notebook's label, so it instead reads DEComposition Book. For a second, it's almost like picking up any other book. The title makes me laugh and I flip to the first page to find it full of tiny, precise print. I fan out the rest of the pages and see that the notebook is completely full. It begins in black ink and ends in blue and, as she started to run out of pages, the last twenty-five or so, she switched to writing on the whole page, margins and all, instead of just on the given lines. I sit cross-legged in the dirt, flip to the first page, and begin to read.

Hello. My name is Ava Addison Brown. If you're reading this, I'm either safe or dead . . .

PART TWO

Bloat: Putrefaction begins. Leaked enzymes begin to produce gasses, which cause the body to bloat, sometimes causing it to double in size. Bacteria causes parts of the skin to change color.

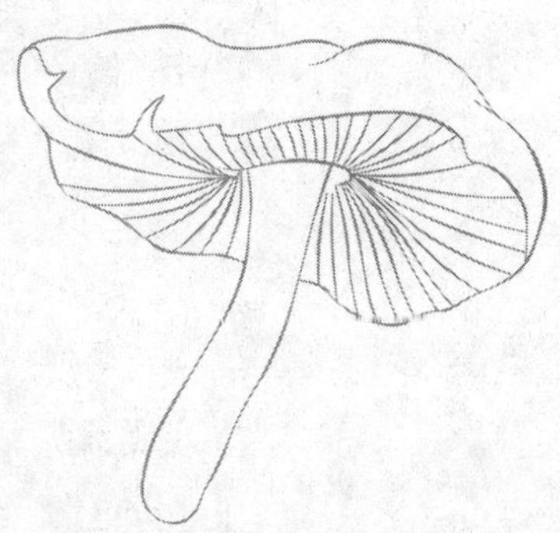

AVA

Chad was reckless to a fault. We found that out the next morning when Megan broke the news that she thought we might be lost over instant coffee and Jimmy Dean breakfast sausages wrapped in the remainder of our hot dog buns. Megan had been near silent all morning, staring into her mug like she was trying to read tea leaves, but when Chad sat up and suggested we go for the waterfalls again, she looked up and said she didn't think that was the best use of our daylight hours.

"Why not?" Chad asked. He said he didn't see any other options that would be equally exciting. But Megan had migrated past caring about excitement. She only cared about getting home safely and on time.

Chad thought we were safe enough. In his world, we had hiked for, what, seven hours yesterday? That meant we were only seven hours from the car. The falls, he said, were even closer geographically to where we'd parked, so really, we would technically be starting to hike back just by continuing to head toward them. It was Sunday, we had all day, and we didn't even have to be back until Monday night.

Megan disagreed. She pointed out that according to him we should have reached the falls yesterday, so who was to say these falls even existed? No. She really thought it would be safer to cut our losses and make the goal of the day retracing our steps back to the car.

He said we wouldn't even need to retrace our steps because we knew where the car was. We would simply go back the way we came. And with that, Megan put down her coffee, crossed her arms over her chest, and said, "Ok. Fine, Chad. Where is the car?"

I swallowed and watched him look around while goose bumps spread across my arms and legs. I looked around too. Megan sat stiff and defiant, staring him down and sipping her coffee, watching as he looked left and right and behind him, eyes narrowing as he tried not to make any faces that would give up just how incompetent and fucked he knew he was.

"Look," he said, "I have a compass. We came from the north. We can just follow the compass back up seven hours, which is how long it took us to get here yesterday, and then I'm sure we'll find the trail and the car."

Megan seemed to relax at the mention of a compass and the knowledge that Chad hadn't simply taken us on a loose gander. Her shoulders dropped and she finally took a bite of her breakfast.

"You have a compass," she repeated more to herself than to Chad.

"Yes."

"And we came from the north?" she asked.

I looked back and forth between them. I remember watching Chad's pupils shudder at the intensity of her eye contact. Megan was really good at holding firm eye contact. Way better than I've ever been.

"Yes."

"Okay."

"Okay."

And so after breakfast we packed up, set a timer for seven hours, and headed north.

~AA Brown

SAVANNAH

THE WHOLE TIME I hold the journal, my hands shake. All I can think about is that I'm holding what is essentially a tangible ghost. This is someone's last words. It's sacred, a handwritten manuscript, an only copy, the first and last edition, and I am overwhelmingly positive that I am going to destroy it somehow. I see myself ripping it to shreds. I see myself throwing it into a bonfire and toasting s'mores over the flames. I see myself tripping too close to a wood chipper. I watch the notebook leave my hands, soar right into the open mouth of the machine, and rain down on the other side like Times Square confetti. Is there a wood chipper nearby? Probably not. But I swear I can sense one. Destroying the notebook is all I can think about—like when you see a baby in a stroller and instead of thinking, *Oh, what a cute baby*, like a normal person, you ponder grabbing it by the only fat tuft of hair it has and launching it in front of an oncoming train.

Hils would say these are just intrusive thoughts and they, if anything, show I'm actually less likely to paint a subway station in baby blood, or take the notebook to the beach and feed it to a shark, but I'm not so sure. Either way, I'm not qualified to handle this. I hold the journal away from my body, pinching it in such a way that I'm touching as little of it as possible, like it's the Declaration of Independence. Then I walk back around the tree so I'm facing the dead girl again. Ava. She has a name now. She's not scary anymore. It makes me think maybe corpses are like penises. The first time you see one, it's the grossest, most disturbing thing you've ever seen. You don't want to touch it and you certainly can't fathom putting it in your mouth, but then after seeing a few more of them or, better yet, seeing the same one repeatedly . . . Huh. I guess corpses are better than penises.

The good news is that I absolutely did NOT kill her. Round of applause for me. But now I have no idea what to do. Call the cops, right? Call the cops. With extreme caution, I tuck the notebook under my arm and go to slide my phone out of the tight pocket of my leggings that straps it to my thigh, but then I remember my phone is in the couch. I feel a rush of relief but I don't know why. It's not like I don't still have to call the cops when I get home. I stare at the ground and try to imagine what I'll do, picturing the keypad of numbers on the screen. I look at number nine. I look at number one. I look at number one again. I look at the numbers harder. I look until they blur. My imaginary thumb hovers, but will not press.

My eyes scroll up until I'm staring at her again. I wonder if it's rude to stare at the dead like it's rude to stare at someone with a deformity. Is there a line I'm crossing or was I just raised in a culture that tells us it's called a shroud for a reason? I've never met a mortician. I'm apparently not a killer. And yet here I am with the same weird backstage pass. The longer I stay here staring at her, the more I can't look away, and the more aware I am of my own body. Just knowing how still she is, inside and out, all I can feel is how still I cannot be. I breathe deep and my diaphragm stretches out long and slow like a cat about to dig its claws into the carpet. Two days ago I felt so small, but I don't feel that way anymore. Was this what I was looking for when I went corpse hunting with Michelle at twelve years old?

Are you seriously trying to talk yourself into corpse hoarding right now? Michelle asks from her home in my head. I need to stop summoning her accidentally, but it's hard to keep her away with so much blood in the water.

Am I corpse hoarding? No, I'm going to call the police at some point; there's just not a huge rush. She's already dead. And she looks peaceful.

Oh my God, you're considering keeping her here, aren't you? That's like ten-year-old-Jeffrey-Dahmer-stabbing-dead-things-with-sticks-level psycho. What are you gonna do next? Lick her neck? Drag her back to the house and prop her up in bed next to you like a zombie Bratz doll?

I'm not keeping her here. I don't know. I just— I feel the spine of the journal pressing softly against my ribs. My heart thumps against it. I just need to know what happened to her. And if I call the cops now, they'll take the journal away as evidence. And doesn't Ava deserve time to rest in peace by herself? She does, right? We all do. I look out at Ava, then in at Michelle, the sand-colored row of freckles on her nose shimmering in a beam of sun. Figures she'd conjure herself a spotlight.

I always knew you were into some freaky shit, she says, and she steps forward, throws her arms out to shove me.

Nothing touches me, of course, but I still flinch and stumble toward the body. I almost face-plant into Ava's lap, but I stop myself from falling. Instead, I take a knee in front of her. I look into her closed-for-good eyes. I shut my eyes and look for Michelle to see what I should do next, a habit from when we were friends. Michelle always decided what I did next. But when I look for her, she's gone. It's just me and the body now. It's me deciding what to do next. Without really thinking about it, I rock back into a seat and crisscross-applesauce my legs. I'm dazed by her deadness and therefore her complete inability to hurt me. I place the journal carefully to the side. Like a shaky puppet propelled forward by a first-time puppeteer, I take one of her hands. I reach out again and hesitate, but in the end I take her other hand, too. In a trance, I draw soft circles into her palms with my thumbs.

Her hands feel so different from my hands, not quite artificial, like mannequin hands, but not quite human, either.

After sitting like this for several minutes, I almost pull back because I'm ashamed, but then I remember there's no one here to witness this weird vigil. It's just us. I look around to confirm and find everything exactly the same as it was. Everything is quiet. Only the trees, as they gather to secure the space for us, can witness this. I put Ava's left hand back down where I found it, and with my free hand, I caress her cheek. I don't drop my hand, but I lean in closer. I can count her eyelashes. I hesitate a couple of times, sputtering forward like a lawn mower engine that won't start for several hard pulls on the string, but I keep going until my warm forehead rests against her cold one. And in this weird moment of one-sided intimacy, something happens that hasn't happened for months: I feel safe.

SAVANNAH

OKAY, SO THE closest thing I have to describe what I'm feeling right now is postnut clarity. You know, like when you stumble into a really suspicious genre of porn and while you're in it it's great and you're screaming and moaning and so turned on, but after you come, all that's left is a cold, wet puddle on your sheets, a weird kink you didn't know you had, and the knowledge that you will go to your grave telling no one you ever enjoyed this. No nutting took place—*obviously.* It's weird but it's not Dahmer weird, regardless of what Michelle may say. The fact it teeters on the edge of Dahmer weird is already starting to chip away at me, though. How fucked-up do your corpse actions have to be to qualify you for jail and general ostracization? How far can you go? If I ever got famous and tweeted about my forehead-to-forehead-with-a-dead-stranger moment, would I get canceled for that? I wouldn't like my odds enough to risk it.

One time, when we were in eighth grade, one of the girls in my school found out that the boy she'd shared her first kiss with was also her first cousin. They'd discovered this after an unfortunate run-in at a family reunion over spring break. When school resumed, word got out and the poor girl quickly discovered that the instant crushing horror she must have felt when she saw her new boyfriend under the arm of her aunt wasn't as bad as it could get. No. The worst was still to come. We school-wide shamed that bitch within an inch of her little life. Michelle led the charge in ensuring that anytime she walked into a room, all the kids inside would erupt with a chorus of "Sweet Home Alabama." She didn't just have to switch schools; she had to switch districts. I think her parents literally packed up and moved out of state in the end. My generation of kids was just too hard to run from. We all had cell phones and none of the adults were quite used to that yet. God, that poor girl. Torturing her just so I could hear Michelle laugh was probably the worst thing I ever did before this. Not that I even know what *this* is yet.

What I do know is that during the weird forehead-touching thing, I was breathing deep, feeling all-powerful and one with life and death and whatnot, when I started hearing this soft, somewhat crunchy fluttering sound, and so I opened my eyes—just in time to watch a fly crawl out from the inside of her nose. And oh the scream that I screampt. The fly was propelled into the air just as I was propelled backward onto my ass. The problem was I didn't remember to let go of Ava's hand, and Ava obviously didn't remember to let go of mine, so when I fell she came with and landed on top of me. She was so stiff that she sort of kept her same shape, crouching over me like a really fucked-up jungle gym. And I screamed and screamed while I swatted and pushed at her body. She was surprisingly heavy for someone who likely died of starvation—and of course she was absolutely no help—and I was fully panicking at that disco, so it took a while to get her fully off me. In the end, I flung her on top of the journal and then proceeded to freak out and scramble to rescue it.

In the end, no journals were harmed and no corpses were desecrated. I even managed to prop Ava back up against the tree in her same pose after several minutes of hyperventilating and a brief vomit scare. I then collected myself, because I am a grown woman, technically, and I am not afraid of a little fly-on-corpse action. She's not even gross yet anyway. I guess I have to call the police, but I haven't yet. The fact that I know now that nobody killed her takes some of the urgency off. I know that when I call the police, it'll be a whole thing and I'll have to turn over everything I found with her, including the journal, and then I'll never have a chance to read the rest of it and find out what happened to her. I only got to the part where they followed that dumbass Chad into the woods. I need to know. Also, that first journal entry makes me feel like she'd want me to know, which is important to me. I don't know her, but I want to do right by her, to give her a good death. So, yes, I will call the cops, but first I'll let her have some peace without the police poking at her and violating her privacy.

I decided all of this and then I gathered her backpack and my backpack and held the journal to my chest all the way home. I left her stuff in the garage for DNA purposes, although I'm not so sure that matters given the whole journal of evidence on my behalf. Then I crossed the threshold into my house and the real world tucked me back into its straitjacket. The shame hit so fast it knocked me back onto my heels and left me breathless.

And now, curled up on the floor of my shower, all I can think about is how I'm sure this is how that girl we bullied in eighth grade must have felt, but for her it was so much worse because everyone knew and because Michelle had a cell phone and I had a cell phone and I wanted to please Michelle. I can almost see Michelle now, kneeling over me, grinning with more teeth than she really has, like a shark or a siren.

What's "Sweet Home Alabama" for corpse fuckers?

"I don't know. Probably something by Adele," I grumble back, but when I look for her again, she's not there. It's just me, small and naked.

Bethany. I think her name was Bethany.

AVA

We definitely went north that time. But we definitely hadn't come from there. Megan stood over Chad's shoulder and back-seat drove the compass for hours while I attempted to recognize absolutely anything that looked more familiar than just another tree. With the elephant of dread slowly lowering its cheeks onto my chest, I stared at everything, picking through my memories, afraid to blink lest I miss something, anything, that looked familiar. But it all looked familiar. It was all just the same thick trees, dense all the way up, with leaves and branches for days! Sometimes I wish we had gotten lost later in the year, sometime around now, because the leaves are gone and even the bark looks skinnier in the winter. I wonder if I could have seen farther without Mother Nature's guts in the way. Then again, I don't think we would've been prepared for winter. Megan and I worked our way up to this together. We were in survival elementary school back then. Now we're in survival college. Well, I am. She flunked out . . .

What? Am I not allowed to make sick jokes anymore?

Anyway, yeah, so I couldn't see more than twenty feet in any direction. I remember taking strained shallow breaths like I was mountain climbing and low on oxygen, because it started to feel like the trees would suffocate me. The more hope I lost, the deeper in trouble we were, the more my chest ached, until I had to stop and squeeze my eyes shut for a minute so I could pretend the hopelessness wasn't real, that it was just a monster under the bed. When I opened my eyes,

I had to rush to catch up to the others, but I don't think they'd even noticed I'd fallen behind. Chad was too busy being pissed that Megan was micromanaging him and Megan was too busy staring that compass down and marching Chad forward like he was walking the plank, holding the point of the sword to his back. I'm not gonna lie—she was pissed. So pissed she was silent, which was almost as unsettling as my life flashing before my eyes in a series of audition dresses I wore but didn't like and PFOs from YAPs.

The thing is, Megan was a personality hire trying to get a promotion. She was rarely quiet, and never like this. I'd seen her quiet like a sleeping puppy, but that day she was a venomous snake waiting to strike. And strike she did. It was late afternoon, humid as all fuck, and not only were we not seeing anything familiar, but also the forest was getting denser. Not a little denser, a LOT, like to the point where Chad had to pull out a hunting knife so large I started to wonder if he brought us out here to serial-kill us. He tried using it to chop through the tangled overgrowth until Megan barked at him that we'd just go around, then marched past muttering that he was an idiot. Only there was no around. *There wasn't really a* through *either. I'd never seen anything like it. The trees were a wall. It was like a garden maze in a movie, impenetrable. The elephant sat, finally resting its full weight on me, and I leaned against the living wall as I struggled to breathe. We couldn't possibly have come from this direction.*

Megan stopped. I caught a glimpse of a change in her eyes that was truly terrifying, and then she turned around very slowly and squared up in front of Chad, hands on hips. The man was a full foot taller than her and holding a big-ass knife, but he still shrank down in response.

"Chad." It was barely a whisper. "How do you know we started north?"

"What?" he asked.

She rolled her eyes. "Jesus Christ. How do you know we came from the north?"

Chad tried to tell her she was being really intense, but that just made her crazier. She started walking toward him, eventually backing him up into a tree, the whole time repeating her question over and over.

"Okay!" Chad yelled. "Fuck." He straightened up. "We came from the north because we came from uphill, right? And then we followed the water down." He made a little motion with his hands like falling water.

I felt my jaw drop and found myself suddenly unable to move, but that was nothing compared to Megan's reaction. She made this incredible sound between a gasp and a honk, like someone had pulled a tube from her throat. Then she simply lay down flat on the ground, staring at the sky with her arms out like she was about to make a snow angel.

"Chad, you're such a fucking idiot and I've been wanting to tell you that for such a long time," she said. And then she closed her eyes and just breathed. I watched her chest rise and fall, surprised I was still capable of thinking how beautiful she was in a moment like this.

"What?" Chad asked, turning to me, the other woman, to explain her behavior like men so often do.

"Downhill doesn't mean you're coming from the north," I said.

"Yeah, dumbass," Megan replied without opening her eyes.

"I really don't think it's necessary for you to keep bullying me like this, Megan, even if I screwed this up a little."

Then she propped herself up on her knees, sat on her heels, dug her white French tips into the earth, rocked back and forth, and absolutely wailed with laughter. Not her normal laugh. This one was deep and raspy with ugly-cry undertones. Chad and I stared. We were captivated. It was a real live mad scene and she was fucking magnificent.

I don't even know how long it was before she got up, but when she did, she wrapped her arms around Chad's shoulders, fingers intertwined on the back of his neck, and looked up like she was going to kiss him.

"How much money do you make?" she asked, batting her eyelashes.

"What?"

"You heard me."

"I just don't see how that's relevant to this situation."

"How much fucking money, Chad?!" she snapped, grabbing the front of his shirt in her little white fist.

"Jesus. Fine. $265,000 a year, plus a Christmas bonus of give or take 20K."

She released him and started pacing the area, muttering "motherfucker" to herself over and over like an incantation. Chad had not gathered that he needed to stop talking, so he tried to be like, Oh I don't know what that has to do with this, *and Megan started cackling again. He looked to me again for help, but I just shrugged and slowly sank to a seat on the ground to watch, wishing we had popcorn. What could I do to save him anyway? Megan was a jack-in-the-box and the music had already started. I wasn't about to put my face directly above it. He said her name again, trying to get the manic laughter to stop. Stupid boy. She turned on him. When she spoke, her voice was so scarily calm that I held my breath without meaning to.*

"Chad. Not that it matters, but I make $47,000 a year to do more than triple the amount of work of you and all your shitty executive homies. In fact, I came out here with the goal of making the kind of take-an-Uber-to-and-from-work-every-day money you get for two emails, a long lunch date with the boys, and a four-hour nap on the couch in your office. I don't even have an office."

Chad opened his mouth to defend himself, but she cut him off, stomping around imitating his stupid man voice. "'Come on this camping trip with me and the boys, Megan. There's gonna be a group of us. We can talk about you moving up to our department, Megan.'

"I knew there were never any boys, Chad. I'm not stupid. That's why she's fucking here!" She pointed a dirty fingernail at me. "No offense, Ava."

I nodded and gave her a thumbs-up. I wasn't offended. I knew why she'd needed me here. I was just honored that she'd asked me to be in her presence instead of that bitch Sally from sales. Chad opened his mouth, but after one harsh look from Megan, he closed it again. He was learning.

"And now—" she gestured around, frustrated tears in her eyes "—because you thought you could get away with getting me to fuck you in a tent for a promotion like some quid pro quo cowgirl, we're going to die out here. But I'm glad you brought your fancy-ass camping supplies, because we're gonna need them."

And she was right.

~AA Brown

SAVANNAH

THERE HAVE TO be rules. It's what keeping exotic pets has in common with running a backyard body farm. Like, if the cobra has to stay in the enclosure, the corpse has to stay in the woods, that sort of thing. I'm off hard drugs for now, so I can't sleep. I miss my Ambien, but I can't get out from under this irrational worry that if I take it again, more and more corpses will start appearing in the woods, like mushrooms after the rain. Unlikely, but I'm not taking any chances. I'm good with my one corpse.

I need to keep busy or else my brain will eat me, so I'm drafting my rules for this endeavor. What's the endeavor? I don't know if I super know yet—please come back in three to five business days. I know I want to know what happens at the end of the notebook, and I'm only a few pages into that. Couldn't I just read it really fast and then turn it into the police tomorrow? Maybe I should be doing that with my time right now instead of this. Sure, I could just chug her journal like an airport paperback and be done with it, but doesn't that seem kind of rude? I'm the last bitch between her and a tag on her toe. Wouldn't she want her story to be savored? I know I would be pissed if someone skimmed through the last known record of me. So I'll take my time with it. I click my pen. I write the first rule.

Rule #1: Maximum of one journal entry per visitation and all journal entries must be read while in her presence for ritual vigil purposes, but not out loud, because she would probably hate that.

What are you doing now? Michelle's voice floats up from the back of my head. I swallow the hard pit of dread that appears in my throat and keep my eyes on the paper. I don't answer her.

You can't be serious. Savage, I knew you were crazy, but I never knew you were this crazy. You can't just keep her like a little pet. You're going to go to jail!

Rule #2: No touching the body without gloves. Try not to touch Ava at all. Ava is a crime scene.

Although, I will say out of everyone, I trust you to be careful to the level of paranoia. You don't let anything slide. You're the queen of worry. Remember that horrible field trip we went on in sixth grade, where we all had to sleep cramped, foot to face, in the hull of that old ship that smelled like ass? We shared a bunk. You were wearing a hoodie and in the middle of the night you found matches in the pocket. And then somehow you convinced yourself that the box of matches would combust any minute and burn down the whole ship. You treated it like a bomb. You didn't want to toss and turn too much, in case the friction ignited one of the matches, and then all of them, until there was a whole boat of children burning alive because of you. You passed the time shaking instead, clenching and unclenching your fists. Your shaking woke me up. Remember?

In my defense, I was on one of my first ever periods at the time.

And then didn't you, like, sneak up to the deck and yeet the matches into the sea like the old lady at the end of Titanic? *I just don't see how you can't handle a book of matches spending the night in your pocket, yet you can live with yourself gatekeeping a whole human corpse. You're still the queen of worry, but you worry about all the wrong things.*

I breathe slowly. One two. In out. She isn't real. She isn't real. My ribs are too tight around my heart, and it bangs against them, trying to knock at least a couple loose. I think it wants to tear its way out of my chest like Bella's baby and be free of me altogether. I get it. I've always been too much, too worried, too weird, just too hard to love. Ava doesn't have to love me; that's why she's safe. I know it can't always be like this. I never said I would keep her forever, and I won't. I just need a second, just a little while of someone who won't leave me. It'll be a symbiotic relationship, a shark and a minnow. I'll even let her be the shark. I'm going to read the journal, give her words the time they deserve, enjoy the weird safety I feel with her, and let her rest in peace for a hot second. That's it. Then I'll call the police.

Rule #3: When her body is bones, you have to call the police. There are other people who need closure.

Okay, well, since you're gonna be a stick in the mud and do this no matter what I say, you at least need to make sure you're keeping a standard of respect for the dead. Don't start thinking you're a mortician, okay? You aren't qualified for shit, so leave her alone.

I squeeze my eyes shut tight, trying not to imagine all the things Michelle thinks I might do with the body. I won't do any of them. I'm crazy, but not like that. I'm not a psychopath—I just have a difficult brain. I'm doing my best. As I open my eyes back up, I picture Michelle rolling hers at me. She always said I make a specific face when I'm spiraling. She said it makes me look retarded. She used to kick me lightly under the table at the mall food court so I'd know to knock it off before she got too embarrassed to be seen with me.

Whatever. Have fun with your Frankenstein shit.

I stare at the empty spot where she was. I close my eyes, then open them, then close them again, then open them. Two full cycles. No Michelle. She's gone, and I'm okay. I write my last rule, shut the notebook, and reach for the bottle of pills on my nightstand. Fuck this.

Rule #4: Don't be weird. Just, don't be weird.

AVA

When Megan was done screaming at Chad and everyone had accepted that we were at least a little bit lost, she said we needed to make an inventory list of the supplies we had on us. Neither of us objected. Chad was still in denial that we were fully lost, but by that point he knew better than to argue with her and began unpacking and laying stuff out for us to sort through. We sorted everything into three piles: food and beverage, home and comfort items, and survival tools. I'll put a folded copy of the list we made in with this page so you can see for yourself what we had.

Consumables:

1 six-pack of chicken-flavored instant ramen
5 protein bars, varying brands
6 packets of apple-cinnamon instant oatmeal
1 tin of instant coffee
3 hot dog buns
½ a family-size pack of BBQ Lays
1 can of root beer
3 cans of beer
3 mostly full packs of gum
1 container of orange Tic Tacs
2 mini Snickers bars

½ bag of Sour Patch Kids
most of a bag of marshmallows
1 bar Hershey's chocolate
½ box of graham crackers
7 loose sugar packets
34 ibuprofen
about an eighth of weed

Home and Comfort:

1 large tent
3 sleeping bags
clothing: 7 panties, 3 boxers, 9 pairs socks, 2 sports bras, 1 pair cargo pants, 4 T-shirts, 2 pairs leggings, 2 pairs pj pants, 1 suspiciously lacy nightgown Megan doesn't want us to speak of, 2 tank tops, 1 hoodie, 1 zip-up jacket, 1 zip-up windbreaker
1 pair hiking boots
2 pairs hiking sneakers
3 travel containers of toothpaste
3 toothbrushes
3 sunscreens—2 mini, 1 normal sized
2 mini bug sprays
4 ChapSticks, 1 Vaseline
1 mini first aid kit with 17 average-sized Band-Aids, 1 set of latex gloves, 1 big gauze, 2 Tylenol, 1 Benadryl, and 8 alcohol pads
2 menstrual cups
2 hairbrushes, 1 comb
3 sticks of deodorant
2 travel-sized face washes
2 travel-sized body washes
2 travel-sized lotions
3 rolls of toilet paper

1 empty composition notebook
1 mostly full pocket notebook
7 pens
1 deck of cards
3 wallets with credit cards and bills and such
4 hair ties
1 sweatband
2 washcloths
1 quick-dry towel
3 backpacks
3 AirPods
2 phone chargers, 1 charging pad
3 iPhones

Survival Tools:

1 Stanley Cup, 1 Hydro Flask, 1 Yeti
1 collapsible pot for boiling water and other things
3 collapsible metal coffee mugs
1 ladle
1 pair kitchen tongs
1 large hunting knife
1 Swiss Army pocket knife
1 tiny shovel
1 cooler
1 wilderness travel guidebook for the Northeast
1 map of the Adirondacks
1 compass
2 flashlights
1 watch
1 flintstone
3 lighters
3 sharp metal stakes we used to roast the weenies and marshmallows

3 spoons, 3 forks, 3 table knives
1 pack of rolling papers and tips
1 pipe
miscellaneous plastic trash

All told, it could have been much worse. We were definitely overprepared for a weekend camping trip, but also definitely underprepared for living in the woods for months. At the time though, we were thinking glass-half-full. At least we had all this stuff. Still, we were scared enough that we each had one beer for dinner that night, and that was it.

~AA Brown

SAVANNAH

"HELLO?"

"Is there a reason I haven't heard from you in two days?"

"Um, not really, no." There is a corpse full of reasons.

"Then why haven't I heard from you?"

"I just forgot to call. I don't know. I was busy."

"Busy doing what?

Like the Grinch, I thought of a lie and I thought of it quick. "I've been doing some spring cleaning. I haven't been here since last summer, so I wanted to go through all the stuff in my closet and see what I was keeping. And the weather was nice, so I went for some walks outside like Hils suggested. I haven't left the property. And, uh, yeah, I just forgot. I'm sorry, Mama."

"I know you haven't left the property. I track your phone. I see that you're outside right now, still on the property, but it doesn't matter. You could be dead at home just as well as you could be dead outside."

I fidget, fighting a sudden urge to smash my phone against the nearest tree and then stomp on it, like they do with burners on TV. I imagine the relief of feeling my mom's knowledge of my location crunch under my foot. It's tempting, but I can't. If she couldn't track me all of a sudden, she would just call the police and send them to my phone's last known location. And that would be worse. I dig my nails into my palms and force myself to do nothing.

"Savannah? Are you there? Are you listening to me?"

"Yes!"

"Okay. Well, you do know that you're only allowed to be there by yourself for your little hiatus because I trust you, and because you insisted that you didn't need someone there babysitting you. But you also said you would call me every day so I would know that you are still breathing. That's the deal. If you aren't planning on calling me every day, I would be more than happy to pack a bag and come stay with you until you come home for the summer. Would you prefer that?"

"Um, no." She cannot come out here. "I'm fine. I promise I will call you every single day from now on. Please don't come out here."

"Why don't you want me coming there? Are you hiding something from me?"

"I'm not hiding anything from you."

"Then why are you trying to keep me from coming to see you?"

"I'm . . ." Fuck. "I'm not trying to keep you from coming out. You can come out if you want to, but I'm literally fine."

There's a pause on the other end of the line. I'm hoping that my inviting her out here throws her off the scent of my guilt, but that only works like 45 percent of the time. I'm a bad liar, mostly because the urge to confess starts to chip at me the second I have anything to hide. I'm glad she can't see me. If she could see me, she would know.

"Fine."

I hold my breath so there's no sigh of relief for her to hear.

"But you better call me."

"I will call you."

I will call her. I pull the phone away from my head and set an alarm to call her every day at 4:00 p.m. My mouth is gritty, like when you bite into some food at the beach only to find it covered in sand.

"I'm not fucking around here, Savannah. Your life is too important to me to be messing around like this. Next time I don't hear from you for more than twenty-four hours, I will be coming out. Okay?"

I picture her coming through the trees into the clearing on one of my visits with Ava, dragging her suitcase with her through the dirt. I picture her pulling out her phone, calling the cops without hesitation, committing me to the hospital, again. I picture my face on the news, the pretty privileged girl with no real problems who decided to have a mental breakdown for no reason and kept a corpse as a friend. I picture the story ending up in the tabloids. I picture Michelle, sitting on a lounge chair by a pool in Cabo, getting the alert on her phone, pulling her Prada shades down her nose to see the screen better, reading about how I'm even crazier than she thought.

"Okay."

"All right, well, honey, I love you but I have to get back to work," she says as if I was the one who called her. "I just wanted to make sure you were okay. Okay? I love you!"

"Okay. I love you, too. Bye!"

When I hang up the phone, the urge to confess is gone, along with the images of what would happen to me if I did confess or if I was caught, and I can breathe again. I double-check to make sure my phone really is hung up. It is. I shouldn't have brought it with me in the first place, but it seemed like a privilege I could afford as long as I had the journal to prove I didn't kill her. I hold the power button until the Apple logo disappears and the screen goes dark, then I stash it between my thighs.

"Sorry," I say to Ava's body. "She's overprotective."

I pull a scrap of skin off my bottom lip with my teeth while Ava says nothing at all, reminding myself that there's no judgment stashed away in her silence. I put my hand against my heart and feel my pulse start to slow with the relief of being around her. I sigh and let my head fall back against the tree. I missed this. It's nice.

I haven't been out here in almost two days. At first, because I was worried that someone would find out where I was going, who I was going to see. And then, because I was worried about how much she might have changed. Two days seems like a lot in corpse time and I started getting concerned about the possibility that I'd waited too long already and would come back to a skeleton or, worse, she would get scavenged by vultures, wolves, or bears—not that I've seen any of those things out here, but for all I know the smell of death summons critters far and wide. Turns out, we're good. She is unscavenged. It doesn't seem right, but maybe all the scavengers who aren't me are simply still asleep for the winter. Lucky them.

She isn't a skeleton, either, but she's changed in little ways. She seems more relaxed than she was when I first saw her. She isn't rigid anymore. She's kind of raggedy looking, actually, beat-up and shriveled, like a stuffed animal that wasn't supposed to go in the dryer but snuck by in the sleeve of a sweater somehow and came out shrunken and scruffy. Her cheeks are sunken in a way they weren't before. Her eyelids slouch inward, grayish and loose, like discarded condoms. I guess the eyeballs go fast. I imagine them as little water balloons full of eye juice that pop and drain back into the skull on the first day. And then what? Does your ability to see drip down your throat? At least you don't have to taste it.

The internet says that morticians actually stab the eyes with little plastic things that look like convex versions of those white tables in pizza boxes; they make it look like there are still eyeballs under the lids. At least Ava never has to get stabbed in the eyes. She's been through enough.

The other difference is that she's splotchy. Her exposed skin has patches of reddish purple, green, and dark blue. It has the same vibes as that condition everyone says Michael Jackson had, but instead of making her look like she's both black and white at the same time, she looks like she's both asleep and a zombie. Along with the eyeball thing, I learned in my 2:00 a.m. googling that this is her blood settling in pools under her skin, as it's no longer being pumped around by the heart.

The smell I was worried about isn't here yet, which I am very grateful for as I take a seat, leaning back against the tree directly across from her, a few feet away. I did bring an N95 with me just in case. When I'm settled in, I put on my gloves, take her journal out of my backpack, and read the third entry. After that, I take the moment of silent appreciation for Doritos and drugs that I believe Ava intended the reader to take. After that, I run out of ritualistic shit to do and it starts to get awkward.

I don't know how to explain how sitting around in the woods with a corpse makes me feel awkward, but it does. I mean, obviously I know she's not judging me or thinking I'm rude for not talking to her, but it does feel rude. She's still too person shaped for me to feel comfortable ignoring her like I would an inanimate object. I wonder if morticians find the silence as awkward as I do. Maybe they're too busy putting lipstick on dead grandmas to notice. I feel pressured to speak, like you do when you're on a long drive with someone you don't know very well and you need the vibe to be literally anything but weird viscous silence, so you start asking bullshit small-talk questions you don't even want the answers to.

"So," I venture, "did you go hiking a lot before this or was this, like, your first time?"

Ava says nothing.

"Yeah, I figured that. I'm sorry I can't help you cover up the splotches. I have this concealer kit that Michelle showed me how to use where you can get rid of dark circles and blemishes and stuff on your face with other colors that you'd think would also look weird on your face, but they end up canceling each other out. I'd bring it out here with some other supplies and clean you up and give you a proper mortuary makeover if I could, but you're kind of a crime scene unfortunately, so I can't touch you.

Not that I want to touch you! You're dead. Just wanna clarify that it's not like that. I respect you and your dead agency. Just wanna make sure you get the primo experience, you know?"

Ava does not indicate that she knows.

"Michelle is my ex–best friend, by the way. You'll probably be hearing about her a lot."

Ava seems fine with that.

"She fucked me up, but that's a story for another day."

Ava doesn't pry.

"Not that I'm trying to compare traumas—I'm not. I know that whatever you went through out here was probably way, way worse. I'm excited to finish your journal and learn more about you and what happened to you. Sorry. Don't take that the wrong way! I don't mean *excited* excited like I'm going to enjoy reading about your suffering. I mean like just from the first few pages I did read, you seem like you were a really cool person and your story is very interesting and I'm happy I get to know you a little."

Ava understands what I mean.

"Okay. Well, good talk. I'll be back tomorrow, so good night and sleep tight—I can't tell you not to let the bedbugs bite, though. In your situation they're probably gonna bite no matter what, but I don't think it'll bother you too much."

I stand and brush the leaves and twigs off me, but then I remember how sad everything is and the sudden sorrow stops me in my tracks. I turn around, just for a minute, and look at her again. My eyes well up and I'm ashamed for a second, because I don't feel like I have the right to cry over someone I didn't even know. She's not mine to mourn, but I do anyway, just for a minute.

"I'm sorry for what happened to you," I say. As I turn to leave, I worry that she'll rot too fast without me, or animals will get her and I won't get a chance to say goodbye.

AVA

The first week wasn't that bad. For the rest of Monday—after we inventoried the supplies but before our dinner beers—we made camp and a plan by the plant wall. It took Megan and I an hour to convince Chad that we really needed to take this seriously, and even then I think he remained mostly in denial. He said he felt stupid acting like he was in a real survival situation when in his mind, in the worst case, he was out of office for a few days and ordering a little more takeout than usual when he got back. Megan and I argued that it would be stupider for us not to take this seriously. It would be stupid to eat all the food way too fast and make reckless choices only to be completely out of resources and screwed within the week with no help coming. Chad tried to insist that help was definitely coming, especially when he didn't show up to an important meeting on Wednesday.

Megan must have seen something in him that softened her, or maybe she was just manipulating him, I don't know, but she started handling him like a little boy after that, speaking in short, gentle sentences. She said of course help was coming. Of course there would be a search party within the week, a big one, but there was no reason we had to be miserable while we waited for help to come. If we rationed correctly, we wouldn't even have to get that hungry. Plus, in the time it took rescue to come, we would play around with our resources and see what we could set up that, hypothetically, could help us survive for a while in the event that rescue took a tiny bit longer to arrive—not much longer, just a little bit. Chad wavered slightly but still didn't seem fully convinced, so she hit him with flattery, saying how much we would appreciate his help—there was so much he could add to our combined skill set.

"Didn't you say you go camping once a year? And you were a Boy Scout, right? You brought all these nice professional supplies, so I just assume you have some knowledge to offer." She rattled off questions, leaning forward into his space, smiling and batting her eyelashes while he nodded along, sitting up taller each time like she was pulling on a rope attached to his head.

On second thought, she was definitely manipulating him. It worked, though! By the time we were drinking our dinner beers, Chad was on board, showing Megan pages of his wilderness guidebook by the light of the fire. I sipped at my warm beer and watched as she nodded along, asking questions just so he could have the pleasure of answering them. Once she looked up and saw me watching, and I swear she threw me a wink—it was so unexpected that I thought for weeks I'd imagined it.

We spent Tuesday in pretty good moods. It was the first day of work we'd all missed. People would be looking for us. We just had to wait it out. Chad mansplained different hunting methods. We found another stream where we could get water. It was wider and deeper than the creek we'd followed originally—not quite a river, but there was enough water that we spotted some fish, so Chad and Megan got to making a fishing basket. I scavenged and found some honeysuckle. We shared a single packet of ramen and a generous handful of chips, sucking small drops of the honeysuckle nectar from the flowers for dessert.

Wednesday was more of the same.

By Thursday we were so fucking hungry. We couldn't speak to each other without bickering. Chad was the worst, oh my god. He kept trying to convince Megan to let us eat the food we had and stop hoarding it. To which she replied through gritted teeth that we weren't hoarding it, we were rationing it. He called her a bitch under his breath, grabbed the knife, and stormed off, muttering something about how this was all bullshit and he was going hunting for some real food. Megan and I drank tons of water to try to stop our stomachs from growling, and when that didn't work, we spent the afternoon sleeping in the shade until it was time to build a fire, too tired to do anything else. Chad came back around seven, just before the sun started to set, with no food and a sunburn. We had a couple s'mores each for dinner and split a protein bar three ways.

Friday morning Chad ate one of the mini Snickers bars without permission. A large fight ensued. Chad fucked off to do whatever Chad did. Megan finished the fishing basket. We went together to find a good place for it and ended up sticking it in the entrance to a corner of water that seemed to operate like a freshwater tide pool. We gathered water, boiled it, and filled our bottles, then filled Chad's bottle, which he for some reason did not have with him. He came back when the sun set, looking like he hadn't wanted to come back at all, but we had all the stuff and the food, so tough shit for him.

Saturday was kind of fun. We found out that Chad's decision not to bring his water bottle was indeed a bad one—he got the shits and had to confess to drinking unboiled water. Megan and I laughed and teased him about it all day and he was a pretty good sport, laughing along with us at his own stupid mistake. Megan and I did all the camp chores again that day while he rested. The fish basket was empty, but I found a big patch of wild blackberries and returned to camp feeling like a rock star, with a purple mouth and a plastic Subway bag full of berries. I opened the bag and everyone cheered. I bowed my well-rehearsed curtain call bow and felt prouder than I ever had on a stage. We feasted on the tiny fruits and passed the pipe around, talking and laughing until we fell asleep.

Sunday, we decided to treat ourselves to something that had become rare: breakfast. We made coffee and cooked up a couple instant oatmeal packets and split them between us, adding more of the fresh blackberries on top. Chad told us about some snares he'd set, and we all went to check them together so Megan and I would know where they were in the future. All were empty, but one of them had been tripped, so we reset it with fingers crossed that next time whatever it was wouldn't be lucky enough to escape. Chad fell asleep super early that night and Megan and I felt we could hold out until morning on just blackberries and a couple sticks of gum, so we just sat around the fire talking, like this was a sleepover. I don't remember most of our conversation, just the last part.

We were getting ready to sleep, lying side by side in our sleeping bags, when Megan turned her whole body around to face me. I rolled over too, and I saw she was crying.

"Are you okay?" I whispered to her between Chad's snores.

She nodded. "I'm just really scared."

"I'm scared too."

"What do you think is taking them so long?"

"I don't know. Big forest, lotta trees. It's not like we wandered into an alternate dimension, and there's no way we went that far. They'll find us," I told her, trying to convince myself at the same time.

"But what if they don't?" Her voice was so soft, like cotton.

I freed my arm from the sleeping bag and she did the same. I took her hand and squeezed it tight. "They'll find us," I repeated.

"You promise?" she asked, scooting her sleeping bag closer to mine and squeezing my hand even tighter. It hurt, but I didn't ask her to let go or loosen her grip.

I couldn't promise—in the same way that surgeons can't promise. I knew that and she knew that. I swallowed hard.

"I promise."

~AA Brown

SAVANNAH

I DON'T MAKE promises I can't keep, and I promised Ava that I'd sit with her through this, so I'm back at it every day. I don't want to say that the rotting corpse in my backyard is helping my overall mental health, because that makes me sound like a psychopath, but since that first day, Michelle stays out of the clearing and Ava's journal distracts me from the sorry state of myself.

It's been about a week since I found her and she looks deader every day, but not as dead as I thought she'd look at this point. Maybe it's still too cold. It's been back to near freezing since I found her. I'm not complaining. It gives me time to adjust to the new look. At first, the greens and blues kept spreading across her skin like mold until there was nothing left that looked normal. But today I showed up to find that the blues and greens have faded into reds, oranges, and yellows, like she got into a ketchup-and-mustard-only food fight while I was asleep. It's fascinating in a disturbing way that sometimes gives me nightmares. A few times, I've brought out my own notepad and colored pencils and tried to draw her to track the changes, but I suck at drawing so I gave up. It's for the best anyway—less evidence.

And the bugs are definitely here now. I knew they were coming, but I didn't expect the Super Bowl crowds. I saw a few ants and some green flies with metallic-looking backs a few days ago and thought that would be the gist of it. I was wrong.

There are so many ants around that I'm afraid to sit down. I keep having to bat the flies away from my face and I'm honestly scared to get too close to her. Maggots freak me out and I don't want to see them. Plus, she smells like a gray steak at room temperature. It's unpleasant—not unbearable, but I don't love the thought of going any closer.

"I hope you aren't offended by the mask," I tell her. "You're starting to smell a little funky. It's okay, though—I know it's not your fault. Don't worry. I won't judge."

She doesn't worry. I search for a topic of conversation. We're running out of the shallow things. I told her about where I went to school and where I was from and showed her pictures of Zelda. Today is a non-journal day or else I would just read, but I can't read the journal every day at the pace this is going or I'll be done with it way before she's done rotting. I'm rationing her words, feeding myself a bit of her at a time. I'm not sure what else to say, so I head toward the only other thing I think about these days: Michelle.

"You know, I can see why you like Megan. She seems like she had a lot of the qualities that I liked in Michelle without being all the way like Michelle."

I shift from foot to foot in the silence before I continue, worrying that I'll somehow annoy Ava by talking about Michelle so much. I know I sound like a broken record. It's why everyone else we knew doesn't want to be around me anymore. I didn't get over it fast enough. My brain glitched. I couldn't process it. I couldn't figure out why. I got stuck in the spiral until she was all I could talk about. It wasn't my fault. My brain became one of those murder walls that crazed detectives have. The crescents under my eyes grew darker and puffier by the day as I stayed up all night, every night, trying to find a string, any string, that I could connect to anything other than the facts in front of me: Michelle loved the thrill of cruelty more than she loved me; Michelle never loved me at all. I still haven't found the string. I did find out that my friends all love her more than me, though, especially once I stopped being fun. Everyone said I should just drop it and move on with my life and maybe she'd come around and we'd be friends again eventually. Maybe it's my fault no one wanted to hear about it. I never did tell anyone what actually happened that night. I couldn't. The words were too heavy to bring up my throat and no one really wanted to hear them anyway, so I let them fall back down until I forgot where to find them, like mismatched socks gathering dust under the couch. I gave up, let everyone but my mom slip quietly out of my life, and pretended I couldn't feel the relief radiating off them as they went. Then I started seeing Michelle, started hearing my intrusive thoughts in her voice like she was the official narrator of OCD. And that's how I ended up alone, worried that with one more sentence about Michelle, Ava will find a way to resurrect just to get away from me, too. Still, I keep talking. She's all I have.

"Michelle was really strong and beautiful and always in charge like Megan was. She would have freaked out at Chad about the compass thing, too, but it would have been way worse. I guess I don't know how bad it actually was—you didn't really go into huge detail about it—but from what you said, it seems like Megan pulled back at the last minute and was able to make him feel safe with her. I respect that. Michelle wouldn't have wanted him to feel safe ever again and she would have made sure he didn't. She would have gotten him to cooperate in the end, too—don't get me wrong, she could shrink a man down and put him in her pocket like you wouldn't believe—but she wouldn't have done it like that. Megan hyped him up until he submitted. Michelle would have shredded him down with her claws until there was nothing left but obedience."

Suddenly it feels like I'm choking, but I make myself breathe through it. I know it's just the words getting snagged on all the pain and shame on the way out, like loose sweater threads. It happens every time I talk about Michelle.

“She, uh, she did that to me, too,” I whisper. I sift through my chest to find my voice and keep going. “She . . . In her defense, with me I don’t think she knew what she was doing. With the men, she knew, but I don’t think—at least not until I told her—I don’t think she knew how much control she had over me. Hils, my therapist, she thinks she knew, but I don’t know. Michelle had to love me more than that. She had to. She told me she loved me so many times over so many years. She couldn’t have known she was doing the same thing as with the men, because she didn’t know she had the same type of power over me. I only told her about the me-maybe-being-a-lesbian thing in December, so she couldn’t have known what she was doing, right?”

I pause. I haven’t said that last part out loud since I tried to tell Michelle that night, not to anyone except my therapist and my mom, but that doesn’t count. I don’t want to fully come out until I’m sure, because what if I come out and then I kiss a girl and it’s bad, or what if I kiss one and it’s fine, but then I can’t handle dating one? Then I’d have to go back in the closet and my mom would be like, *See, Savannah, I told you you’re not gay.* And then the gays would think I was trying to appropriate them and I’d have to scrape all traces of rainbows from all my social media accounts like all the major corporations do on the first of July and it would be so embarrassing. It’s already so embarrassing. If I try to squeeze even a drop more shame into my body, my skin will rip. It just can’t fit. No. Before I come out to the world, I have to be sure. But Ava can’t laugh at me on Twitter. There’s no safer audience to come out to than a corpse. You could come out as trans to J.K. Rowling’s corpse and still be totally fine. And so I continue.

“So that’s the other thing. I’m gay. Or at least I think I’m gay. It’s like I already know how to date men, so it’s still easier for me to date men. Like . . . Okay. So when I dated men, I would almost date them like I was hunting for sport. I liked that they were obvious about wanting me when they looked at me. I knew I had power over them, because they wanted in my pants but I didn't necessarily need to be in theirs, which is how I assumed all straight women thought, by the way! Apparently not. Apparently some of them actually like the dicks, which is insane, because have you seen one of those? Sylvia Plath was right, turkey neck and turkey gizzards all the way—oh my God, why have we been touching those for centuries? But see, Ava, that's what I thought the game was. I thought the job of a woman was to secure a man and provide him with her body and house labor in exchange for extra money, security, and maybe some friendship sometimes? My parents didn't like each other, so that's what it looked like to me. But I don't think a man could ever break me like Michelle did. I don't think I could want one like that, either. Women are just better, like—"

I make the curve of a woman's torso in the air between us with my hands. This would be easier to explain if Ava still had eyeballs.

"I always knew I could have sex with a woman—that's not the problem. But I've never dated one. I don't even know how. Who even pays? I think I might have to, though. Date women from now on, I mean, not pay for the dates. I'm fine paying for the dates. I just . . . I wasn't fully convinced I was gay, because I didn't think emotionally I could ever feel that way about a woman. I convinced myself that the women I wanted to be with were just women I wanted to be like. But it's looking more and more like whenever I said I want to be her, I meant I wanted to be with her. I used to want to be like Michelle."

As soon as the sentence is out, I get that punched-in-the-heart feeling that's happening way too often lately, and I have to stop. My face goes warm as my hands go cold. I press both palms to my chest. I close my eyes and breathe into my hands until I'm not winded anymore. It's a good thing Ava is such a gracious listener; anyone else would think I'm acting ridiculous.

Finally, I croak out, "I think I'm heartbroken."

I sink to the ground. Something crawls up my shoe and I remember the ants. I guess the price I pay for this therapy session is having to strip at the door when I get home and spend the whole night paranoid that they're still on me—or in me. Ambien today, for sure. Nevertheless, she persists.

"I have to be heartbroken, right? I don't see what else could feel this bad. Ava, I feel like I'm dying. Sorry. That was insensitive. I know I'm not actually dying, but it really does feel like that! I have chest pain. My mom literally took me to the ER about a month after Michelle left because she thought I could be having a pulmonary embolism or something. That's how I got thrown in the psych ward the second time. Doctors are so nosy."

I haul myself up, brush a handful of ants from my calves, and start pacing.

"But that's the thing, that's why I think I might have just been gay all along. There's no way a man could ever make me feel this much pain. I used to read books with heartbreak in them and think that kind of pain was just for fiction, but it's not. This is what all these bitches are writing about! Heartbreak isn't when some obsessed-with-his-own-abs political science major named Patrick ghosts you and you have one big, frustrated cry and then stomp around the house for a few days, angry that you lost control over your minion." I wrap my arms around myself. My next words come out in a shudder. "It's this. Heartbreak is this."

I stop pacing and stare at my feet, waiting for my throat to loosen up. I can see Ava's feet, too, encased in very scuffed-up brown leather hiking boots that look like they came from the men's section of the store.

I sniffle and watch my tears hit the dirt between our feet until I start to feel normal enough to remember this is an insane activity. The more I'm out here, the more I'm getting used to this feeling at the end of our sessions. It's fine. It's probably good to keep a healthy level of shame about this. It feels no worse than anything else going on right now anyway, but the onset of this feeling does mean it's time to go. That, and there's an ant that's managed to migrate all the way to boob height. I flick the ant in Ava's direction.

"I'm sorry about flicking that ant onto you just now. I don't know what the proper etiquette is with the bugs. I'm also sorry about all the trauma dumping. I'll get it back together pretty soon, hopefully, but thank you for listening."

I swipe the remaining tears off my cheeks with the back of my hand and roll my head around on my shoulders because my neck hurts from being so tense all the time. The sky is orange between the tree branches. The sun must be setting. Perfect timing.

"Good night, Ava," I say. "Rest well."

AVA

When we ran out of food was when Chad started to get serious*. I guess we all have our motivators. It was the beginning of week three and we were down to our last pack of gum, about 15 Tic Tacs, still a pretty good amount of coffee (thank god), and a half handful of Sour Patch Kids. Megan had been using the candy as little treats to get Chad to do stuff for us. We figured it would be really sad when we ran out and had to do everything useful ourselves, but it turned out that Chad was activated by desperation. I'm telling you, it was like some weird patriarchal hunter instinct awakened within him and he became determined to thrive.*

At first it was kind of annoying, because he kept suggesting shit that could get him, or all of us, killed. He wanted to hunt snakes to harvest their fangs for fishing hooks by sticking his hand into random holes and yanking the snake out when it bit him, because "there's only one venomous snake in the region and it's a very specific kind of rattlesnake that we likely won't encounter." He wanted to follow the bear tracks we saw sometimes, because "the bears probably know where the food is!"

A day or so into foodlessness, he suggested he climb the plant wall. Megan was making coffee. I was propped up against a tree next to her, rereading the wilderness guidebook. (Now I'm re-re-re-re-rereading it.) Chad was fidgeting around the perimeter of our little camp, coming closer to the plant wall, heading away and looking up to the top of it, approaching again to grab at it in various places, shaking it occasionally so the leaves rattled. I wondered what he was up to, but I was more amused than worried it was something stupid, so I just let him go, like he was a house cat on a mission in a pretty cat-safed house. Megan did the same for a while, not intervening, just turning to mouth What the fuck? *at me while pointing at him. I just shrugged and handed her the ladle because the water was boiling. She ladled the boiling water into our crusty metal cups and stirred in the tiny rations of instant coffee. I watched her make mine, salivating as the grounds turned the water the thin brown of a tragically weak cup of black coffee. It tasted like coffee's ghost (and I miss it so much). She handed the cup to me with a smile and I cradled it, sipping at it, blissed out with my eyes closed like I was the star of a Folgers commercial. Similar to Folgers, it tasted just civilized enough.*

Megan stood holding the other two cups and walked over to Chad. "So what's going on over here?" she asked as she handed him his coffee. He thanked her and then revealed that he wanted to climb the wall.

"That wall?" I asked stupidly, looking up. Of course he meant that wall, but the thing was huge, a group of massive, ancient trees enmeshed in a tangle of branches and leaves like a giant head of matted hair. It had to be twenty, thirty feet to the top.

"If I can get to the top, I can see farther out, get us some information on where we are."

I chewed on the idea. Megan looked very unconvinced. She came back with "Right, but that's also super risky. If you fall and break anything out here, you're dead. The most we can fix on our own is, like, I don't know, a broken finger or a rib maybe since you just have to wait on those anyway. But if you break an arm, a leg, god forbid your spine, we might as well just put you down like a dog, because otherwise it's a slow and painful death from infection."

"Well, thank you for the confidence, Megan. Encouraging as usual."

I chuckled into my cup because I didn't want Megan to see. They both had a point.

"Look, I'm just saying that we don't know how sturdy this thing is." She went to the wall and started pushing leaves aside to reveal the structure of it. "See? It's a lot of small branches tangled together. There's very little in here that seems thick enough to support a grown man."

"A pretty skinny grown man," Chad said with a grin. Nobody laughed. Megan continued picking through the foliage like a monkey checking a friend for fleas. I lamented that I was going to have to stand up for this, but I figured I should go see, if for nothing else than to say I saw enough to form an educated opinion. I met them at the wall and pawed at it while they continued to bicker through the pros and cons. Some of the branches were brittle and dead and I could break them with one hand, but others were so sturdy they could probably hold two of us at once.

In the end, we put it to a vote. Since there were three of us, it was easy to vote on all major decisions. Megan voted no. Chad voted yes. I voted yes.

"Ava, really?" Megan whirled on me.

Chad went for a high five, which I ignored.

"If the wall isn't going to support him, we'll know before he gets high enough up that a fall can do serious damage. And it would be useful to see from up there. What if there's a campsite close enough to walk to and we just can't see it through the trees?"

Megan sighed and shook her head. She wasn't convinced, but we'd voted. The vote was final. She stared up at the wall.

"We at least need to spend a little time planning a route up that won't kill you."

"Fair enough," Chad said, putting his free hand up like he was swearing an oath.

We spent the next couple hours doing just that. We looked around until we found an area where a tree was actually supporting the wall. We reasoned that the tree would provide extra support to all the branches and vines around it, making them sturdier. Megan was the lightest of us, and I was the heaviest. We made up this very scientific process where we would all pull and stomp on possible handholds and footholds in the area. Anything that didn't give way on the pull test, we'd have Megan hang from or stand on. If it held for Megan, I would try it. If it held for me, we would mark the spot by tying some bright red foil around the hold. We'd gotten the red foil by slicing the empty Doritos bag into thin strips. We did this until Megan and I could both go up about ten feet. From there, we'd just have to wing it.

Then it was time to send Chad up. Megan and I took up residence at the base to guide Chad to the top like we were standing outside a car, trying to help him parallel park. Chad would mark new handholds as he went, to ensure he could find them again on the way down. The first ten feet were easy, as we knew they would be. After that, we quickly realized that we could do almost nothing to help him from the ground. Over the next hour, he worked his way up the remaining fifteen or so feet, stretching out one arm at a time and testing handholds by pulling on them.

Below him, we clutched each other, tense for the possible fall. Megan dug her grown-out nails into my forearm. We alternated between holding our breath and gasping every time a branch broke. We could see Chad's arm shaking as he tried to hang on to one handhold while struggling to find the next place that could support his weight. As he neared the top and it became more and more likely that he would live through this, I started to let myself dream. I saw us laughing this off at someone's campground, telling the story of our stupidity to the strangers who helped us. In the end, I guess I shouldn't have hoped for that much, because when he did reach the top, all we heard from him was "Fuck."

"Nothing?" I yelled up, my throat dry.

"Nothing," he shouted back, winded.

"Okay, come down!" was all Megan had to say.

Megan and I were actually pretty useful on the way down, at least, because we could see the markers before he could. We prompted him with "no!" "okay, yes" "no, farther left" "yes, there!" all the way to the ground, where we found that his palms were red and scratched to bits from how hard he'd been gripping the handholds. Megan had to pry his fingers open slowly. They were almost stuck in a claw shape. She cleaned the biggest wounds with boiled water, because he wasn't scratched up bad enough to justify an alcohol wipe, and then wrapped them in bits of fabric cut from the inner lining of a jacket, because the Band-Aids weren't big enough to keep the whole palm covered but the wounds weren't bad enough to use up the gauze.

And that was that. That was how we found out we'd wandered into the middle of nowhere, confirmed. It was good teamwork though! As I fell asleep that night, I remember thinking it was like an extreme version of one of those corporate training exercises. You know? Those ones where they bring in special team-building "experts" and you spend the day wasting your time on office scavenger hunts or making Twister-like shapes with your bodies in small groups of coworkers. I smiled into the dark as I thought, if only those corporate team-building people could have seen us. They would have thrown us a conference room pizza party. I shouldn't have said that. Now I want pizza.

~AA Brown

SAVANNAH

WHEN I WAS nine, I was really into Ancient Egypt, so much so that the other kids started calling me Mrs. Tut. They did it so relentlessly that I had to move schools. That's how I met Michelle. She was the first person to talk to me at my new school—she liked my pink velvet pencil case. After the transfer, I learned my lesson and kept my obsession under wraps, pretending to everyone I'd gotten over it while poring over books about Nefertiti in the middle of the night when I was supposed to be asleep. It fascinated me how much of a life the archaeologists could put together from only a tomb. I want to do the same with Ava and try to piece together who she was as a person—I'll use what I have and what I can find out with some light sleuthing. The job should be easier than an Egyptologist's, because Ava had the internet while she was alive.

I pour myself a glass of wine—white, because I am very paranoid about staining this already very dirty book—and then kidnap Zelda from where she is peacefully sleeping on her cat tree to make her sit in bed with me instead. I get out a fresh notebook of my own and a pink pen, put on my book-reading gloves, take two deep breaths, and get out Ava's journal. In order not to violate my own rules, I have the spot where I left off, after Megan yelled at Chad and dug her nails into the dirt, earmarked with a Post-it, and I won't go past that spot unless I'm in my official reading space with Ava. My plan is to go through the parts I've already read and make note of any facts Ava has told me about herself so far, as well as anything she says that makes sense to her but not to me. I also need to figure out what the deal is with the words on Ava's arm so I can fully appreciate them before they're gone.

At the top of the page I write *Ava Addison Brown*. Under her name I write *vissi d'arte*. It looks like a tribute. It also makes me miss school. Weird combo. I run my gloved fingers down the pages of her journal line by line, collecting little snippets of her.

I write *poor.* I write *artist.* I put a colon next to *artist.* I write *opera singer.* I write *lesbian.* I write *in love with coworker Megan.* I write *watches Discovery Channel.* I write *watches Naked and Afraid.* I put a star next to *watches Naked and Afraid* and *watches the Discovery Channel* and, hesitantly, *lesbian*. These are the things we have in common. I write *died for pussy.* I almost put a star next to *died for pussy*, but I don't, because her case is a little more serious than mine. I write *lost since Labor Day.* I write *liked Doritos.* I write *420 friendly.* I add a star for both. I write *yellow gold not white gold* because of her jewelry. I write *black hair.* I write *PFO* with a question mark next to it. I write *YAP* with a question mark next to it. I write *worked in office* with a question mark next to it. I write *not vegetarian.* I write *especially not anymore*, but then I cross it out because that seems insensitive. I write *seemed nice.*

I sit back and admire my work, watching the puzzle of her come together. I put Ava's journal down and side-eye Zelda while she sniffs at it, then pull out my laptop to head over to Google. I hit Zelda with the "ah! ah!" before she can get too comfortable, and she backs off and starts licking her paw.

I don't look up Ava's name right away, because that's venturing outside the little bubble I've built for us where keeping her has no consequences, but I know in reality she probably has family and friends looking for her. I know that when I google her name, I'll have to look her personhood in the eye for the first time. I'm not saying I regret what I'm doing. I mean, I do regret it in short tsunamis of guilt that bring me to my knees, but I don't regret it enough to call the police right now.

I finish my glass and pour another. When I type in pfo, I get some medical info about hearts with holes in them. From context, I don't think that's right, so I type in pfo yap instead. Same heart thing. My last try is pfo yap opera. Bingo. Something called a Yap Tracker pops up, so I click through that and discover that YAP stands for Young Artist Program.

Apparently, when opera singers are like twenty-two to thirty, they audition for these programs where they train and perform while donors pay a pittance that they call a living stipend. Allegedly, you're supposed to be able to do the program and focus full-time on your studies. And it seems like you kind of have to do them, because if you don't, there's no way for people to notice you. The website is bleak and has very little free information, so it's hard to snoop for more than the basics. No forums or nothin'. It looks like it hasn't been updated since it was built in 2005, and it's decorated like it wants your dreams to die. I'd have to pay fifty-nine dollars to access the whole site, so I return to Google, search up a list of well-known YAPs, and pick a couple at random.

I type PFO Merola. More weird heart condition PSAs. I type in got PFO from Merola. This time the first result is a tweet from someone called Maggie the Mezzo that reads Whelp. Just got my pfo from Merola. Tis the season! with an upside-down smiley-face emoji and a shrugging-brunette emoji. Thank God I'm in the generation that's good at the internet. I click on the tweet. Maggie looks to be about my age, maybe a year or two older. There's a quote tweet from an account named Papageno whose profile picture is a man dressed as a giant bird. The tweet says brb finding out if birds have loins so i can gird mine. I smile. I follow the bird man. There are a couple of comments on his quote tweet, one of which catches my eye. What's pfo stand for? Thank you so much to Twitter user Lil Broke Menace for asking. And somebody even replied! Please fuck off:) the reply says. I'm picking up my pen to write *young artist program* next to *YAP* and *please fuck off* next to *PFO* when I catch a glimpse of the replier's account name: Ava Is Anxious.

"No fucking way," I say loud enough that one of sleeping Zelda's ears bends back toward me.

My heart pounds like it hasn't since that one time Michelle dared me to drink four Red Bulls back to back when we were twelve. I spent the night wide-awake worried that my heart would explode all over my lavender bedroom walls and then my mom would be mad at me for having to repaint. I'm talking myself down, telling myself there must be at least a few opera people named Ava, when I notice her handle: @missavaaddison. It has to be her.

I click into her account. Her bio says, i sing better than you:). I smile when I read it. I like Ava so far. Her birthday is May 3. She's thirty-three. I write *birthday: May 3rd, 33*. She lives in New York, New York. I write *~~lives~~ lived in NYC*. It's weird looking at Ava's Twitter like this, scrolling through tweets about work and politics and times the MTA wasn't working right. It's all so normal looking that it's unsettling. If you don't look at the dates, it's like she's still here. It makes me think about how many ghost profiles must be haunting the internet by now.

Her last tweet is the only thing that signifies what happened, because it has a ton of comments underneath. Hundreds. It's just a picture of some trees on the side of the road with the caption Upstate! from September 2. There are one or two early comments like so pretty! and enjoy!, but the vast majority are things like:

We miss you!

You have been on my mind all of these weeks

RIP Queen!

Praying for you guys!

Heard you sing a few years back, hope someday we all get to hear from you again!

love you, hope you're safe wherever you are:)

don't worry, we're still looking for you guys

Heartbroken </3

I glance sideways at the notebook. I don't think she knew that she was loved enough for all of these people to be worried about her, but I wish she had. Maybe then she would have found the will to make it just a little longer and then I could have helped her. I would have helped her.

I shiver as the guilt hits. I know, I know. It's bad. I'm keeping answers from all these people. I drag my finger across the cursor, doomscrolling, feeling sicker with every comment I read until I get dizzy and have to stop. I close my eyes as tight as they'll go, like a kid pulling the covers over their head in the night so they can't see the monster when it comes out from under the bed. Like somehow what I can't see can't hurt me. But all closing my eyes does is evict the tears that have apparently been forming and leave me batting at my face with a cat-hair-covered blanket.

I backtrack out of the consequences-of-my-actions comments section and read over my list again, piecing Ava together like a blind person running their hand over a face. I add a couple of things I learned from the tweets I skimmed. I write *likes pink* (there was a tweet of a pink MacBook and a pink notebook and a pink coffee mug on a desk, so I think it's safe to assume). I write *fan of NYT crossword puzzle*, because there are a lot of screenshots of the comments section of the *NYT* crossword. The middle-aged seem to be taking that shit very seriously.

I realize that I've been avoiding looking at her profile picture, like she was Medusa or something. You'd think seeing her alive would be easy now that I've seen her dead so many times, but when I finally do decide to click on her profile picture to get a good look, I really have to hype myself up. I'm starting to think I might be broken inside, because most people prefer seeing the living version of the people in their lives. I guess I just prefer seeing whatever version I saw first.

Hils would say this is an example of my aversion to change, but I disagree: my Ava changes all the time. And this Ava—her life before the woods—is so foreign to me that it reminds me she's a stranger. If there's a funeral, no one will invite me. I never heard her laugh. I never spent the night talking to her on the phone about nothing. But she feels so much like a friend that I'm scared it'll break my heart, seeing a version of her I don't recognize at all. Ava as she died is my friend and I know her better than anyone, but Ava as she lived wouldn't have even crossed my path, which makes me a friendless loser, trying to possess her without her consent, no better than your average psychotic asshole. The shame creeps across my skin like a rash.

When I make myself look at her picture, it's a form of penance. Honestly, she held up to the woods pretty well. She's a good forty or fifty pounds heavier than the Ava I found. Her hair is a couple of inches shorter, styled in a fluffy black pixie. Her cheeks are pink and round. Her skin is clean and white. Her mouth is thin, but her lips are full, berry red and glossy with a couple of layers of lipstick, and curled slightly upward in a close-lipped smile. In her ears are the earrings she's still wearing now.

This is my Ava. Was. I spread my fingers apart against the screen to zoom in on her eyes, which I've never seen. They were green, with little flecks of gold and hints of darker brown near the pupils. They're adorned with simple makeup, just black liner that barely forms a wing, mascara, and a touch of soft gold glitter. Life makes her look so shiny and loud. My Ava, but as seen through those glasses that can cure color blindness. In the picture, she's wearing a silky black blazer with nothing underneath. She's leaning forward, her elbow propped up on a table we can't see, her chin resting on a hand dressed in many rings. Something about her makes me lean in, too. She was magnetic. Something wet splats on my mouse pad and I realize I'm crying now because I never got to meet her.

She was really beautiful.

AVA

Okay, this is irrelevant to the plot, but every time I think back on this story it makes me smile. Megan's going to hate me for putting it here though.

It was one of those freak scorching-hot days in late September and we were all lying around in this mossy area near our camp where the ground was softer and cooler. Chad was reading the guidebook, his head propped up on a smooth rock covered in thick moss. I was flat on my back, staring up, counting leaves on branches and wishing they were chicken nuggets. Megan, next to me, kept fidgeting, shifting her hips from side to side like her ass was a windshield wiper. I asked her if she was okay, but she just smiled at me, said she was fine, and stopped fidgeting for ten minutes. When she started up again, I just pretended I didn't notice for the next half hour of silence. And then the snoring started. I looked over and Chad had fallen asleep, mouth wide open, guidebook splayed on his chest. I poked Megan in the arm with two fingers.

"Chad's knocked out!" I told her, pointing out the funny expression on his face. Asleep, he looked like a kid. I wondered if this was what he looked like when he was a Boy Scout.

Megan smiled and said something like "Yeah, that's cute," but her eyes seemed far away, distracted and a little distressed. I sat up and she mirrored me.

"Are you sure you're okay?" I asked her.

She looked around frantically, her big blue eyes even wider than usual. Then she glanced at Chad again. She sighed, her shoulders fell, and she looked to me in defeat, little pools of tears forming on her bottom lashes but not spilling over. "I think I've been wiping my ass with poison ivy," she whispered finally. She smacked me in the shoulder when I burst out laughing immediately, but what else was I supposed to do?

"It's not funny!" she hissed, scooting back and forth against the moss like a dog scratching its butt on the carpet.

"It's pretty funny."

"It hurts!"

"I know, I'm sorry!" I did know. At least three of my siblings had run-ins with poison ivy when we were growing up. I spent many a long night rubbing ointment onto rashy body parts while the afflicted squirmed in my arms and cried about how much it hurt.

"I don't know what to do—it's so fucking itchy!" she said, tears in her eyes.

"Well, first you have to stop scratching it." I motioned to how she was scooting back and forth.

"I'm trying." She said the words between scoots. I bit the inside of my cheeks to keep from smiling. "Sorry, I know I look ridiculous."

I thought she looked adorable, but instead of revealing that, I just shook my head and said, "Nah, you're fine. You should probably switch to using the moss that grows in the water though. It's softer and the water coming off it makes it feel a little cleaner, like a bidet, kind of." We had run out of toilet paper two weeks prior and had left alternatives up to individual choice.

"Thanks for the recommendation," she grumbled. "Do you think it'll get infected?"

"Probably not. Just keep it clean and we'll figure something out if you think it's getting worse," I told her.

But by later that night, it was pretty clear it was getting worse. She paced and paced in front of the fire, grumbling the whole time, while

Chad and I watched, drinking tea for dinner and pretending it was soup, our eyes following her like the ball in a tennis match.

Chad cleared his throat. "Everything okay, Megan?"

"I'm fine," she said through gritted teeth.

"You don't seem fine."

And then I made an executive decision. "She wiped her ass with poison ivy," I told him.

"Ava!" Megan snapped at me at the same time as Chad's face broke into a mile-wide grin. "Don't laugh at me, Chad!"

"I'm not laughing," he said, hands up, palms forward. To his credit, he wasn't laughing, but the corners of his mouth were about to touch his eyes, he was smiling so hard.

"I think you'll be more comfortable in the long run if you can just be uncomfortable freely and let us help you with stuff, and if that's going to happen, he needs to know what's going on too."

"I hate you both," she said, glaring into the dirt.

"Why don't you let me take a look at it?" I offered, then watched her face go through every stage of grief from mortified all the way to resigned.

"You only," she said. "Not Chad!"

"I wasn't going to ask," Chad said. "That would be an HR violation."

Megan rolled her eyes at him. "Alright, fine, Ava can look, but I'm gonna go wash off first."

She grabbed one of the flashlights and stomped into the night. When she returned, we banished Chad twenty paces into the trees to wait until he was summoned back, and I went into the tent with her. She knelt in front of me, doggy style, so I could see. I shined the flashlight down onto her angry-looking ass. She flinched when the light touched her.

"I'm sorry," she groaned up at me.

"It's okay," I said. "It's not my first rodeo. My siblings used to get this rash all the time. Definitely poison ivy. Is it okay if I wipe it down

with one of the alcohol wipes and then maybe rub some Vaseline on it? I think that will help the pain while it heals."

"You can do whatever you want as long as you make it stop."

So I suited up my hands in the latex gloves from the first aid kit, wiped down the rash with alcohol, and then spread on the Vaseline mixed with some sunscreen, which had aloe vera in it. She moaned a soft "mmm" and relaxed a little when the Vaseline mixture hit. "That feels nice," she said, lowering herself to her stomach and closing her eyes.

"I'll cover you up, but you should maybe stay like that and just let it breathe while you sleep. Don't rub at it."

"Stay exposed??!"

I went out and explained the situation to Chad. To his credit, he offered to sleep outside so she'd be more comfortable. It was a warm clear night anyway, so he was fine. I stayed in the tent with Megan, reapplying my homemade ointment every couple hours whenever she started squirming again. It didn't get infected, thank god. The only real price she had to pay for it was Chad calling her Poison Ivy for two weeks afterward—whenever she snapped at him about it he claimed he was talking about the Marvel character and it was a compliment.

That, and the embarrassment of it all. She told me once that if I ever told anyone about this, she would haunt me when she died. Your move, Megan. Your move.

~AA Brown

SAVANNAH

I READ ALL her tweets. I peruse her website. I zoom in on every picture in her gallery. When those aren't enough, I find her Instagram. I click into every picture and read every caption, careful not to like anything. I watch her YouTube channel, including the instructional videos aimed toward children from when she taught baby music classes in her mid-twenties. I rewatch the ones of her singing. I imagined her voice would be like a hug, but it's more of a hard slap in the face. The kind that's so forceful it almost cracks your neck. A beautiful scream.

I get out my big over-the-ear AirPods for the occasion, turn the volume all the way up, and play every recording I can find of hers on repeat. I go for a Google Maps walk through her neighborhood in Washington Heights. I find an old Zillow listing of her apartment and take a virtual tour. She had a blog ten years ago, before she left the church. It's a scarier read than the *Decomposition Book*. I've always found religious people unsettling. They have the same energy as hardcore Disney adults.

I also read all the news articles and amateur sleuths' Reddit posts I can find about her group's disappearance and come across some theories I don't expect. Most people seem to agree that the three simply went on a hike and got lost. But there's a subset of very adamant people who don't think that's what happened at all. They think if that had happened, there's no way the rescue efforts wouldn't have found any traces of them.

Apparently, the rescue efforts were huge. Literally thousands of people looked for them, officially and unofficially, for months, including experienced hikers, friends and family, campground rangers, police, official search and rescue groups, and, with enough pressure on the HR department of their joint workplace, even their office staff was given the option of taking paid days off if those days were used to help with the search. They sent helicopters. They sent cadaver dogs. Nothing. It was like the wilderness ate and digested them. The lack of concrete answers sent people speculating. The white women with true crime podcasts started alleging that Chad murdered the two women, disposed of their bodies like a pro, and now was on the run, likely already having fled to Canada. I think of the clueless man that Ava describes in her journal and burst out laughing. He couldn't even follow a compass let alone commit a flawless double murder and fake his own death, but I guess these people wouldn't know that. For them it's *no body, yes crime.*

Ava has a lot of people looking for her. She was very popular at work for always getting her shit done on time, being kind and generous to everyone in the office, and bringing doughnuts on Mondays. She always brought coffee for Megan, too, but not for anyone else. The coworkers they interviewed said Ava and Megan were good friends and shared a cubicle, which has since become a small office memorial. There are pictures of it in *The New York Times* article: two gray desks covered in flowers and pictures of the two of them—together, and separately—at office parties. Megan was also very beautiful, effortlessly wavy dirty-blond hair that fell past her shoulders, giant blue eyes, full pink lips, and a body of soft curves. She looked like she could have been an influencer. I zoom in on her hand in one photo of her holding a glass of wine on a rooftop to see the clean, almond-shaped French tips that Ava described in the journal.

Ava also had a lot of outside-the-office friends, mostly gathered through singing gigs around the city. A few of them built a website dedicated to the search, with a hotline, and hosted concerts to fundraise donations, which largely kept the efforts going even after the officials gave up hope and stopped pouring taxpayer dollars into it. There isn't much effort from most of her family, save for her oldest sister, who is just as involved with the search as her singer friends. She moved to New York temporarily and is staying in Ava's apartment, paying her rent with the help of her friends, hoping she'll come home. The rest of them—and there are many, eight siblings at least—don't seem to care at all. I guess they're very religious and don't approve of her being gay. A reporter found her mom in Utah and interviewed her. He described her as distant and disinterested. All she's quoted as saying is, "We're praying for her, as we always have."

What a cunt.

My notebook is overflowing with information now. My brain is stuffed and strained trying to hold it all. I can feel it sizzling against my skull like an overheated laptop. I take a break and call my mom.

"Mom," I say, "thank you for actually caring about me."

"Are you losing your mind?" my mom asks.

"What?"

"Are you okay? That came out of nowhere. Are you sure you're not going a little nuts there by yourself?"

"What? No, I just wanted you to know that I appreciate you!"

"I appreciate you, too, baby. I love you very much. Are you sure you're okay?"

"Yes, Mom! I'm fine. I'm just trying to be grateful!"

"Okay, jeez. I get it, Savannah, you're grateful, thank you very much. Don't yell at me for checking on you. This book I've been reading on audiobook says that we're supposed to monitor you for signs you might be tying up loose ends in your life just in case—"

"Mom, I'm not suicidal!"

"The bill in my mailbox from your 5150 says otherwise. Besides, I thought you said it was a good thing that I give a fuck about you."

I sigh and think of Ava's shitty mom. "You're right, thank you for caring, but I am very much okay."

I stare at the detritus on my bed, my horizontal murder wall, where I'm pulling Ava's life apart bit by bit in a way that makes me wonder if I'm not worse than the maggots, and it makes me think, *God, am I really okay, though?*

And because my mom can smell guilt on me like a bloodhound, she asks, "What are you doing?"

I say, "Just doing some research. I'm gonna watch an opera later, I think."

"An opera? Like the Phantom? Where did that come from?"

"It's a project my friend is doing for school. I'm helping her. She doesn't have time to watch all three of the operas that her professor wants her to, so I offered to watch one and give her the key points."

My mom perks up. She loves it when I appear to have made a non-Michelle friend. "Oh! What friend? New friend? Do I know her? Is it, um—" she lowers her voice "—a girlfriend?"

"No! Mom! No! It's not, it's, um, it's my friend, uhhhhh . . . Ava?"

Fuck!

"From school?"

"Yep, Ava from my American Lit class. We wrote a paper on *Moby Dick* together." My mom does not know enough about an English degree to know that we don't write collaborative papers.

"Oh, very nice," she says, satisfied. I mute myself so I can exhale without giving it away.

"I actually have to go now," I say, eager to get the hell out before I can bury myself any deeper in lies. "Ava's thing is due soon and she's calling me for my rundown in a few hours, so I have to get on this opera. Operas are long." Are they? They are, right? That's why old people like them. They have all that retirement time to take up.

"Okay, honey, I'm proud of you for branching out! That's great! Enjoy your opera!"

Oof. I can already tell I'm going to freak out about this whole conversation in the middle of the night.

"Okay! I will! Love you, bye!"

I hang up. Yikes. Hopefully she forgets about "my friend Ava" within a few days or I'll have to gaslight her.

I turn my attention back to the notebook. One thing is left circled. The words on Ava's dagger tattoo, *vissi d'arte*. I looked it up and apparently it's the title of a song in an opera called *Tosca*. I've never seen an opera. I've never even *thought* about going to see an opera. Not on purpose—it's just not really on my generation's radar as an activity, but I'll do it for her. I'm kind of excited about it, actually. I liked Ava's YouTube clips a lot, so I think maybe I underestimated opera.

She talks about singing the role of Tosca on her Twitter. In an Instagram caption on a picture of her tattoo from last year, she says she got it because she'd acquired her first *Tosca* contract at Des Moines Metro Opera in Iowa. Now their website has a picture of her on the *Tosca* page with an announcement that states:

> **Ava Brown has had to pull out of the role of Tosca due to unforeseen, still unexplained circumstances. Our thoughts and prayers are with Ava and her family at this time, and we wish her a safe return. She will be replaced in this production by soprano Jennifer Green.**

God, all that work just to get replaced by a Jennifer, who I decide I do not like in solidarity. Poor Ava. I don't really know what I want yet, and the only thing I have to compare it to is all the work I did to love Michelle and earn her love back only for her to drop me like I was nothing. I get it enough for my heart to hurt for us both. I drag my mouse across Ava's picture like I'm running my hand across her cheek. When I watch the opera, I will imagine her singing it.

I make it a whole thing in her honor. I scoop up Zelda and my laptop and relocate us all to the couch downstairs. I pop popcorn to share with Zelda as a bribe to keep her sitting with me. I pop a bottle of champagne, too. Zelda's tail is puffed but she does not get off the couch because there's popcorn in a little pile beneath her face. I find the opera on YouTube, subtitles and everything. I guess piracy law is less strict when the people with the copyright are long dead. I was right—opera is long, longer than a movie, so it's a good thing I set up camp.

I'm sure Michelle would think this is stupid. She always thought that about any activity or hobby that I didn't submit to her for approval in advance. In the third grade, my grandmother showed me how to knit, and I was really proud of my new skill and fascinated by the concept of making a whole wearable thing with my hands. I spent all Christmas break knitting Michelle a magenta scarf; at the time magenta was her favorite color. When I showed up to school, beaming, with the lumpy gift-wrapped scarf held out in my little hands, she just laughed and said it was dumb, that I wasted my whole two weeks knitting like an old lady, but that's why she loved me, because I was weird like that.

She never wore the scarf. Said it was crooked and she had better ones from the store. It was the first and last thing I ever made. When I close my eyes to sleep, sometimes I can still see her twisting the scarf around in her fists while I wished she would be more gentle with it, inspecting it with a contorted expression on her face like it was a worm. Only, for some reason, in my head she's not nine years old; she's grown up and in her eyes I can see the decade more of experience she has in hurting me now.

I wish I still thought she was only trying to break me down and build me back up until I was good enough for her, good enough to be loved the way I loved her. I can't accept that all

I ever was to her was useful. I gave her so many little gifts like that scarf to show my love, but they were never enough. I gave her offerings like she was a god, but like a god, she never actually touched them or thanked me.

Michelle would go to the opera, sure, but not to try to feel anything about it. She'd go just to wear a pretty dress and take pictures of herself holding a champagne flute to post with a non-opera-related caption, and she'd leave after intermission, laughing, complaining loudly all the way out that she was so bored she almost fell asleep like three times. And I'd follow behind her, stuttering soft apologies at the ushers, wishing we'd stayed until the end, but happy my hand was in hers as she tugged me toward the door.

Michelle was so loud in her distaste that I've made a life for myself, for years, not doing anything that she would see as stupid. So when I press Play on the opera, it feels like an act of rebellion. It makes me nervous, guilty, afraid of getting caught. I think of her catching me like this, drunk and frumpy, watching an opera to learn more about my favorite stranger's corpse. In my head, her catching me like this will also lead me to tell her everything about Ava. I think of all the ways it will happen. Zelda will manage to press the FaceTime button with one of her tiny toe beans or I will skim it with a blanket or someone in the opera will sing something that sounds like "Hey Siri, FaceTime Michelle!" and Siri will call her, because it will be the one time Siri listens, and then Michelle will see me and I will see her and I will tell her everything, because I always tell Michelle everything, and then she'll tell everyone and people will think I'm a necrophiliac even though I've never once been a necrophiliac.

Thinking about how she would react makes me feel like I need to confess; it's like being locked in the box with the world's bitchiest priest. I miss most of the first act checking my phone over and over again to make sure that I am not accidentally calling Michelle to confess, then I check my recent calls to make sure I haven't just missed it. I peek over my shoulder, twice, just in case she's somehow behind me. I check my phone again. I turn it off. I check to see that it's off. I make myself stop, because Hils wouldn't like it, and fidget through the rest of Act I, drinking, alternating petting Zelda and scratching the skin off the top of my right foot, wishing I still had those knitting needles so I could use them to stab myself.

I catch enough of the plot. Tosca's boyfriend fucked up and harbored a fugitive and now the OG dirty cops are mad at them. They're torturing him and she's negotiating, but it's not going well because this universe's proof that politicians haven't changed in hundreds of years is trying to rape her in exchange for her man back. Typical. He's on top of her screaming, "Mine!" and she's pinned to a couch, screaming, "No! Help!" It's violent enough to make me pull my head out of my ass and really watch. Huh. I tilt my head to the side like a curious puppy. Opera's kind of metal. Tosca's sort of saved when some drums start playing in the background and the politician gets off her and goes to the window to check it out. It's still not good, though. He says the drums just mean they're getting ready to execute her boyfriend. He says she has an hour to let him fuck her or she dies. Tosca slumps on the couch and it all goes quiet. I'm thinking, weird place for a commercial, and I'm getting ready to get a refill on my champagne when I hear it. Still half lying across the bad man's couch alone in the silence, Tosca opens her mouth, and a very tiny *"vissi d'arte"* comes out.

"Oh shit! Zelda! Wake up! It's happening!" Zelda opens one angry eye, then closes it.

I sit up and lean forward so I can make sure I'm catching all of the subtitles. *I lived for art. I lived for love. I've never harmed anyone.* She sits up and stares down, palms up and shaky on her lap. She hides her face in her hands and cries while a cello plays in the background. She lists the ways she's been a good and devout person and stays down for a second, rocking back and forth and crying while she asks God why he would repay her like this. I nod along with her. I agree, it's bullshit. The words *perché perché, Signor—Why, why, God?*—are on her lips over and over again as she gets up, only to fall to her knees with one last beautiful, desperate scream. *Why do you repay me this way?* She whimpers these last words at the floor. Somehow even the soft parts are loud enough for everyone to hear, even though she has no microphone. But maybe the audience feels the tightness in their chests right about now like me, realizing they've been so quiet because she's the only one in the room breathing.

When the bad guy comes back to collect, she stabs him, repeatedly, with a knife she found, asking with her whole chest if he's choking on his blood yet. It's a bad bitch move and I cheer for her so hard that Zelda finally decides she's fed up and slinks upstairs for some peace. I'm confident heading into the end that one, this won't be my last opera, and two, my girl Tosca has got this.

I am dead wrong, at least on the second part. Tosca's boyfriend dies anyway. The rapist gets the last laugh from beyond the grave. And Tosca throws herself from the parapet of a church. I watch the bows and clap for the woman who sang Tosca even though she can't hear me and sit for a second after the screen goes black, staring at nothing while I finish the bottle of champagne. I think of Michelle, getting ready for the spring break trip to Miami that I was supposed to be on with her. I think of Ava, rotting against a tree in my backyard when she's supposed to be on a stage. The world has always been better to the villains. At least Tosca took one out with her.

SAVANNAH

I THINK I missed a crucial PSA about the decomposition process. It's my fault for not being out here for two days and for underestimating the power of the weather when it comes to rotting flesh. In my defense, on my first day with Ava, it was about this temperature, sixty-two-ish, but back then she was fresh, only a little bit dead, like an octopus at a fancy sushi restaurant that they stab in the head in front of you and serve up still squirming. Since that first day, it's been cold again, in the thirties, at most forty, until yesterday when it shot back up to the sixties and stayed there. And that temperature change has really set everything off.

For the first time, I'm having the Hollywood corpse experience. I smell her before I see her. It's so strong it makes me back up a couple of steps and question my life's choices before I even reach her spot. I strap my mask on before I keep moving, but it doesn't help as much as it used to.

The smell is thick, like a fog you can't see through. It smells like a pile of trash on the street outside a surf-and-turf restaurant in July, if all the garbagemen in the city forgot about it for a few Tuesdays and the trash pile was getting bigger all the time and every day someone came by and sprayed it with citrus-scented Febreze. It makes my eyes water. I force myself to get closer, and the smell gets thicker. I can't help but imagine it sticking to me more and more as I walk, like if someone had thrown her into a wood chipper I happened to be standing in front of, and I kept stepping forward to shower in the chunky rotten mist. Okay, maybe that's a little dramatic, but the smell is *brutal*. Trust.

When I see her, it's even worse. I was never afraid to die before, but now I am. All that skin care she must have done to look that good in her headshots, and now all that hard work's been decimated. She's puffed up, almost double her original size in some places, her stomach and chest especially. My brain searches for some frame of reference for what I'm seeing and the only thing that comes up is that scene in *Shrek* where Shrek and Fiona blow into live woodland creatures to float on strings like balloons. Ava is what would happen if Shrek blew up the ass of a zombie. The green and purple splotches on her skin are a cursed moldy pizza dough, stretched out thin and yellowing at the edges. Her lips and the area just around them are black and vibrating with maggots, and the undulating layers of bugs make it look like she's blowing raspberries at me. I gulp through a wave of gags until I'm squirming, too, tears running down my face as I try not to puke.

I was planning on a lot today. I wanted to tell her about my experience watching an opera for the first time and hearing her sing and learning all the things I've learned, but I wasn't anticipating this. I can't even keep my eyes on her without at the very least dry heaving, and the smell is choking me. I breathe through my mouth in small, quick gasps, but I swear I can taste the smell. It feels like I'm chewing on chunks of her just by being here. My chest is tight. This will have to be a very quick visit.

Luckily I thought it would be colder so I'm already wearing gloves; I don't want the smell to get on any unnecessarily exposed bare skin. I don't want to stay here a second longer than I have to. I fish Ava's journal out as fast as I can and pull it open to the page I'm glad I bookmarked. I feel bad, but I'm fighting a full-body urge to get all the way the fuck out of here that I'm sure is some sort of innate survival instinct. I get that this situation involves seeing the reality of death up close and confronting mortality and all that, but this is mortality beating my ass in a way I was not ready for and couldn't even fully comprehend until now.

I force myself to read every word without skimming, but bless Ava for making this a short entry. In the notebook it barely takes up a whole page, just a couple of paragraphs accompanied by a folded-up piece of paper—a smaller page, from a different notebook, spiral bound, judging by the feather-like flecks of paper still gripping the left edge of the page. It's an inventory list of all the supplies they had on hand when they first realized they were lost. The small paper is full, front and back, some of the handwriting different than Ava's. The letters Ava didn't write are bigger and rounder than hers. I'm assuming the new handwriting is Megan's. It's too girlie to be Chad's. I let myself skim the list. I'll study it later, when I'm out of here. Right now I just need to be away from the smell. My chest is starting to hurt from holding my breath.

I try to look at her again before I leave, out of obligation. I feel bad that all I've done is sit here gagging at the smell and turning away at the sight of her. The bloat strains against her clothes, making her look a bit like an old sausage in a too-tight casing. She's wearing two layers of jackets. The outer one is a green windbreaker. The inner one is a fitted workout jacket that's zipped up to her neck, where the flesh puffs out like a misplaced muffin top, begging for just a little more space. I debate pulling down the zipper to give her some extra room to decompose. I hover above her body, holding my breath, thinking about it. I picture myself bending down and trying to tug the zipper. The zipper is stuck. I pull harder. The zipper comes down, taking a wet chunk of Ava's chest with it. Okay, nope. I won't be doing that today. I stare again at where her purple neck strains against the fabric. If I stay here, is she going to explode on me?

I swallow the bile that floods my mouth at the thought of it and jump back. Yep. That's extremely enough for today. I run home, choking and crying like I've been tear-gassed. When I get to the house I stand outside, not knowing what to do. I just know the smell's clinging to me. I'm still wearing the gloves. I'm desperate to get everything off, but so grossed out that I don't even want to touch me. Shuddering, I start with the gloves, dumping them in the trash by the garage even though they aren't the disposable kind. I never want to see them again. I know I didn't actually touch her, but my brain keeps telling me that I did and somehow forgot. I press the button that opens the garage, put down my backpack, and strip entirely, leaving my clothes, mask, and shoes in a big pile on the floor to be burned at a later date. I shower for an hour and emerge red and raw from head to toe like a seafood boiled crawdad. I still don't feel clean. I may never feel clean again.

AVA

"Ugh, I'm never going to feel clean again," Megan said, scrubbing at one of her armpits with a wet rag. I watched, trying not to look like I was watching—seeing her with armpit hair made it easier to fathom I had a shot. Megan and I took once-or-twice-a-week baths with a bit of soap, but you can never come out of river water feeling like you actually showered.

"I'm embracing it," Chad said.

"Oh, we know," Megan replied, and I laughed.

He was propped up on a rock, sunning, taking a break from trying to make fishing hooks. We'd had a couple lucky finds: some discarded and hopelessly tangled fishing line, and five safety pins that I'd forgotten I'd pinned to the inside of my bag after leaving a costume fitting. I was on untangling duty that day. We'd been taking turns for days because the task was so frustrating. I was determined to be done, so I was working extra hard at it. Chad was using the shitty pliers on the Swiss Army knife to bend the safety pins into hooks. Our plan was to attach the line to the little metal circle already looped into the base of the pin.

It had been five weeks, and it was another one of those sticky humid days where you can't step two feet down the street before feeling like you need to go back home and shower. That day, we were hanging out by the fattest stream we could find to beat the heat. We'd been mapping the area, going out in groups of two when we had the energy while one person remained behind to tend the camp—boiling water, cutting firewood, inventorying the supplies, and tidying up as much as possible. We still couldn't find the first stream we'd followed out here, but maybe it dried up. It was, after all, much smaller and shallower than the one we'd set up camp by.

"Chad?" Megan asked.

"Yup?"

"Fuck you for not getting us lost in the tropics. A sea breeze and some coconuts would be amazing right about now."

Chad snorted. "Yeah, like you have beach money."

"Damn," I said, chuckling as Megan's mouth formed a surprised little O. "He got you there."

Chad grinned. We still had toothpaste, and his teeth looked too bright against the dirty scruffy beard he'd grown. He was starting to look older. We all were. Too much sun and too little moisturizer. The lack of food and resulting rapid weight loss made our skin slouch on our faces like reverse Botox. When I dared to use a metal object or a phone screen as a mirror, I saw someone I probably would have avoided eye contact with in a subway station. I mostly tried not to look. Later, I'd use Megan as my mirror instead, because she described me like I was the most beautiful thing in the world no matter the grim reality. Now I don't know. I haven't seen my reflection in months. I'm afraid to look without Megan here to convince me that I'm still beautiful somehow.

Anyway, after one last hour of some of the deepest, most frustrating suffering I'd been through at that point, I finally got the fishing line untangled. I held that fucker up like Simba and the other two cheered like I'd found a tree that grew bottles of hard liquor. We worked to keep up a pretty decent morale in those early days, celebrating and savoring every win to the fullest. I miss that. We thought we were just surviving, but we were closer to thriving than any of us realized. I miss having a team. It really helped.

I handed off the line to Chad so he could thread it with a hook and then helped Megan lift up rocks to look for worms or slugs or anything we could use as bait—things we weren't quite starving enough to want to eat ourselves.

We found a good handful and walked the banks until we scouted a calm area of water where we saw the glimmer of fish scales gliding under the surface. And then we found out Chad was actually a pretty decent fisherman. A couple hours of us sitting dead silent and watching the water, and the line bobbed. We held our breath and waited. It bobbed again, a stronger pull this time. Chad started to coax the line, giving the smallest, gentlest tugs until the fish was visible, shimmering as it bounced just below the surface. Then, with one last big tug, it was on the ground, flopping and gasping and gorgeous. We screamed like straight dudes in dive bars when their team scores in the Super Bowl. I didn't even cringe when Chad beat his chest and roared like Tarzan. Megan smacked the fish over the head twice with a rock, apologizing the whole time. When it was dead, Chad scooped it up and dangled it upside down like a trophy. It was a picture I'd seen and rolled my eyes at a thousand times before, but I'd never been happier to see a white man holding a fish.

~AA Brown

SAVANNAH

SHE'S LAS VEGAS for maggots. They're everywhere, feasting at the all-you-can-eat buffet that is her corpse. They're a blanket so thick that I can barely see her underneath. I'm better prepared this time, at least. I double-masked and put some VapoRub in and around my nostrils for the smell. I also brought a lawn chair from the garage so I don't have to sit in all the Ava-stuffed bugs that are slumping off her body to relax into their food comas.

I set up my chair in my usual spot, sit down, and fish the journal out of my backpack. My brand-new box of surgical-grade latex gloves came in from Amazon today. I put on a pair and packed a spare pair in my bag before leaving the house. Like I said, I'm ready to go today, unlike last time. I pop an AirPod in each ear to drown out the sound of the flies. I put on my regular playlist, which now includes some opera, on shuffle. I tell Ava "No offense" before I hold the notebook high in front of my face so I don't have to look at all the unfortunate things happening to her right now. They are for sure right when they say there's no dignity in death.

I read through their first week in the woods while Cardi B's "WAP" plays in the background. I think I'm getting too comfortable. I'm sure there was a time in my life, not too long ago, where I would be physically unable to happily listen to "WAP" while reading my little book like a tourist sunning on a beach, knowingly two feet from a woman's decomposing body. If someone were to stumble upon me right now, I'd look insane. I'd look like a real-life version of that room at the end of the line for Haunted Mansion at Disneyland, where at first glance all the portraits look tame, like the one of a peaceful, pretty woman in a nice dress holding an umbrella on a sunny day. But when the wall around the portrait stretches out to reveal the whole thing, she's standing on a tightrope over an open-mouthed crocodile.

I finish reading and put the book away. I'm glad I'm making the effort to read it out here. Otherwise, I think I would forget that what I'm reading about is real life. Reading Ava's story in front of her helps me remember that she was real. That she *is* real. A tragedy I can smell. I think I'm learning empathy.

Michelle always said I had no empathy. She mostly said this when I didn't agree with her or whenever she was having a hard time and I didn't sympathize enough, like when the people she bullied would stand up to her. Michelle could dish it out, but she couldn't take it, and part of me was always a little bit on the side of her victims even when I was complicit in hurting them. Michelle would freak out, say it was unfair, say she didn't even really do anything, cry and bitch for days, and I would just nod along because I couldn't bring myself to fully feel sorry for her. When she would notice I wasn't crying along with her, she'd say I have no empathy. Maybe I don't. It's not like I'm demonstrating a whole lot of it now.

It can't all be my fault. It's a generational problem. Corpses have been walking in and out of my life as long as I can remember: 9/11 as a baby, true crime docs always on the TV, the news, live-streamed wars, that Reddit video of a cartel beheading that went around my middle school, Twitter . . . One time the high school next to mine got shot up and we just went back to school the next day like nothing had happened. But with Ava, I have to feel something. She's not just a story; she was a life. I have her voice. I have her handwriting. I have her body. I have something real, for once, in a world where everything unpleasant can just be scrolled past.

I just wish she wouldn't change so quickly. I wish the bugs would eat her slower. I wish the weather would stay colder. I wish I could put her back the way she was and have her as something shaped like a friend again. But I can't stop time, so just like everything and everyone else, she's going away and then I won't have anywhere to go or anyone else to focus on and nobody I can trust not to leave me, except my mom, which is just sad. She's obligated to care about me even when no one else does.

Michelle still has friends, though. Michelle has all the friends I used to have. They chose her in the divorce. She's less sad. She's still fun. She's not the one who's constantly face-planting into some new what-if question she came up with out of nowhere. My former friends are all preparing for spring break with her right now. One of them has been promoted, I'm sure, to my place—to best friend. I think it's Leah. She never did like me.

"What do you think?" I ask Ava. "Do you think it's fucking Leah?"

Ava does not know who Leah is.

"I think it's fucking Leah," I grumble. I pick a stick up off the ground and start snapping it into little pieces, just to have something to do with my hands.

"I'm sorry about your mom. She sounds like a real piece of work. But your sister definitely loves you and you have some pretty loyal friends, so I think you can be proud of yourself even if you never got to live your biggest dreams. I mean, shit. Look. I don't have any friends, and I also don't know what I'm doing with my life. I bet you're thinking how we should have traded places. Or you would be thinking that if you still had a brain. It would have been better if it were me there, right? I'm useless. You already had a purpose and people and a whole life. I'd trade you if it were up to me. I saw *Tosca*, by the way. First opera! I thought it was really good, actually, 'Vissi d'arte' slaps; I see why you got a whole tattoo about it. Love the reference with the dagger. I don't have any tattoos, but maybe I'll get one to remind me of you so you can tell the other ghosts that you had at least one fan and can prove it. Speaking of, I saw your stuff, too, on YouTube. You're really good! See, I know what you are—were—worth. But me? I'm nothing. I'd trade places with you in a second. I'm already as lonely as you look. And loneliness suits death better than it does life, you know?"

I tap my fingers on my knees. It's hard keeping the conversation going when it's just me talking, but nothing comes out of Ava's mouth except maggots. I wish she'd say something, maybe tell me that I'm okay and it'll all be fine, that I'll get through this and make new friends who don't know how many times I've been institutionalized or who Michelle is, that I'll finish school and figure out what I'm meant to do with my life, that I'll date a nice girl who I'll never tell about any of this. I need an adult in my life who isn't my therapist or my mom. I need a friend, someone kind, someone sane.

"I wish you could talk," I say.

I gather my things and stand up. Time to return to the fresh, clear air where my anxiety lives.

"Bye, Ava, see you tomorrow!" I tell her, putting my AirPods back in and shouldering my bag.

"Fat Bottomed Girls" by Queen plays me out.

AVA

There must have been a fall hurricane or something, because it poured for days. Good thing it was still warm enough that if we stayed dry and huddled up at night we didn't need a fire, because there was no dry firewood to be had. Everything was drenched. But the tent was good and waterproof, so we just packed up and moved to higher ground when the first big clouds rolled in, secured everything really well, and hunkered down inside with all our stuff, only leaving to pee or collect a cup of rainwater.

We passed the time playing poker, the tent illuminated by propped-up flashlights. We had a deck of cards, and for chips we used real money, which I'd never done before. Every one of my paychecks had been pre-allocated to cover my basic needs. Sometimes, I'd splurge on something nice, just like everyone else, but I never saw the point in gambling. My resources have always been too precious and precarious to risk. I used to fantasize about it though—about being the kind of unburdened person who could throw money around on a table for fun, not really caring about winning or losing. I guess you could say I was living the dream in that tent, throwing money around. I wonder if billionaires feel about money the way that I felt that night, like it's not even real. We had about $600 cash between us (very much mostly Chad, for emergencies, he said) and it felt like Monopoly money. We pooled the contents of our wallets in the middle of the floor and divided it evenly at the beginning of the game.

We played for hours, passing around bits of smoked fish and berries, the real precious resources. Everyone lost all their money several times, but it didn't matter. When we got to a point where we had a winner and one person had all the money, we would just throw everything back in a pile and split it up again. I tried my best to lose first, so I could watch Megan stare Chad down, nose scrunched, eyes squinted to slits, inspecting the crevices of his face for crumbs of a lie. Two out of three times, she was right, but one time Chad laid down his cards to reveal a full house against her three of a kind. She threw her money down on the sleeping bag, pouting while he cheered and jeered and asked her, "How's it feel to lose, Poison Ivy?" He taunted her so loud that we could barely hear the rain pounding all around us.

"Whatever," she said with an eye roll, counting everything back up into three $200 piles, and he grinned ear to ear, promising a royal flush next time. They'd developed a sibling-like relationship that was sweet to watch, always teasing each other, always bickering, but always joking too, always there for each other at the end of the day. I miss it. I miss having both of them. I miss playing poker in a tent in the rain. I miss the goddamn smoked fish we were so tired of. I miss smiling. I miss laughing. I miss hope. I miss it all.

I don't know. Our little poker night might not seem like much when you look in on us from out there, but that night means a lot to me. I can't remember what we talked about. I can't remember how many games we played. I can remember that it was the last time it was all three of us, as happy and peaceful as we could be in our situation. I think about that night all the time. Looking back on the memory feels like looking at a photo you know was taken moments before a disaster killed every smiling person in the frame. If I'd known what was coming next, I would go back and tell us all not to go to sleep, to stay awake as long as possible, to savor the sweet taste of the berries, to snuggle in a little closer together against the rain—because after that night, shit got real. After that night, we were never that happy again.

~AA Brown

SAVANNAH

I KNOW IT'S going to be a bad night. I knew it when I was in the clearing and the act of talking to Ava wasn't doing enough to combat the loneliness that's been picking at me all day. I've been alone for months, I know. I should be used to it by now. And mostly I am, but some days it gnaws on me. I feel it on my skin like goose bumps.

By the time I get home, I'm restless everywhere like a pair of legs after they've walked for hours. When the door of my house shuts behind me, it feels like the first shovelful of dirt on my coffin. Claustrophobia presses on my chest. I take my slow deep breaths in twos. I almost want to turn around and bolt back out the door, spend the night in the dirt beside Ava, getting chewed up by her bugs instead of by my thoughts. I look around my living room, which is too dark already. I hate the night. It's so much worse at night.

"It's okay," I tell myself out loud. "It's okay. Just need to get to midnight. At midnight there are drugs."

I glance at the clock on the oven: 7:15 p.m.—great. When I blink, I see Michelle filing her nails, taunting me by saying nothing, by making me wait for it. Activities. I need activities. If I have something to do, the time will go by faster. *Routine*. I hear Hils's voice from my sessions. *Routine is your friend*. Okay. I'm still in my Ava clothes, so I should shower. I strip in the kitchen and walk my clothes straight to the washer, a habit I've developed since Ava got really stinky. I head upstairs, turn the knob of the shower, and sit on the edge of the bathtub to wait while the water warms up. I get in when it's hot and stand under the faucet, hugging myself, shivering despite the water. I turn it hotter until it's much too hot. I stand under it and let my skin turn red. I wonder if this is a little bit like what happens to lobsters.

The bathroom fills with steam at the same pace that I fill with dread. I don't even know what I'm dreading yet. It's just a feeling, but it's a loud feeling. It's like when you're being followed, an overwhelming itch to run until you're somewhere safe, but there is nowhere safe. I can't run from inside of myself. I check over my shoulder for the cause of the feeling, but there's nothing concrete there, just a pile of stuff that could happen. My mom could die, then no one would care about me. Some other hiker could find Ava and have her removed before I have the chance to say goodbye. Michelle could find out, somehow, that I see her sometimes even when she's not there; she could use that information to back all the rumors she spread that I'm crazy. I can see her now, making a viral series in which she bats her doe eyes and tells the world her ex–best friend was a psycho, that I dragged her into my insanity, made her do all the crazy things my brain thought up, tried to convince her that she loved me when she didn't, tried to seduce her against her will.

I see her making Twitter posts about the word *enmeshment*, twisting everything to make me the toxic one, telling everyone I was the one who instigated everything that night, that I was just pretending to be a victim for the clout of it. I see strangers believing her without knowing me, spamming me with DMs about how it's so wrong that I pretended to be a victim of something like that, that I made it harder for the real victims to be believed with my tall stack of lies. I see myself, paralyzed into silence, still too fragile to talk about the truth, too afraid that if I expose the wound, all the world will do is stick their salt-covered fingers in the hole and rub in the pain.

And what if anyone ever finds out that I found and kept Ava's body here just so I could have someone to talk to? Then Michelle will triple down and Ava will be even more evidence, the best evidence yet, that I'm clinically insane, poisonous to whoever dares to befriend me, and I won't have a prayer. I see the YouTubers I follow covering the story, referring to me in sentences that start or end with the word *allegedly.* I see this year extending out into the rest of my life, escalating into a situation that will braid itself into my reputation and follow me through the world until finally, mercifully, I die.

I get out of the shower. I dry off. I put on my favorite little cotton shorts-and-camisole pajama set to make myself feel better. It doesn't work. The silence is too loud. It's making me itch. I sit on the side of the bed and scratch at my ankle until it bleeds. I dab at the blood with a towel and watch it stain. I don't bother with a Band-Aid. Drops of blood slide down my foot when I walk.

I yell for Alexa to shuffle my playlist. Alexa does. I go downstairs. I turn on all the lights. I check the time again: 7:48 p.m. I pour myself a glass of white wine from a half-empty bottle in the fridge and chug it. I wipe my mouth with the back of my hand and fill the glass back up with the rest of the bottle. I throw the bottle in the recycling and sit at my kitchen island to sip at the wine while I decide what's next.

I look around, analyzing my surroundings like this is an escape room and I'm in a rush to find the exit. I could clean, but I stayed up most of the night cleaning when I was outrunning my brain yesterday. I wonder if normal people can handle being bored without their thoughts eating them like the bugs are eating Ava. Must be nice.

At 7:57 p.m. I pick up my phone, open TikTok, and start scrolling. I make it a drinking game and take a sip every time I scroll. Chrome nail tutorial. Sip. Clip from the newest season of *Love Is Blind*. Sip. Aesthetic dorm room restock video. Sip. News of another school shooting in Texas. Sip. Makeup tutorial. Sip. New strain of COVID officially made it to New York. Sip. Kitten screaming at itself in a mirror. Sip. Ad for lingerie bundle on TikTok shop. Sip. Trump's being sued again. Sip. Recipe for an easy weeknight pasta dinner . . .

My stomach gurgles watching the noodles hit some garlic oil in a pan on my screen. I guess I could cook something. All I've had today is half a bag of chocolate-covered pretzels and two glasses of cold brew with vanilla creamer. I could cook something. I could make this pasta, probably. It looks easy enough. I get up to check that I have the ingredients. It's just garlic, olive oil, red pepper flakes, salt, pepper, spaghetti, butter, pasta water, fresh parsley, and lemon, the zest and the juice. I have everything except the lemon and the parsley. I decide to sub them out for lemon pepper and dried parsley. I see the time again when I put the water on the stove to boil: 8:22. Fuck me, it's been five minutes.

Okay. Pasta. Only think about the pasta. I watch the video again and slice my garlic thin like the hands on the screen do. The water's boiling, so I drop the pasta in and stir it around until it's submerged. In another pan, I put the oil, the garlic, the pepper flakes, and the regular pepper. It sizzles and the smell drifts up. My stomach growls, but then my brain decides to choose this moment to remind me what we smell like when we die. The rot and the garlic mix together in a horrifying sweet way that makes me feel sick. I have to squeeze my eyes shut and breathe through the nausea until the image goes away. I count to two over and over again until it does. *One two one two*. Everything's fine. My brain is just like this. I open my eyes. 8:43. The pasta's done. I strain it and put it in the pan with the garlic oil. I toss in slices of butter, the parsley, salt, and lemon pepper, and stir. I did not remember to save the pasta water because I am not a real adult. I turn off the stove, then check twice that it's off. I finish my wine and pop a new bottle. I get myself a new glass because this one feels dirty now. I inspect the new glass. The glass is clean, but I have to wash it again before I'm happy with it because I don't remember when I washed it last. I plate up my pasta. I check that the stove is off again. Twice. 8:47.

I take my bowl and my glass to the couch and put on a thirty-eight-minute YouTube video that I only eat during the first seven minutes of. The pasta slaps, at least. When I get up to get my second bowl, the time is 8:59, which feels personal. I check to see that the stove is off. Then I stare at the clock until it turns to 9:00, then return to the couch. I finish my second bowl, clean the kitchen, check to see that the stove is off, play with Zelda, half watch two episodes of *Bob's Burgers*, and finish the second bottle of wine—and somehow it's still only 10:21. I switch from wine to Sprite and vodka and rewatch the first *Twilight* movie because it's on. I wonder if Edward ever turned Bella's Diva Cup into a shot glass, for a little treat. The movie ends at 12:42. I pat myself on the back for managing to make it past midnight as I wobble up the stairs, even though the only reason I made it this far was by being so drunk I forgot about time.

When I get upstairs, I reach for the bottle of Ambien. I'm untwisting the cap when I remember what happened last time. I really want the pill, but every time I try to justify it to myself, I see some new unhinged thing I could do while sleepwalking, so eventually I sigh and put the bottle down. Instead, I reach for the CBD+melatonin gummies my mom sent me. The jar says to take one. I take five. Fifteen minutes that feel like forty-five go by and I reach for my vibrator, hoping maybe an orgasm will help me sleep. It works on men. I turn on the toy, close my eyes, and immediately think of Michelle. I shake my head, trying to think of someone else. Nope. It's Michelle, Michelle, Michelle.

I grab my phone and pull up some porn. The girl touching herself on my screen looks nothing like Michelle. She's a chubby brunette and Michelle is a skinny blonde, but still she manages to morph into her before the image hits my mind. First, Michelle on the bed in the video, fingering herself. But then it's Michelle leaning over the bed from that night. Michelle in the baby-blue angel outfit she wore. The pain spreads in my chest as I start to panic. I swear if I ever have a heart attack, I'll be dead before I know it's even a problem. I turn off the vibrator, toss it to the other side of the bed, close my eyes, and count my breaths in twos. *One, two. In, out.* The room spins from all the alcohol and I grip the sheets in tight fists for stability. *One, two. In, out. One. Two.*

I'M FINALLY ASLEEP when I feel the shadow of something tapping on my thigh. At first I ignore it, thinking it's Zelda trying to gaslight me into believing it's time for a snack even if the timer on her automatic feeder says otherwise, but instead of the insistent little meows I'm waiting for, I hear urgent whispers.

"Hey!" the voice says. "Hey, baby, wake up."

The sleep makes the words sound far away, like they're floating at me through water. The poking hand forms a cup around my upper thigh and squeezes, jiggling the fat back and forth.

"Do you know where we are?"

"My house," I mumble back without opening my eyes just to play along. I assume I'm dreaming, because I have to be. I don't even have neighbors.

"What? Megan, please, wake up and tell me where we are."

Megan? I guess the journal haunts my dreams now, too. Fair enough. I turn my face down, into the pillow. The hand bites down on my thigh.

Ugh, God, fine. With all the melatonin sitting on my eyes, I can only wake up a little. I squint through my curtain of hair expecting to see absolutely nothing and instead find a woman sitting on the edge of my bed.

"Jesus Christ!" I shout, scrambling back against my headboard. I grab for the string that controls my bedroom lamp and pull. I close my eyes just before the room floods with light, half hoping the woman only exists in the dark. But when I open my eyes she's still there, flinching away from me the same way I flinched away from her.

"Who are you?" she yells, her back against my bedroom wall.

"Who am I? What do you mean who am I?! I live here; this is my house. Who are—" And then the adrenaline shoves the remaining weight of the melatonin off me and I can see again and her face registers. "Wait. Ava?!"

"How do you know who I am? Who are you? Where's Megan?"

"I—I'm Savannah."

"Okay, nice to meet you, Savannah. That tells me nothing. How do you know who I am? Why am I here? Where is Megan?"

"I, um, well, these are all very good questions. Maybe you should sit down?" I'm stalling. I don't know what to tell her. How do you tell a ghost that she's dead? Is she even a ghost? Or is she a hallucination? How do I know what she remembers? She doesn't even seem to remember that Megan is dead. She doesn't sit down, doesn't move away from the wall. I wonder if she even can sit, or if she would sink right through the bed if she tried. She crosses her arms over her chest. I study the way her limbs look when she moves. Regular, human, solid. It's weird to me that she's solid. I feel like a ghost should be a little bit see-through, but she's not.

"I'm fine. I just need to know what's going on."

"Well . . ."

"Do you not know what's going on, either?"

"No, I do. I just think maybe you should sit down . . . if you can?"

I hope I'm handling this okay. This is what doctors do when they tell people bad news, right? Have them sit down first and prepare?

"I'll sit when you tell me if you know where Megan is and who you are."

"Okay." I gulp. I worry that I will laugh by accident when I tell her even though it's not funny and I don't want to; I wonder if doctors also worry if they will laugh. In the end, I just spit it out. "I'm so sorry, Ava, but Megan's dead."

"I know Megan's dead," she says, "but if I'm somewhere that's not a cave in the middle of the woods, then that must mean I'm dead, too, which means Megan must be somewhere around here."

"Oh good, you know you're dead," I blurt and then regret it at record speed. "Not that it's good that you're dead, or that Megan's dead or anything like that. It's just good that you know that, because it's a lot less to explain. Not that I would mind having to explain!"

She stares at me and I get insecure about the way I'm handling this—she deserves a real adult right now and I'm just not one.

"Okay." I take a big breath and let it out slowly. Here goes nothing. "So, my name is Savannah. This is my family's lake house in upstate New York. I don't know where Megan is, but, as for you, I, uh, I found your body in the woods behind my house and my best guess is that your spirit got stuck around here, but I don't know any more than that. I'm so sorry."

I don't tell her that I have her journal. I definitely don't tell her that I have her body. I try to tell myself that the reason I don't tell her these details is that it would be too much for one day. I'll tell her tomorrow, if there's even a tomorrow; I could just be dreaming. I'm probably just dreaming. I hope I am, because if I'm not, then I'll have to tell her the truth, and the real reason I'm not telling her now is that I'm worried if she knows the truth, she'll hate me and I'll lose a friend in record time, even for me.

"Okay." She drops her arms and lowers herself back down onto the edge of the bed. The bed supports her just like it supports me. She can sit.

"Yeah. I'm sorry," I say again.

We sit in silence for a minute and I take her in. She's got her pre-woods body back, clean and manicured. She's wearing a dark purple satin slip like one I saw her in on her Instagram. It was one of her opera costumes. She stares at my closet door, contemplating, hands in her lap. I stare at the floor, trying to give her some privacy. She's barefoot and there's no polish on her toes or fingernails.

"How long have I been dead?" she asks.

I think of the maggots, slurping brown ooze from her puffy gray neck. "For a couple of weeks now."

"Weeks? Then why am I only here just now?"

"I don't know. I'm sorry."

"It's okay. It's not your fault you don't know," she says.

She's being so nice to me that it's making me feel worse. I remind myself that she's just a dream, that in the morning there won't be anything left to feel guilty about—except for everything else that there is to feel guilty about.

"This is a lot," she says after several seconds of her contemplating and me fresh out of things I can say that won't sound stupid or useless.

Her voice is so tight that I start reaching my hand out to touch her, but then I pull back, worried that touching her would be the wrong thing, too. She doesn't know me like I know her, and I don't want to intrude. A few tears race each other down her face and drip onto her lap. I look away and let her grieve herself. We sit like that for a while until she's not crying anymore and her shoulders have slouched into a soft acceptance and I feel like it's safe to speak.

"You thought I was Megan?" I ask.

She nods. "You look like her, kind of. Less so now that I can see all of the details, like, her eyes were blue and yours are brown, but you have almost the same hair, same general shape. You look enough like her that it was hard to tell in the dark when I couldn't see your face."

"I'm sorry I'm not her," I say. I'm loose with *I'm sorrys*. I apologize all the time. I always feel like I should, even if all I've done is be alive near somebody else. At least now I have a good excuse. I bet she wishes she was haunting a different house, the house of someone who knew how to do a lesbian-hunting seance maybe.

"It's okay," she says. "It's not your fault."

She accepts things really fast. Probably too fast. Fast enough that I'm still mostly sure she's a dream. I find myself nodding back at her anyway, marveling at the bright green of her eyes up close, staring at the rise and fall of her chest. If this is a dream, I like it. I like her. I hope I dream of her again.

"You look young," she says. "You said you live here by yourself? Sorry! I didn't mean for that to sound as creepy as it did. I'm not really used to talking to strangers anymore."

I almost flinch at being called a stranger, but then I remember that, to her, I am.

"I'm a senior in college, but I don't think I'll graduate this year. I'm kind of taking the semester off. My parents let me stay at the lake house since it's closer to my school than home. I'm from California." I chew my lip, ashamed to be young, ashamed to be taking a semester off, ashamed that my parents have a lake house, ashamed to be from California . . .

"Yeah, don't worry about rushing it. The outside world sucks to be honest. I miss school. How do you know who I am, anyway?"

"I, um . . ." I stop for a second to gulp and stare down hard at my hands. It's just now dawning on me that she might not love this next part. "So I read some of your journal, the *Decomposition Book*—it was with your bag. Sorry. I didn't mean to invade your privacy or anything."

She shrugs. "I mean, I was a corpse to you at the time. I would have read it, too, I'm sure."

We sit in silence again. It's somehow less awkward when she's in corpse form. I feel like I should fill the silence with something, but I don't want to say too much and then have her say nothing else at all, because then I would feel more stupid than I already do.

"So . . . what now?" she asks finally.

I was going to ask her the same thing. I figure since she's the one who has to deal with being dead and trapped in my house all of a sudden, it should be her call. "What do you want to do?"

I hope she doesn't say that she wants to talk a bunch more. She seems nice, but I don't know what I would say and I would worry the whole time about saying the wrong thing by accident and making the weight of her death harder to bear. And I'm not at my best or brightest—my brain's foggy with night. Still, if she wants to talk, I'll do it. I brace myself against the guilt of imagining what we would have to talk about. I can't decide if the dream is becoming a nightmare or not.

"Sleep?" she asks. "It's pretty late, right? We can figure it all out in the morning."

"Do ghosts sleep?"

"I have no idea, but I guess we're about to find out. Do you have, like, a couch I can crash on? I'll sleep anywhere, to be clear—the floor, even! Anything would be better than where I've been, trust me."

I scoop up an extra pillow and motion to her to follow me. She does. Her footsteps make almost no sound, so I keep turning my head and looking back, checking to see that she's still there. Every time I look, I'm shocked to see her, padding along after me like it's nothing. We're halfway down the stairs when I remember that my parents aren't here and the primary bedroom exists. Finally. Something I can offer that's not stupid and useless.

I turn to Ava, grinning. "Guess what?"

"What?"

When I throw open the door at the top of the stairs and gesture for her to look inside, her composure breaks all at once and she makes a running leap for the bed. I jump back, startled by the sudden enthusiasm.

"Oh my God," she groans. Her voice is muffled by all the pillows she has her face buried in, so it sounds like "ermahgerd." I watch her from the shelter of the doorway. She doesn't move for a minute. Her arms and legs are flopped flat out like an upside-down starfish. "I'm just gonna stay like this. Don't mind me," she says without removing her face from the pillows.

I start to tell her good night, but then I remember she's probably just a figment of melatonin's imagination, decide to preserve what little dignity I have left by not talking to the air, and ease the door shut.

When I get back to my room, I toss and turn for hours thinking of all the possible ways this could just be me going more crazy. I finally do manage to sleep by telling myself over and over that it was just a dream. That she'll be gone in the morning and everything will go back to normal and I'll laugh about this and tell her corpse I dreamt of her. It's all going to be back to normal tomorrow. It's just a dream. It's just a dream. It's just a dream.

But when I wake up the next morning, she's still there.

SAVANNAH

I STAND JUST inside the bedroom doorway and watch her sleep, harnessing my inner Edward Cullen. I take a step forward, then another, rolling my bare feet out heel to toe to be extra quiet, like I learned to do in the year of competitive marching band that I did because Michelle was in color guard.

Ava's so pink and peaceful, soft and warm with life. But she seems to be out cold, so I bend next to the bed. I kneel but don't sit all the way. If she woke up, I would look like a perverted meerkat. She looks like her headshot without the makeup, her body fuller, hair cut the way she wore it in the picture—a black pixie cut that's short on the back and the sides and fluffy on the top. She's still in the purple slip she was wearing last night, but one of the straps has slipped off her shoulder. I look away fast because I don't want to look away at all. Her mouth is slightly open and she's breathing deeply in and out. I follow her breath down to her chest and watch it rise and fall like a cat would watch a yo-yo.

The same thing that compelled me to touch my forehead to hers in the woods that first day wants my hand to move, wants it to go to the side of her face and trace a finger down her cheek, wants it to place the strap back on her shoulder so she wakes feeling covered and safe. My hand lifts and drifts forward until I'm slapped across the wrist by the sound of Michelle's voice.

Don't touch her!

I put both hands in the pockets of my robe to hide the evidence that I ever even thought about it. Michelle might be right. I don't want to wake her up, and I'm being weird. I have a rule that I'm not supposed to be weird. Michelle laughs. I stand, getting ready to run even though there's nowhere to go.

Oh, I'm not worried about you waking her up.

I wonder what she's worried about even though I know it's a wonder I'll regret.

You're not worried that if you touch her, she'll disappear? You're not worried that she's not real at all?

I remember the squeeze of Ava's hand on my thigh trying to wake me up. It's okay. I'm not crazy. I'm not crazy.

You're not?

I'm not *that* crazy. I'm crazy enough to keep a dead body as a friend, *temporarily*, but not so crazy that I could hallucinate a whole person.

But what about me? You're not worried she's just like me? One of your fake women you wish would love you?

I squeeze my eyes shut tight so I can stop seeing Michelle. She blurs until she's just little white spots against the blackness. I tell myself that it's not true, that Ava isn't like Michelle. I look for the logic in it. I cannot touch Michelle, but I felt Ava squeeze my thigh—I *know* I did. I'm good at imagining things, but I'm not so good at imagining things that I could invent a whole person that looks and feels like flesh and blood. And it's not *impossible* that she's a ghost. Plenty of sane adults believe in ghosts! My mom believes in ghosts; my dad believes in ghosts; my middle school biology teacher believed in ghosts.

I don't believe in ghosts. And I'm not one. And she might not be one, either. But sure, reach out and touch her if you want. But if you touch her and your hand goes through, won't you know that I'm right and you're crazier than you thought? How will you handle that?

I'll die of shame, probably. Or maybe I won't. Just because

your hand goes through a ghost doesn't mean it's not a real ghost. People's hands go through Hollywood ghosts all the time. Why should mine be any different? And if I am crazy, then it depends on how many people find out how crazy I went and whether or not I have doctor-patient confidentiality with all of them. If this was all just in front of Hils, I think I'd be okay.

Could you live with it, though? Well, maybe you could. You live with yourself every day you visit her definitely real corpse.

Michelle walks out of the blackness behind my eyes and I can see her again, so bright and loud compared to everything else my brain has to offer, so determined to be the only part of myself I can see or hear or know. I keep my eyes on Ava as Michelle drowns me in her voice. I'm shocked Ava hasn't woken up yet, shocked she can't hear how loud it all is. I take a deep breath, trying to nudge the tightness in my chest loose. I let the air fall out in a rush and it blows aside a strand of Ava's hair. I collapse a little with relief. See, she could be real.

I don't know, Michelle says. Her voice sounds lighter, like she's so thrilled that she's about to burst into song out of nowhere like a Disney princess. *If I were you, I would be worried. I would be worried about what it means you are if she's not real. Because what would that mean for you? That her corpse wasn't enough, that her words weren't enough, that you needed to colonize her in some way, come up with an AI chatbot version of her that you could own, a version you could force to love you in the night, like you're a rapist.*

I'm not a rapist. I'm not. I won't force her to love me in the night. I don't even know why she's here. I wouldn't force her to do anything without her consent. I close my eyes to see Michelle, shrugging, leaning back against a wall I can't see. Her shoulders look like windshield wipers at night sliding up and down the darkness. She smiles a soft smile, with no teeth at all, and it's somehow scarier than her big cruel ones.

You know what I'm going to say, don't you?

I do. I do know. I wrap my arms around my sick stomach and surrender. There's nothing I can say to her that will make her not say it. If I try to talk back, she'll only say it worse.

You already are. You're already forcing her body to be with you without her consent. You visit your little hostage every day in the hopes she's finally developed enough Stockholm syndrome to love you back.

I can't do anything but chew holes in my cheeks and bow my head under the weight of the shame. I swallow a mouthful of guilt-flavored bile. I will my heart to stop, but it doesn't. It knows life in prison is a worse punishment than death.

Think of the headlines you'd make if anyone found out about this. She drags an open palm across the air in front of her face, like she wants me to fill the space with an image of something horrible, and I do. I see the headlines:

LOCAL GIRL SAYS LOST HIKER'S
BODY IS HER FRIEND

CORPSE HOARDING CO-ED PLEADS INSANITY,
CLAIMS GHOST ENCOURAGED HER

I wonder if other girls my age will make TikTok videos of themselves spilling the fucked-up details of the case to their followers while doing their makeup to go out. I think about how much more ruined my life would be after that happened. I wouldn't have any shot left at moving on from this year or making new friends. I'd probably have to hop on a lease with Casey Anthony if I ever needed a roommate.

I run out of the room and brace myself against the railing at the top of the stairs, trying to breathe. I wonder if it's already too late for me after this, if I can ever really move past this year after what I've done. If Michelle's right and I've made up her ghost, it'll be even worse. I turn and look through the open door into the bedroom again. Ava stirs and the sheets shift with her movement. My heart shivers with relief. The sheets moved when she did—that means she's solid enough to shift matter. If she's solid enough to shift matter, then she's real. And there was the hair that moved when I breathed. There was the squeeze of the hand on my thigh. And Michelle isn't outside of me like this. Michelle's not so solid and lifelike. Michelle's just more me and she knows it. Ava's not like that so far. Ava's vivid with an amount of life I'm almost sure I couldn't create.

Are you, though? Are you sure? Sure enough to bet on what happens when it falls apart? No offense, but you're kind of hanging by a thread already.

I swallow more bile. I lie flat on the floor, flat on my stomach in the hopes that it will stop hurting. It doesn't and it won't. I negotiate a compromise so my brain doesn't kill me. I promise I will not treat the ghost as real until I know she most likely is real. I promise to investigate. I promise to hold on to my last shred of sanity. I promise I'm trying my best. I promise, I promise, I promise. I curl into a ball and pick at the scabs on my feet, waiting for my promises to buy me some pity, some mercy, but mercy never comes.

SAVANNAH

I'VE DECIDED TO make it my full-time job to be suspicious of the ghost. I need to be sure. That's the only way to make Michelle shut up about this: certainty. Hils wouldn't like it. She says I need to start trying to tolerate uncertainty, but I feel like I should be allowed to make an exception to investigate a ghost. Hils wouldn't want me talking to a fake ghost, either.

Ava's ghost comes down the stairs about thirty minutes after I manage to haul myself up off the floor, giving me time to splash cold water on my face, brush my teeth, brush my hair . . . I know I don't know if she's real or not, but just in case, I'd rather her not see me looking like a mentally ill gremlin, because then she'll really want to haunt a different house. I'm sitting on the couch with a cup of coffee when I hear her. I crouch low behind the cushion and watch her move, like I'm an alligator. Just like last night, her footsteps make almost no sound, but she seems otherwise solid. Gravity still applies. When she walks, she doesn't drift; she steps just like me. She's in a different outfit, green sweats and a long-sleeved black T-shirt. I wonder where she got it.

"Hi," I say, sitting up as she gets to the bottom step.

She seems to have forgotten I'm here, startling a bit at the sound of my voice. She turns, looking for the source of the sound. "Oh. Hi!" she says when she sees me. The politeness in her voice reminds me of waking up with roommates on my first day of college. She walks a little faster until she's standing up against the back of the couch.

"Savannah?" she asks. "Sorry if I'm wrong; bad with names."

"No, it's okay, you got it. I'm Savannah. Sorry, you already said that. You're Ava?" I don't give her time to answer the question; instead I babble about being awkward last night, or too drugged up, and then I apologize for saying that I was too drugged up and explain that it was just melatonin and alcohol and that I'm not addicted to drugs—but also I'm okay with it if she's addicted to drugs. I'm not used to seeing her so upright and awake, and when I'm nervous I can't shut up. "Sorry," I say at the end, already going over everything I just said in my head and regretting it all. I hope she doesn't think I'm addicted to drugs.

But she just laughs. "It's okay," she reassures. "It's a weird situation."

There's a stability to her that I can't even fathom.

"I'm Ava, nice to meet you, officially." She sticks out her hand for me to shake. I stare at it.

What if she's not real? What if my hand goes right through? What if my hand doesn't go through, but all that means is that I am also dead somehow and I missed it?

I shake. She's solid enough. My hand doesn't go through. I hold her hand for a while by accident, because the softness of it surprises me, because it feels so normal, because I haven't been touched in too long.

"Am I dead?" I blurt. I shouldn't be making this about me, but of course I am. I make everything about me—my mom tells me all the time.

She laughs. "I don't think so. Do you remember dying?"

"Do *you* remember dying?" I feel bad for asking that, too. It's not a good question for small talk; I've never been good at small talk. Michelle says it's one of the reasons people think I'm too much. I'm always spilling out over my own edges.

Ava doesn't seem to mind. There's no dark, sudden, suffocating silence glomming up the space between us like there usually is when I've done something wrong, when I've said way too much. Like with her corpse, I feel too safe too fast, like I could tell her anything and be okay. It's making it hard to be suspicious of her, although I am trying.

She chuckles and gestures to the couch. "Mind if I sit?"

My cheeks get hot. My mom's voice in my head tells me that it's rude I didn't offer sooner, that she taught me to be a better hostess than this, that I should have already been in the kitchen, making her something to drink.

"Do you want something to drink?"

She laughs. "I can sit?"

I nod too many times, guilty for forgetting to ask her if she wanted to sit. Incredibly, she doesn't seem bothered by my awkwardness, just amused, like she doesn't think I'm being rude at all. She comes around the back of the couch and sits. I swear I see the cushions move to accommodate her, maybe not by much, but enough to be evidence. She bends her knee, and there's the sound of fabric on fabric as her leg brushes against the couch. I add one more point in favor of real to the scoreboard in my brain.

"So, do you want something to drink?" I ask.

She shakes her head. "I think I can get it myself, maybe? I got the clothes by myself."

"I was going to ask you!" I tell myself it's fine that I spoke, that this is a conversation and so far she's been okay with hearing my voice, too, that this is my house, even though secretly I've already yielded it to the one of us who feels more like a real adult.

"Yeah, I just wanted different clothes and they showed up. I'm not quite sure how it works."

"That's nice, though, at least! Sorry. I don't mean to say 'at least' like that, like it's okay that you're dead because at least you get free outfits. It's not like— I'm not trying to minimize. I'm—" Going to shut up now, I hope. "Sorry."

"You're fine, don't worry," she says, in a way that makes me believe for half a second that I really am. Her eyes shimmer when she looks at me, or maybe it's just the sun streaming through the windows, lighting up the gold flecks in the green around her pupils in a way that makes me feel special. I hold my mug a little less tight.

"So do you remember dying?" I ask again, and this time my voice is more sure of itself.

She rests her elbow on her bent knee, then her chin on her fist. She thinks about it for a second. Her eyes drift past me.

"Not really," she says finally. "Not in detail. It was like a dream. I was in the woods, walking, too tired, so I sat down by a tree to have a rest. I think maybe a small part of me knew I was dying. I wasn't scared of it exactly—you get kind of used to the concept of death when it's been sitting behind you for months. Still, I tried to fight it. I remember treating it like when you have a concussion and you aren't supposed to fall asleep. I was sitting against that tree like, 'Don't fall asleep, don't fall asleep,' holding on like that for a while. I didn't move. I couldn't. The exhaustion was thorough, paralyzing. A part of me wondered if rest would help, a part of me worried that if I let myself rest, I'd never wake up, so instead I just sat, staring straight ahead for hours."

I nod along with an expression I really hope is earnest enough. "And somewhere in there you died?"

"And then a woman with long, dirty-blond hair wandered out in front of me in the darkness in a white silk nightgown. It was so dark that I never got a good glimpse of her face and she never looked at me, but the hair was the same. At that moment, I thought it was Megan, but that was impossible—Megan was dead. Unless it was just my time to go, too, and she had come to collect me. And I was only really putting off dying at that point because I knew Megan wanted me to live. When I saw her, I thought she was telling me it was okay, that I could fold, that it was over. I closed my eyes and then I was here. When I saw you lying in bed, your hair spread out over your face, I started shaking you awake, because I thought you were Megan. But I'm starting to realize it probably never was Megan. Was it you in the woods, too?"

When I open my mouth to respond, I start crying. The guilt's everywhere all at once like fruit flies in July. I regret that I asked. I regret existing. I regret that I'm the one crying when I don't deserve to be the one crying because she deserves to be the one crying because I killed her.

"It was me," I babble. "I promise I'm not addicted to drugs, I've just been going through some shit and it was one hard night and I chased a bottle of wine with an Ambien and I don't remember what happened, but when I woke up the next morning I was lying on the ground next to you and you were dead already. I'm sorry, Ava—I'm so, so sorry. I didn't mean to. I'm sorry." I bury my face in my hands so I don't have to see how sad my confession makes her. But she just starts laughing—not the controlled chuckles she's been giving me, but big and full and bouncing off the walls like a runaway rubber ball.

I look up, mopping tears and snot off my face with the hem of my shirt. When she finally stops laughing, she's bent over her lap, gasping. "Sorry," she says, breathless. "It just figures that that's how I'd die. Death by accidental catfishing! Ha!"

"I'm, again, *so* sorry." One day I will need to get a better word than *sorry* to hate myself with, but for now it's all I have. I hold my stomach to try to squish the guilt down before it starts to hurt too much. I stare at the couch instead of her, tears still dripping from my chin.

I only look up when a thumb slides down the side of my face—her thumb.

"I'm sorry," I say again, determined to say it until it feels like I've said it enough, determined to say it forever.

"Hey, it's okay."

I look up into her eyes; they're full of a grace I would never give myself.

"You're just doing your best," she continues, holding one side of my face in her so-soft hand. "And before you, there was months in the woods, and gross water, and no food. You're not why I died. You just happened to be there. It's not your fault. I was so weak by that point, I doubt you could have helped me. Even sober."

"You don't have to say that." I sniffle. "You don't have to make me feel like it's okay and I'm okay if it's not and I'm not."

She shrugs with only her right shoulder. "Well, maybe it is okay, and maybe you are, too. You don't have to give me a place to crash while we figure this out, either, but I hope you will."

I nod more than once, more than twice. I'm not suspicious enough, I know, but I already want her to stay forever with her full-of-grace eyes and her so-soft hands. "Of course you can stay," I tell her. "Of course. It's the least I can do."

In my head, my mom is proud of me for my hospitality. Ava drops my face and I wish she would pick it back up. Her softness makes me sleepy, and I want to lay my head in her lap.

"Thank you," she says, smiling. "I'll try to get out of your space soon enough."

"No rush," I say, not suspicious at all. I start convincing myself of her realness so I can keep her love in my life. I tell myself that if she weren't real, she would be meaner to me, like Michelle. I decide to test it again, just to be sure. I do something that Michelle finds annoying: I ask for reassurance that I already got.

"Are you sure I'm okay? It's all okay? For sure?"

"Oh, for sure, for sure. Double for sure."

I love that she said it twice.

"It's a little weird for us both, but it's okay. It could always be worse." She gestures to the woods out the window and I laugh.

Well, I could still end up Casey Anthony's equally questionable roommate, but at least until then I'll have someone. If she's not real, I just have the same amount of no one as before. If none of this is real, all the fallout is for nothing and I can't handle that right now. I sip at my coffee and stare at the rise and fall of her stomach as she breathes. I stash my suspicions in a closet in the corner of my mind and start to ease the door shut.

If she's not real, that's tomorrow's problem.

AVA

After poker night, when it finally stopped raining, everything was just a tiny bit harder. The little stream we were getting water from had swollen up into more of a river, flooding the areas around it. All the fish must have gotten washed downstream or something, because we weren't catching anything with our fishing baskets or our fishing line. We ran out of berries too and, while we went out foraging a lot with the wilderness guidebook to try to identify more edible plants, we didn't have much luck at finding anything we were comfortable eating. We were always arguing with each other over this or that tuber or familiar-looking leafy green. In the end, we decided that maybe our area just wasn't ideal for us anymore. Best-case scenario, hiking to a new location would end with us stumbling across someone's hunting cabin, a campground, or maybe even a beautiful paved road with a gas station at the end of it. Worst case: just more of this.

Megan and I were packing up camp when Chad called us over to see the mushrooms. The second we heard the word mushrooms, *we shot each other a worried look and dropped what we were doing. Having Chad with us at this stage was a bit like parenting a toddler; we were always trying to keep him from putting random, potentially dangerous, things in his mouth. We didn't have to go far to find him, and thank god for that, because I had entered a stage of chronic exhaustion. Every few steps winded me. Megan too. I knew, logically, that every little incline shouldn't feel like Everest and yet there we were, facing the reality of what the situation had done to our bodies already. Like I said, I was glad he was close. We found him around the back of one of those big-ass trees that has to be hundreds of years old, with roots for days. He pointed down at the roots, where a small patch of mushrooms was growing. At first glance, they looked almost like button mushrooms, with thick white stems and tan phallic heads.*

"What do you think?" Chad asked with a grin. "Just like the ones in the store, right?"

Megan squatted down to look closer. "I don't know. They look fine, but they're still mushrooms. We have to be careful with mushrooms."

I flipped to the mushroom page of the guidebook, which I always brought to possible food finds. They didn't not *look like button mushrooms, but they also didn't look* exactly *like button mushrooms. The caps weren't thick enough, and when I asked Megan to pick one and flip it upside down, which she did after covering her hand with her sleeve just in case, there wasn't as much flesh underneath the cap as there was on the button. The stems were also longer comparatively. I remember thinking that maybe they cut the stems short before they put them on the shelf in the store for aesthetic purposes. They also didn't look like any of the super deadly mushrooms listed on the page. Still, I quickly decided against eating them and shook my head at Megan. She nodded, silently agreeing to back me.*

"I don't think it's a good idea." I flipped the book and showed him the button mushrooms on the page, pointing out the discrepancies.

Megan stood up while I explained, and when I was done—before Chad had a chance to speak—she chimed in to agree with me. She told him it was better safe than sorry, but Chad just stared at the mushrooms like Gollum stared at the ring. I exchanged a worried glance with Megan. We both doubled down, telling him we would look for different mushrooms. There were weirder-looking ones that would be easier to identify in the area. We would go hunting. We would go fishing. We would dig up roots and pretend they were potatoes. Nothing could convince him. He just kept staring at the mushrooms.

"Okay, how about this? You two don't have to eat them."

"Nobody should be eating them," Megan interjected, but Chad ignored her.

"You don't have to eat them. I'll be the test subject. I'll take a little tiny nibble of one and then we'll wait like six hours and if I'm still fine, I get to eat more. Once again for the Megans in the back: you two still don't have to have any at that point, but I get to eat more if I'm fine later."

"Are you sure it's worth the risk?" I asked. "Chad, there are no doctors out here if you fuck up."

He waved a dismissive hand at me. "I'll stick my finger down my throat if it's bad, but I don't think it will be. Look at them. They're just like the ones in the little blue cartons in the store."

"They're not. I already pointed out how they're not, but okay."

"You're going to let him do it?!" Megan turned to me.

"I'm not 'letting' him. I maintain that this is a bad and very reckless idea, but I don't think he's going to listen to me. It's his grave. Let him dig it if he wants."

Megan sighed. "Chad, I really do not think you should eat any of this, even if it's just a small piece. I don't think you fully get just how badly eating the wrong mushroom could end for you."

"I get it," he insisted. "I just don't think these ones are going to be bad. Ava said they don't look like any of the bad ones in her book."

"I said we can't be sure," I clarified.

"That's why I said it would just be a little piece at first. Jeez, you two. It's going to be like a millimeter of mushroom. What's the worst that could happen?"

"You could die!" we both shouted simultaneously.

He grinned, kneeling down in front of the mushroom patch. "But I won't." He broke off a tiny jagged triangle from the cap of one.

"Chad, seriously?" Megan asked again.

"My body, my choice," he replied.

Megan rolled her eyes. "Fine. Your fucking funeral."

She turned around and stomped back to camp.

"Are you sure?" I asked one last time, looking down at him.

In response he just put the piece in his mouth, chewed, swallowed, and smiled.

"Ok," I said. "Check your watch. What time is it?"

He glanced at his wrist. "9 am."

I did some quick math. "Let's regroup about this at 3."

We went back to camp together. Megan didn't speak to Chad for the rest of the morning, but I saw her glancing at him every twenty minutes or so, looking for signs of illness. But he was fine. He was fine all six hours. And at the end of those six hours, he made a huge show of dancing around saying he told us so before eating three more mushrooms. But it wasn't the sixth hour that got him—it was the tenth. At 6 pm, he started looking a little woozy. When he saw us watching him, he muttered some excuse and disappeared for a while. He came back at sunset looking pale.

"Are you ok?" Megan asked.

"I'm fine," he insisted. "Just a little tired. Long day."

But it hadn't been a long day. None of us had done much of anything. Megan and I exchanged worried looks.

"Okayyyy," Megan said, dragging out the word to show she knew something was off. "Why don't we just call it a night, then? Go to bed early?"

"Sure," Chad replied, looking a little green. "Sounds good. Just give me one second. I'll be right back."

He stood and hobbled off into the trees as fast as his sick little legs could carry him.

"He's totally going off to throw up or shit his brains out, right?" Megan asked.

"Oh, most definitely."

"How serious do you think this is?"

"I don't know. It could be nothing. The mushrooms didn't look like the really bad ones in the book, so maybe he'll be okay and a hard night of shitting and puking will finally teach him a lesson."

She nodded a lot but wouldn't look straight at me, her eyes were very far away.

By the time Chad dragged himself back, looking like a ragged ghost, the sun was just about gone from the sky and Megan and I had set everything up for bed in the tent. I'd also made a few trips down to the water, bringing back as much as I could carry in our containers while Megan boiled it in batches. Our thinking was, if he was about to be really sick, it'd be good to have extra water on hand and ready to go. Keeping him hydrated would be crucial. Sure enough, we were woken up around 4 am by him going in and out of the tent over and over to throw up or have diarrhea, probably both based on how ragged and scared he looked.

"How are those mushrooms treating you?" Megan asked on his fifth or sixth trip back inside, switching on a flashlight and shining it at him, smirking.

And then he did something neither of us expected: he broke down in tears and started apologizing profusely, begging Megan to help him. It'd been over a month and a half and Megan and I had cried a dozen times each in front of him, but we'd never seen him cry before. He'd been holding on to that last shred of societal masculine bullshit for dear life and the world of hurt those mushrooms put him in had scared him straight. I stared. I had no idea how to handle the sudden emotion or the incredibly high stakes of the situation. Megan was ready though. She threw one arm around his shoulders and assured him over and over that it would be okay, that it was probably minor and would pass. At the same time, she flung her other arm back toward me and wiggled her fingers. At first, I extended my arm forward, confused but thinking maybe she needed someone to hold her hand too, but she shook me off and I realized she was asking for the water we'd prepared. I snatched up a bottle and passed it to her. I watched as she made him drink it, feeling helpless, but I followed Megan's lead and offered little assurances wherever I could. The rest of the night we sat with him like that, force-feeding him water in between bathroom breaks.

Finally, when there had been nothing left for him to purge for hours and we'd stopped trying to force water in favor of rest, we all crashed. Megan and I were back up by noon, but Chad slept until midnight. When he woke up, we made him drink water, crossed our fingers, and sent him back to sleep. In the morning he seemed fine—I swear he did. We were all so relieved I can't even tell you. Everything was going to be okay after all! We joked about mushrooms all morning and afternoon, going back to our normal business. We even caught some shrimpy-looking things in one of our fishing baskets and had a really bland, really small seafood boil. But Megan and I could keep the fish down perfectly well and Chad couldn't. He said his pee was dark brown despite our constant rehydrating. When he was empty again, he curled up into a little ball on the floor of the tent, shaking. He looked so much like a child. It was horrible. We didn't know what to do. He declined our repeated attempts to shove the little bit of pain medication we had down his throat, shaking his head, his skin a pale yellow and shining with sweat, saying we would need it when he was gone and he'd just throw it up anyway.

We couldn't do anything, so we just sat with him and kept him warm. Megan held his hand and I rubbed his back and he used the last of his voice to make jokes for our sakes about how this was an ideal way to go, with two babes doting on him. He fell asleep and we couldn't wake him up. He slept one day. Then two, his skin getting yellower all the time. We couldn't make him drink. And then the next day, really early in the morning, I woke up to the sound of Megan screaming so horrifically I lunged for the knife first, because I thought she must be getting mauled by a bear. But there was no bear. There was only Megan—screaming, sobbing, throwing her body up and down to give chest compressions, plugging Chad's nose to blow air into his mouth. I froze. I could only move my hand slowly forward to grab for his wrist. When I touched him, I just swallowed hard and let go. He was cold and stiff already, very much gone.

"Megan," I said. Her name came out so soft it was almost just a breath. I searched everywhere for my voice and tried again. "Megan!"

She didn't look at me. Didn't stop.

"Megan, he's dead!" I tried, loud.

She didn't seem to hear me. I remembered I had a body and not just a voice. I scooted up behind her, wrapped both arms around her waist, and yanked her backward into me. I said, "He's gone, Megan, he's gone, he's dead," over and over again into her ear, so that maybe at some point I would believe it too. I stared at his wax replica of a body while she cried and clawed at my arms and screamed at me over and over again to let her go, but I held on until she went limp against my chest.

Because we had to, we eventually went outside to take care of the business half of death. In that truly terrible discussion, we decided we couldn't and probably shouldn't bury him—better he be somewhere someone might find him. We would drag him to a nearby spot with lots of wildflowers and leave him there. We would take him out of his sleeping bag and take his jacket and boots, but leave him clothed otherwise. We would take the rest of his possessions with us to bring to his family if we didn't die too. We would have a small funeral where both of us would speak. Then we would gather our fishing baskets, disable our snares, and rest up to leave and move a ways down the water. We couldn't stay there for the winter anyway—it was too open, and the cold would have gotten us fast. So that's what we did. Really bad few days. We barely spoke. Megan cried herself to sleep every night. I stopped sleeping altogether. I wondered all night, every night, if we should have done anything differently, if we could have. But that's what we did and I'm sorry if anyone is reading this and thinks we should have done something else.

When we left that campsite for good at the end of those horrible haunted days, we hiked past the remaining mushrooms. I didn't point them out to Megan—she'd suffered enough and I could tell by the way she pressed forward staring hard ahead that she was trying not to look, but I glanced at them again and noticed they'd matured. The tops had become flat and wide and pale with little white skirts growing underneath. Now that they were grown up, I recognized them easily from a picture I'd been sure to study extra hard just in case. Death caps. The deadliest mushroom in the world. Had we waited a week, we would have known immediately and without a doubt that eating them was a hard no, but, like I said, Chad was reckless to a fault.

~AA Brown

PART THREE

Active Decay: Indicated by fluids beginning to drain through orifices. The body liquifies and loses most of its mass.

SAVANNAH

r/AmItheAsshole · 0 mins ago

throwawayaccount080300

AITA for ~~Keeping Not Reporting~~ Waiting to Report ~~my Ghost Friend's~~ a Body to the Police?

A couple of weeks ago I ~~woke up next to~~ found a ~~woman's~~ body in the woods behind my house. I didn't call the police at first because I thought maybe I killed ~~her~~ this person. I didn't, though, just to clarify! ~~I was just on drugs at the time. I found~~ I can't rcally get into how I know lhal, bul I deflnltely did not murder anyone. The thing is, I still haven't reported the body. I will report it! I only haven't ~~because I've gotten used to having her~~ because they didn't die by violence, so it's not like a crime scene for real ~~and I love her and I need her and she's all I have~~ and I thought ~~she~~ they deserved some time to truly rest in peace before the whole world came poking around.

At first this didn't seem like such a big deal, but ~~now that her ghost has shown up at my house and I have real~~ feelings ~~about her and real interactions with her~~ now that it's been over two weeks, I'm starting to feel bad and I don't know if I'm doing the right thing. It's not like I can ask this person what they would want, because ~~then she might hate me and~~

~~I'd really have no one~~ obviously the body can't talk. I will still report it. I want to give the friends and family that closure, but if I turn in the body before it's bones, ~~I'll miss her too much and I risk losing my ghost friend and I'm not ready~~ then there will be a whole bunch of autopsies and news stations and a whole crime scene investigation even though there wasn't a crime, and that's so invasive for no reason. I visit the resting place every day. I'm very respectful. This person isn't alone or unsafe, just decomposing peacefully and naturally and I'm trying to do right by them. I just don't know if I really am doing the right thing~~, or just the selfish thing~~. Help?

I WRITE AND rewrite my post for hours just to delete it before it can even develop a real time stamp. I need help, but it's impossible to get it without sounding crazy—even from strangers on lawless Reddit. I can imagine the TikTok girlies picking the post apart now, laughing in the comments section about how I must be so sick in the head. And I can't risk the post going viral and someone figuring out who I am or where I am or who the body is. That's jail, right? It's gotta be jail. I check to make sure the post is really deleted. It is.

God, I'm so stupid, I didn't even put myself on a VPN. I can't tell Ava, because she doesn't know what I'm doing about her body yet, or at least I don't think she does. I hope not. It's only been two days since she appeared; I don't know her super well yet. I don't even fully know if she's real, but again, that's tomorrow's problem, and it's not tomorrow yet. I do feel really really bad for not reporting it now that I'm looking at her lost little soul moping around my house all the time. I like her. She's nice and warm and she keeps me company and now it's even harder to think about letting go of her body. I check again to make sure the post is really deleted. It is. I google to see if Reddit has a recently deleted folder that I'm missing, but it doesn't seem like it does. I check again. The post is gone. I probably shouldn't be checking this so many times. The uncertainty itches. I go back to worrying about Ava while scratching the fresh scabs off my foot.

What if the only reason I have access to her ghost is that I have access to her body? When I report her body, won't I lose them both? Not that she'll want to be around me anyway once she finds out I'm holding her corpse hostage, or maybe she will, I don't know. It doesn't seem worth the Russian roulette of it all to tell her and find out. I'll still have to tell her eventually. And I will tell her! I also will turn her body into the police, when she's bones, like I said. And I have time—it got cold again outside. It snowed, even. She's probably a stinky ice sculpture right now. I wouldn't know, though; I haven't been out since the snow and Ava's ghost came on the same night. I'll have to figure out how to sneak out of my own house to check on her body. I'm itching to see her. She's become a confession booth without the threat of a priest, and I desperately need somewhere to go with all of this, but obviously that somewhere can't be the internet. I can't tell ghost Ava what I've been up to, and I can't go to my mom or my therapist or my nonexistent friends; I'm stuck. Her corpse still feels like the only place I can be honest.

All real people would do is yell at me that I'm crazy. And maybe I am, but I'm worried I might be too fragile to hear it.

AVA

It took a week for us to find a spot that would be suitable to stick out much colder weather in if needed. When we did find a place, it was actually pretty cool at first, a real-life cave set in the side of a rock face. The cave isn't huge, only a bit bigger than the tent. It's deep set in the woods, surrounded by trees on all sides, which we hoped would mean less wind could get to us. The entrance is small and, at 5'11", I have to duck low to get in and out.

We found that we could build a tiny fire at the front against a wall and funnel the smoke out through the entryway if we needed to. Mostly, we did this in the early evening, got the cave as hot as possible over a few hours, then put out the fire and used a door we'd made out of woven trees and leaves, a few layers of folded-up tent, and tent poles for structure to plug up the entrance and camouflage where we were from whatever was outside. It's a pretty neat setup and we were proud of it. The only thing was that the cave is farther from the water than we were used to at the time, so we'd try to go together once a day in the morning and take back as much as we could carry.

We didn't talk about Chad. To talk about it would have killed whatever morale we had left, which probably would have killed us, so he became a painful gap in our vocabulary. Megan didn't acknowledge that she cried at night and I didn't complain that I couldn't sleep. We made silent adjustments around each other's pain. After several nights staring at the ceiling, pretending that I didn't hear Megan crying so I wouldn't embarrass her or make it worse, I shimmied out of my sleeping bag and asked if I could crawl into hers. I didn't say it was because I couldn't sleep or mention her tears. I just said that I was cold. She nodded rapidly, warm relief flooding her little wet face, and started yanking frantically at the zipper. I squeezed into the small space beside her and she turned around so her back was to me. I wrapped my arms around her and held on tight. She was like an oven and I was sweating like crazy, but she stopped crying and I fell asleep and stayed asleep for the first time since Chad died. After that, it wasn't a question. We crawled into the same sleeping bag at night and snuggled some peace into each other.

With the shelter situation settled and the two of us sleeping again, we channeled everything we had into becoming full-time winter prep employees. The Mormons are big preppers, so getting ready for the winter shouldn't have been a big deal for me. The problem was that we didn't have any of the right materials. I know how to can, but we didn't have jars or anything to put in them. What we could do was smoke meat. Until the cold came and the plants died, we would limit our protein, opting for a primarily vegetarian diet whenever possible, preserving most of the meat and saving it for the coldest months.

Megan once saw some survivalists on a TV show build a smoker in the base of a hollow tree to make jerky, so we went on a hollow-tree hunt. When we found one, I was worried that Megan was going to start a forest fire. She argued that at least a forest fire would lead someone to us, which shut me right up. Within the hour of finding said tree, I was building a wooden rack to go inside of it following her specifications. Smoker finished, sun setting, we stood back and admired our work.

"Damn," she said. "I wish we had something to smoke in it."

I stuck out my arm. "Cut it off. I wanna see it work."

She laughed and pressed my arm back down to my side. "Somehow I don't think we've made it all the way to cannibalism."

I disagreed but followed her home anyway, watching my new toy fade into the distance. She caught me looking and promised she'd find me something to smoke. And she did! We hung out for days by the water. She fished with the line. I made a new fishing basket and found a perfect place for it. We got pretty good, and the new area had more fish. Every day we got at least a few little shrimps or mollusks. Every other day we got a whole fish. She'd always kill it, because she had this thing about holding herself responsible for the lives she took. When they were dead, I would gut them and smoke them. Then we'd have a few bites each and store the rest away. She set snares too, but it was rare that we caught anything in those, so we didn't depend on them. I became head forager, because Megan was too messed up about Chad to do it herself. If I found mushrooms, I had to be absolutely sure, then I had to prepare them myself, away from her, and I had to feed them to her without telling her they were mushrooms. The first two times it happened were rough. Both times she cried because she could tell they were mushrooms, and begged me to confirm they were. I refused because she was the one who'd made the rule. And both times, we were fine. After that, she trusted me. She did not trust herself though. Not with the plants. Except for once! We were fishing together on a sunny afternoon the second week in our new spot when she gasped.

"Holy fuck, it's katniss!" she screamed.

I lounged against my favorite rock, eyes closed, feeling a smile spread across my face. "Everdeen? Yeah, manifest that. She'd be helpful right about now."

"No, look!" she said again, her voice farther away. I opened my eyes to see her hunched over some plants. She waved at me to come over. I did not want to get up, but begrudgingly obliged because she looked thrilled. "Look!" she said again when I got there. She was absolutely beaming proud. "Katniss, the plant she was named after—little white flowers, grows by the water. I looked it up when I read the books and it looked just like this!"

"Oh shit, you're right!" I high-fived her. "The tubers are edible, right? Like potatoes?"

She nodded repeatedly, mouth stretched wide, hair bouncing like the ears of a golden retriever on the way back from a round of fetch. I knew I loved her right then, but instead of telling her, I just helped her dig up katniss in happy silence. With too much to carry in our hands, we filled the front of our shirts and brought them back that way, feeling absolutely Bezos wealthy. And it got even better! Because on the way back to the cave, we checked a snare and saw that a squirrel had triggered it and taken a rock to the head. Megan was very glad the snare had done the killing for her. Squirrels are cute. I gutted it and we decided to treat ourselves instead of taking it to the smoker. We stewed it low and slow with the katniss tubers—like Irish stew with potatoes. We cried happy tears all through dinner, and that night, for once, we went to bed full.

Thank you. Thank you, Katniss Everdeen.

~AA Brown

SAVANNAH

I GET UP super early and go to the woods while Ava is still sleeping. The snow is thick on the ground and I bundle up tight to trudge through it. I shiver out into the icy wind, trying to remind myself to be grateful that the snow has prolonged my time with her and not mad at the sea of inconvenience powder. I can't manage one solid step without sinking. By the time I reach her body, I'm soaked, shivering, tired, and I want to go home. I take deep breaths and remind myself this is a first-world problem that I created. Some of us actually did have to survive these conditions for real. I get to go back to my warm little house after this and fix everything with a hot shower and a cozy blanket. I know I couldn't survive out here; I really hate the snow.

She's half buried in it, icy and ghoulish, like one of those bodies that the sick fucks climbing Everest use as a landmark. It's still dark and the image of her in the glow of my flashlight covered in frozen ooze is definitely going to give me nightmares, but I'll just have to accept that as punishment for my own sus actions. I kick my snow-covered chair to the side and huddle back against my tree to block the wind. I'd rather stand than have a cold wet butt. Shivering, I point my flashlight at the pages of Ava's journal and read through the part where Chad climbs the wall. I'm glad he didn't fall until I remember that it doesn't matter. I can't get attached to any of these people. They're all backed against a clock. It's not *if*; it's *when*.

I guess it's never actually *if*. It's *when* for me, too. I'm just delulu enough to be able to spend this much time with a corpse and still think it couldn't be me.

I put the book in my bag before it can get wet or blow away, then I turn off my flashlight. Like a virgin on her wedding night, I've decided this will be easier in the dark.

"So I don't know if you're aware, but your ghost is in my house and she's really nice, but I feel like now my keeping you here might be a problem, ethically. She doesn't remember anything before arriving at my house. The way she puts it, it's like she was dying and then like two weeks went by where she was just chillin' in the dark, but she couldn't feel time. She says dying was like being put under anesthesia for surgery. You fall asleep in one place and then have the thickest nap and wake up in another place.

"The last thing she remembers is sitting against this tree when I wandered out here on drugs. She says she only let herself go because she thought I was Megan, which is fucked, right? Maybe that means if I hadn't taken the stupid Ambien and sleepwalked out here at that exact moment, maybe she would have kept up her will to live through the night and been able to make it to my house alive the next morning. And if she doesn't remember anything else in that whole two-week gap, then she must not know I'm keeping you. I literally had to sneak out of my own house to be here today. I could just tell her. I know. But if I tell her, I run the risk of her being pissed at me and then I lose the only friend-shaped person I've had in months. No offense."

I turn my flashlight back on so I can pace. I wish I smoked cigarettes. This feels like a good time for a cigarette.

"I could also just report you before she finds out, but if the police come, she'll find out what I've been hiding anyway. I guess I could just beg forgiveness after showing that I am capable of doing the right thing. But also, does it matter? She's still dead. It's not like you're a real crime scene. No one killed you; you just died. We know this. I'd only be rushing the inevitable to get answers to your family, which, okay, yes, I know the way I handled this is a bit fucked-up, but don't you deserve a little rest in peace before the whole world is on you? And wouldn't it be better if I explained everything to her on my own without the cops hovering? Maybe if I called the cops, I wouldn't even have time to explain myself. Maybe the second the police come and get you, she'll just disappear and then I'll be all alone again. That would be the worst case. Then I'd have no Ava *and* she'd be mad at me. Okay, so I definitely can't do that . . ."

I pace faster. The flashlight passes over her corpse again and again, illuminating her in brief flashes, like a strobe light in a haunted house. She doesn't scare me anymore, though. I'm not a guest; I fucking work here. I stop and whirl to face her, shining the light straight through her almost-empty eye sockets like the police do when a person is asleep in their car.

"Goddammit, why can't you be the sentient one?! I need advice!"

Silence. I sigh and drop my hands to my sides.

"I'm sorry for yelling. There just really doesn't seem to be a perfect answer here and I'm in too deep now to leave it alone. I had a plan, but I didn't plan for a ghost in my face to remind me that I low-key suck for this."

I stare at my boots and her boots—Chad's boots, I've learned from the list of supplies folded up inside her journal.

"Okay, how about this? I will tell her. I'll definitely tell her. I will. I promise. Not today, but I will tell her." I stop and sift around in my brain for a timeline that feels both responsible and not torturous. There isn't one. Do I have to tell her? Yes, I'm going to tell her. I watch my breath puff out in front of me in little white clouds made of guilt, and I make a decision. "I'll give it a few more days so she can get to know me and see that I'm not literally the worst and then maybe she'll trust me more when I have to break the news about you. She'll hear me out. Sure, she might be a little pissed, but she'll give me the benefit of the doubt. And then we can have a calm discussion about this like actual adults and I can ask her what she wants me to do and I'll respect her wishes whatever she says. There. Yeah. That's a good plan. Solid plan. I almost feel better about this." I'm lying. I do not feel better about this. "Okay. Bye bye, Ava! Enjoy your little break from decomposing, but I'm gonna go get warm."

By the time I manage to wade home through the snow, the sun is up and so is Ava, sitting at my counter drinking coffee. I remind myself not to be jealous of the fact that she can manifest little comforts for herself but not for me. Yes, I still have to make my own coffee, but mine is better, apparently. She says hers tastes like the memory of coffee, almost the real thing but not quite. I imagine it tasting a little weaker, like it was made with one of the OG Keurigs, or like when you get an iced latte delivered and by the time the driver gets to your house, the ice is melted, which doesn't seem so bad. I guess I'll find out when I'm dead.

"Hey!" she says when I walk in. "I thought you were still asleep. You usually are around this time."

I wonder if she already knows, if she's trying to guilt me into telling her.

"Yeah, I couldn't sleep and went for a walk."

She glances out the window behind the sink. "In this?"

A tree branch slams against the window in the wind just to prove her point.

"I like how the cold feels on my skin," I say, tensing up my muscles to stop shivering. I decide to give her something true to hide my lie. "It reminds me that I'm real."

She throws me a little half smile. "Do you often feel like you're not real?"

"You sound like my therapist," I tell her.

She laughs. "Am I at least cheaper?"

I blush and I don't know why. She scans me up and down. I know she notices something is off. I can't decide if it's the guilt or if it's that she noticed I'm blushing. If she asks about it, I can always say the cold makes my face red. Gaslight, gatekeep, girlboss. I wait for her to pick at me like a scab, but she doesn't say anything.

"Anyway," I say, panicking for no reason, backing toward the stairs before she can smell her own corpse on me, before she can think too hard about the blush. "It was a bad idea to go outside. You're right. Way too cold. Even for me. And I definitely love the cold. It's great. I'm feeling *soooo* real right now. But I'm gonna take a shower and warm up."

She opens her mouth to say something, looking very concerned about my sudden retraction, but I cut her off by shouting "Bye!" and sprinting up the stairs before she can say anything at all.

AVA

A few nights later, fat and happy on our newfound katniss supply, we'd just tucked ourselves into bed when I heard rustling outside. I'm practical by nature, so I dismissed it as the wind at first. But the rustling got louder and closer until I was able to pick out the rhythmic thump of heavy footsteps and the crunch of branches breaking under them. I reached for the flashlight. We kept it in the sleeping bag with us at one of our hips. We had to—otherwise we'd never find it in the dark. Before this, I don't think I knew what true pitch black was, but being awake in the night out here is closer to the experience of blindness than darkness. When I clicked on the flashlight, Megan turned around in the bag to face me and sat up.

"What's wrong?" she asked.

"Do you hear that?"

She paused to listen. Outside, the sound was coming closer. Along with the large thumping footsteps, I could now hear the animal breathing in thick wet huffs.

"Oh fuck," Megan said. I felt her body tense next to mine. "What do you think it is?"

I could tell by the fear in her voice that she knew what it was, but I said it anyway. "A bear. Has to be. There's nothing else big enough out here to sound like that."

"It's coming closer," she whispered.

It was. The breathing was getting louder, the footsteps heavier. It was coming right toward us. My own breath caught in a ball in my throat.

"It's the fish," I managed to whisper back. We'd been doing pretty well in our fishing ventures, and we had a little over a pound of smoked fish in the cave with us that we were saving for winter.

"What do we do?"

This caught me off guard. Usually Megan came up with the plans, but I guess she drew the line at bears coming to steal our food in the night.

"Hand me the knife."

"You're going to fight the bear?!" she hissed back at me.

"Ideally no, but don't you think we should be prepared?"

She passed me the knife. By this point, the huffing breaths were right outside. The footsteps stopped. I unsheathed the blade and sat straight, pushing Megan behind me with my free hand. She pressed herself against my back, unwilling to be pushed all the way out of the action. I could feel her breath on my neck, accidentally in sync with the bear's. Our makeshift door began to shake, the leaves we put up for insulation shivering and falling off as the bear put its snout against it from the outside, sniffing and pressing forward until it encountered the thin material of the tent that separated us. I gripped the knife, and Megan gripped me, digging her nails into my shoulders.

The bear's mouth opened against the fabric and chomped down. It was trying to bite its way inside. I could feel Megan's heartbeat on my back. My own pounded in my ears. I've never felt so alive and so close to death at the same time. I knew I had to do something. If I froze, the bear would get in here eventually. If it got in, we couldn't fight it off. We had no chance without a gun. I combed my brain for everything I've ever learned about bears and remembered a documentary where the guy said that bears won't try to fight you if they think you're bigger and scarier. If confronted by a bear, he said, you should get big and loud. Big I could not do. The cave isn't even big enough for me to stand. I have to bend in half by the waist to enter. Loud though . . .

I took a big breath and set up the scream. Finally, a practical use for all the money I spent on grad school. I opened my mouth and sound poured out. Lots of it. Over and over again I yelled. My screaming bounced against the back of the cave, amplified, and flooded the space. Megan caught on to what I was trying to do and joined in. Together we sang the ugliest, loudest duet of all time. Outside, the sniffing paused. The bear pawed at the fabric again. We screamed even louder. The snout pressed and then hesitated and pulled back. I tried to tune us out and listen to the small sounds under us. Footsteps again outside.

"It's working! Don't stop!"

We didn't stop until the bear turned and ran. I could hear it crashing through the trees, duped into thinking this was a fight it couldn't win. I went quiet first and held up my hand for Megan to do the same. We stewed in the silence, listening. After several minutes of hearing only our own heartbeats and breaths, I lowered the knife and put it down, within reach. Megan scooted out from behind me. We got back into the sleeping bag. I left the flashlight on, propping it up against one of our water bottles so it stayed pointed at the ceiling, illuminating the whole space. We lay there, face-to-face, nose-to-nose. Her chest was pressed against mine and our too-strong heartbeats slammed into each other like competing drum kits.

"We're okay," I said.

"We're okay," she repeated back at me.

She wrapped her arm around me and pulled me forward, less like a hug and more like an attempt to merge into one body. Our hearts beat harder somehow. I wrapped my arm around her too, reflexively, understanding the need to spread all the fear and adrenaline out over both our bodies to make it seem like less overall. She wrapped her leg around me and pressed her hips forward into mine. I traced the curve of her waist and settled on her hip. We stared at each other, our noses millimeters from touching. Then she grabbed my thigh and slipped it between her legs. She let her hand wander my torso.

I stared at her, frozen, doing gay math, trying to figure out if what she was doing was indeed what I thought she was doing. I felt a twitch below the belt in spite of my efforts to think respectful thoughts, just in case this was somehow a straight girl activity, like sleepovers. I didn't want to move first. I just kept my hold on her hip and stared at her, trying to read her eyes, which was difficult because her face was so close to mine, her eyes looked merged together like a cyclops. Then she closed them. She rocked her pelvis lightly against my leg for a second then stopped herself, her body tense again, her breathing ragged. Her eyes popped open and she pulled back so she could really look at me. I couldn't decide what to do so I just waited, hesitant to make any sudden moves and ruin it. With the hand that wasn't between my thighs, she reached around and cupped the back of my head, pulling her fingers through my hair and scratching my scalp. I tried not to moan or give any other sign of how much I loved it. My gay calculations were looking correct, but I was not about to jinx it. Finally, she spoke.

"So, I know we're both really gross, but if you're interested . . ." She dragged her hand a little farther up my thigh.

I was interested. I was very interested. I was so interested that I lunged forward and kissed her before she could say anything else. She moaned into my mouth and kissed me back. I don't remember getting undressed, but suddenly my clothes were gone and so were hers and I was kissing my way across every available surface while she mapped out my body with her hands. She grabbed at my boobs, my hips, my back, my stomach, my thighs. She reached down and I rocked against her palm for a bit before I put my mouth to her neck and kissed my way down. She stretched out and sucked her fingers as I went, spreading her legs wide to welcome me. I wrapped my arms around her thighs, brought my face to one of her knees and kissed my way back up, where I found her wet and ready, juicy and delicious. And I was starving.

~AA Brown

SAVANNAH

"WOULD YOU LIKE to tell me why you haven't been to therapy in two weeks?'

"Well, hello to you, too, Mom."

My mom sighs. "Savannah, this is serious. Don't start with me right now."

"I'm not starting with you. I'm fine. You don't need to roll up all aggressive about me not going to therapy."

"I'm sorry, did you just call me aggressive? Did you forget who you're talking to?"

I gulp on reflex. Adult Savannah, twenty-one-year-old fear-no-corpse Savannah, is not afraid when she hears this. It's ten-year-old Savannah that's the problem. Her massive guilty conscience might have been too big for her own tiny body, but it fits perfectly in mine. She fears her mother and is overwhelmed instantly with a need to confess. She wins. I fold. I don't confess, but I do scurry back like a shadow confronted with a light.

"I'm sorry. You're not aggressive. It's only been two weeks. I didn't mean to scare you by not going. I'm sorry. It's just that I was fine. I didn't think I needed it. I—" I bite my cheeks to keep myself from tripping over any more short sentences.

I glance sideways at Ava. I worry she can smell the shame that coats me all of a sudden like a bad perfume. I don't like that she's seeing me interact with my mom like this, acting like I'm fifteen trying not to get my phone taken away. I hope she still sees me as a sort of adult after this. I can't believe I managed to get publicly humiliated in my own house.

"You what, Savannah? What is it now?"

Whenever she asks me this, it makes me feel like the OCD was right. *See? You are too much for anyone but the dead. You're too much for even a mother to love all the way.* I guess it's only a matter of time before Ava starts saying that to me, too, now that she's walking around with feelings of her own. *What is it now, Savannah? How much more reassurance could you possibly need, Savannah? When are you going to stop spinning stories in your head, Savannah?* I fight the urge to ask my mom if she still loves me.

"Nothing," I say. "It's nothing. I'm not avoiding therapy. I'll go this week, it's fine. I've just been trying to experience life, like Hils says to. I've been hanging out online with my new friend, Ava, remember? The one with the school project?" Out of the corner of my eye I see Ava raise an eyebrow at me, but I ignore it. One thing at a time. Tomorrow's problem. "I promise I will email Hils and set up an appointment for this week, but I'm fine. Really. Everything is fine."

I don't even believe me, so I don't see how my mom will. I fight the urge to double down and keep telling myself that everything is fine, because I think if I double down too much it'll seem more suspicious and tip her off to what's really going on here. Well, maybe not exactly that; it would be hard for anyone to guess the specifics. But what if she could? We sit for a tense minute. I stare at a tiny gray dot of a stain on the rug to avoid Ava's eyes, grateful that Ava's usually merciful.

My mom sighs. "Are you sure you're okay?"

Are you sure you still love me? "Yes."

"And you will go to your therapy appointment this week?"

Sure, I don't know what I'll tell her, but I'll go. "Yes."

"And you're really putting yourself out there and finding new friends?"

Well . . . "Yes."

"Okay. You better not be lying to me."

"I'm not lying—I'll go to therapy." I'm not lying. At least there's that.

If my mom were in the room, it would be a stare-down, but instead it's a tense silence. And then she relaxes and the tension breaks.

"Well, honey, I'm really glad to see you working on doing better."

"Yeah." It's a stupid word, but I can't find another one.

"What are you going to do today?"

Hope on my hands and knees that anyone in the world still loves me, even you, because no matter how many times you tell me, I don't believe you when you say it. "Nothing much. Just hang out at the house." I hesitate, debating my next words. In the end I decide to say them, because I think they'll make me seem more okay to her, even if they feel batshit crazy in my mouth. "I think Ava and I are going to watch a movie later."

I am drenched in regret. I cannot look at Ava under any circumstances. I stare so hard at the spot on the rug, I half expect to remove the stain with the force of my eyes, but I worry slightly that this would summon Billy Mays's ghost and then I would have to avoid eye contact with two of them.

"Oh, Ava is coming there?"

"No, we're watching over FaceTime. Ava is still in Manhattan." Jesus.

"What do you mean over FaceTime? You can do that?"

"Yeah, it's like a party feature that connects your devices so you can watch at the same time."

She's not good with technology. Hopefully this will sound too complicated for her and she will drop it.

"That sounds too complicated for me, but you two have fun."

"We will!"

"Okay, well, go do what you need to do. Thank you for picking up the phone every day."

"No problem, Mom." I hesitate. "I love you."

She doesn't hesitate. "I love you, too."

I relax all the way. The reassurance has partially healed me for the next three seconds.

I hang up. Then I double-check that I hung up. I throw my phone down on the couch next to me and slump against the cushion.

"Soooo, how's your mom?" Ava asks.

"I'm going to pretend you didn't hear most of that." I already know I'm going to think about this in the middle of the night, every night, for a long time.

"It sounds like she's just looking out for you."

"She treats me like a child."

Ava looks at me in a way that makes me self-conscious, like she's trying to guess if I'm actually just three kids stacked in a trench coat. I tell myself I'm probably just projecting that onto her, that she doesn't really think that, but she'd be right. I've never even had a job. I brace myself to hear her say that my mom treats me like a child because I am a child, but she doesn't.

"She's just worried," she says instead. "You're vulnerable right now and you're insisting on seeing yourself through it. She's respecting your wishes on that, but she's still going to worry."

I don't know if making me call her every day—or else—and policing the frequency of my therapy appointments is respecting my wishes to be left alone, but Ava doesn't have a mom who worries about her and she actually did die out there on her own, so I probably should just shut up and eat my food.

"I know she's worried. I just wish she wasn't so aggressive about it." I check my phone to make sure I hung up, just in case.

Ava shrugs. "Some people are aggressive when they're scared."

"I'm not," I mutter, quiet enough that I don't know if she even heard me. It's true, though. My mom's fight-or-flight response is definitely fight, but I don't know if mine is. Maybe fawning? Probably not. Michelle says I don't have the empathy for that. I don't fight. I don't run. But I don't see a fourth option for those of us who, instead of fighting or fleeing or fawning, simply stand and wait for the scary thing to give us what we know we deserve. That's what I do. I fold. I don't get up afterward, either. Instead I lie there like a dead thing until someone beautiful comes to poke me with a stick and check if I'm okay. It's what I'm doing right now. It's why instead of saying anything else I pick at a loose thread on my blanket and leave the silence for Ava to fill.

"You should listen to her" is what she finally says. I appreciate that about this version of her. In the woods, I always have to talk first.

"Listen to her and go back to therapy or listen to her and let her come out here and hover over me to the absolute max like the mom in *Black Swan*?"

She chuckles even though it wasn't funny, and I appreciate her for that, too. Her laugh is nice. It's what pixie dust would sound like as it fell, little bells that make you fly.

"You should go back to therapy," she says.

I pull the blanket up to my neck and scoot backward.

"What?" she says.

"I don't know, it just feels weird going back to therapy with everything."

I don't want her to think that I see her as a burden, or think that she's keeping me out of therapy because I'm hanging out with her, although that's sort of true. I just need less therapy when I'm with her, because she's such a calm and reassuring presence and I feel safer than usual now. I can't say that, though, because then she will think I'm a freak who gets overly attached too fast, which I am.

"Am I everything now? I'm flattered!"

I resist the urge to pull the blanket up over my blush. Instead, I chew on the insides of my cheeks until they bleed. I think I'm starting to find the taste of blood comforting. I wonder if vampires think of it like that, like comfort food.

"No. I mean, you're great! You're very . . . I'm really glad to have you here. It's not that. I just feel like I've been thinking about you so much that I don't have much to say to my therapist."

"You've been thinking about me for two weeks?"

Fuck. Fuck fuck fuck fuck fuck.

"No! Yes. I mean, the two weeks before I found you were just really boring, and then finding you was a big shock and I would probably want to talk about that, but that's not really what my therapist is looking for. She's got a very specific realm of problems she wants to stay within."

Ava laughs. "I don't think that's how it works. Her agenda is just you, you know? Whatever it is that week that you feel like talking about will be fine with her; she's not the trauma police."

"My mom would disagree. She *definitely* wants Hils to stay focused on fixing me ASAP, so she can have the perfect-daughter version of me back, the version that's useful to her, the version that worked hard and got into a decent school, the one she can brag about to her friends."

I'm starting to worry that Hils will never be able to fix me, that nobody can. I don't know what it's like to experience a brain other than my own. And when I try to think my way out of myself, it only gets worse.

"Well, your mom doesn't get to know what happens in your session, just that you went, and that'll have to be good enough for her. And I'm sure you're good enough to brag about either way."

It's refreshing to be in the company of someone who doesn't know how much of a PR disaster I am lately.

"Right."

I munch on my bottom lip. I don't want to go back to therapy. It feels inconvenient now. I have too much to do. Two whole separate Avas and I can't tell Hils about either of them.

"If you're worried about me overhearing, I can be in another room. I won't invade any space you don't want me to. I know you didn't exactly invite me here, but I don't think either of us know how to get me all the way out of this house, so another room might be the best I can offer. Or outside! I can go outside!"

She cannot go outside. I do not need her finding out what's outside.

"You don't have to go outside!" I say it too quick and she flinches, startled.

"I don't mean to make a big deal out of it. We don't have to talk about your therapy schedule at all. I just want to make sure you have privacy. I don't want to be the reason you don't go."

"It's not that. Staying in another room is plenty. I'm just nervous, but it's okay, that's not because of you." I try to force a smile that doesn't look forced. Forced smiles are obvious on me. I look like a doll with a sewn-on face. "I'll go back to therapy."

SAVANNAH

HILS IS NOT my therapist's real name. I call her Hils because she looks like Hilary Duff. She lets me so I think it's fine, although sometimes in the middle of the night I worry that she hates me for it, that she thinks I stole her identity and gave it to Hilary Duff. My mom tried a short run of male therapists on me before her, because my mom prefers a male therapist, but I wouldn't open up to a man. I didn't think it was a man's business to be creeping on my secrets and I couldn't bring myself to respect any of them enough to want to listen to anything they had to say.

My appointment is a Zoom-ish meeting two days after I relented to Ava and my mom and agreed to go back. I say Zoom-ish, because it's like a therapist-sanctioned knockoff of Zoom that Hils has that complies with HIPAA or something. I don't know what I'm going to say. I just know I can't tell her anything that's the truth.

Hils says hello and asks how I am.

I say I am doing well. As I say it, I think of all the nights before Ava's ghost came, the ones where I struggled not to die waiting for midnight. Comparatively, I am doing well. The bar for doing well is low in this house.

She asks what I've been up to.

I don't know what to say. Again, I can't tell her I've been hanging out with a dead body; she'd have to report that. I could tell her about all the things I do to get myself to midnight, but since Ava's ghost showed up, it hasn't actually been that hard. She's a full-time distraction and I love her for it, a reassurance machine. But if I tell Hils about that, she's going to report me, which wouldn't be her fault—she just has to, I think. Is it just murder that your therapist has to report you for or does that responsibility also extend to corpse hoarding? I don't feel confident enough one way or the other to chance it.

I do wish I could tell Hils about this. I need advice!!! But nope, I can't go there. I can't risk it. In the end, I settle on the most boring, neutral version of my life I can find, my publicist-approved answer.

I tell her I've just been chilling, not much going on without school, spending too much time on TikTok, watching Zelda grow from a kitten into a whole cat. I stop myself before I tell her I've been taking walks in the woods. I want to keep the information I give as far away from Ava as possible, just in case when I actually do report the body, Hils deduces that I've been lying to her this whole time. She'll know I wouldn't have just missed a rotting body during all those walks. She'll know I've been showing up less because I've been cheating on her: one therapy session paid here, one therapy session free out there with a corpse.

Hils asks if there's anything else I've been doing. I analyze her face before I try to answer. I think I see a slight change in the position of her pupils. Does she know that I gave her a PR answer? She must know I gave her a PR answer.

I swallow. It's over; I start coming up with ways she could have found out. Maybe Ava's ghost emailed her an SOS or maybe I already said something that tipped her off. Maybe she already knows about my walks in the woods. What if she can smell the corpse on me through the screen? What if I wrote it on my forehead and then somehow forgot I wrote it on my forehead and it's still on my forehead and she's reading my forehead and she's about to be like "So do you want to tell me about what's on your forehead?"

Yep. She figured it out.

I panic and look for something else I can throw her as a decoy—a fake explanation for the guilt tattooed on every inch of skin.

"I think I have a drinking problem!" I blurt all at once, a cork popping out of a bottle.

She starts to laugh and then stops and apologizes for almost laughing, but I wish she had laughed all the way.

"Sorry," she says. "It's not the drinking problem, it's just the way you said it. We should talk about that, if you think you have a drinking problem. Why do you think you have a drinking problem?"

"I mean, I've been drinking . . . a little more than usual?"

"How much more is a little more than usual?"

"I—"

Okay, well, I can't give her the real number, because then she'll make me stop drinking, and I can't even handle California sober right now.

"Like a few, or four maybe, glasses of wine a week, a glass almost every night . . . But I used to drink, like, no glasses of wine! Zero wines."

She makes a face like she a little bit doesn't believe me, which is fair. "Well," she says, "*if* it's only a few glasses of wine a week, then that's better than I expected. But still, keep an eye on it. You don't want to get in the habit of using alcohol to cope with the OCD. But tell me if you do find yourself coping with alcohol, because we should talk about that."

Hils, my entire recycling bin is full of wine bottles.

"Yeah, no, it's okay, it's not, like, *that much*."

"You're not mixing it with the Ambien?"

"No." I am about to spontaneously combust with the violent urge to confess all of my sins, corpse related or otherwise.

"Okay. Good. Make sure you're not doing that, obviously."

"I won't."

"And about how many times a week are you taking the Ambien?"

How many days are there in a week? Well, actually, no. Lately I've been doing better about the Ambien because I have Ava. It's wayyyy more emergency-use now that all I want to do is stay up and talk to her.

"One or two."

"Okay, that's also better than I thought you might say. Good job."

I swallow. "Thank you. I'm a star."

"So is the drinking problem the main worry this week? Or has there been something else?" She knows and she's trying to get me to say it.

I shake my head no and dig my nails into my palms, bracing for her to tell me that she will have to contact the proper authorities about this, but then she moves on and asks me if I've been using the word *maybe* to try to combat the spirals like she asked me to at the end of last session, my homework. I'm supposed to be answering all my what-if questions with *maybe* to help me accept all the uncertainties that come with living life without getting trapped under the weight of them.

What if Hils finds out I've been hiding Ava from all the people who have been looking for her for almost three weeks? Maybe.

What if my mom puts two and two together after Hils rats me out and figures out that Ava the body and Ava my friend are the same person? Maybe.

I try to remember what I was spiraling about during my last session.

What if Michelle never loved me, not even as a friend? Maybe.

What if I think of her every day and she never thinks of me at all? Maybe.

What if she was good to me the whole time and I just imagined that night and made it all up and she's right to call me crazy now and she was right to leave me there and it's all my fault? Maybe.

What if it's because of this, because I can't stop thinking about all the what-ifs? I know it's exhausting to tolerate, because it's exhausting to me, because it's endless, because by the time I tunnel my way out from under one ambush of what-ifs, there's always more coming around the corner to bury me again. What if the reason Michelle did what she did was to punish me for tiring her out with my constant spiraling and endless need for reassurance? Maybe.

I worry it's never going to feel like it's working. I worry that it will be endless maybes for me, with nothing in return. I tell Hils this. All of the old what-ifs are still there, too, no matter what I do, cluttering the corners of my consciousness, getting dusty waiting for their turn to pop back into the rotation. Even if I did answer all the questions with *maybe*, they'd still be there, stacking up like all the books I buy and then forget to read.

And *maybe* just opens up a new realm of possibility, because if it's maybe true, then maybe there's more to spiral about; maybe it's worse. And when my brain hands me the thing that's worse, I'm still supposed to just say *maybe*. I wish she could at least give me something better to say to myself than *maybe* . . . I'd feel better about *probably*. *Probably* has a crumb of certainty in it that I can lick off the plate. *Maybe* shouldn't count as an acceptable answer. I tell Hils all of this, too, but she says that's the point. The *maybe* makes the answer uncertain. I'm supposed to be able to accept the uncertainty and move on, without dwelling and allowing the original thought to snowball until I'm crushed under the avalanche of every possible thing that could go wrong. I ask her if normal people can accept all that uncertainty and move right on with just a *maybe* and a shrug.

She says that neurotypical people also struggle with uncertainty, just not to the extent that people with OCD do; that's what she diagnosed me with a few months ago after I crashed out.

I squint at her. That can't be true. I'm sure it's easier for everyone else than she says. Either that or I'm weaker than she thinks I am. I tell her this and then we go back and forth for a few minutes about how it's not that I'm weaker than she thinks I am; it's that trying to tread water in the thought spiral will only trap me there until I'm drowning in a whirlpool of my own unfortunate what-ifs.

Half listening, I stare past my screen at the vanity/desk in the corner of my room. The surface is coated in a thin, slightly glittery mixture of dust, eyeshadow, and powder foundation that I have yet to wipe off. I wish I'd gotten the version of OCD that makes you cleanly and not the one that makes you crazy, but I guess I can't have nice things. I clock back in to catch the end of her spiel. It's the same spiel I usually get. The one where repetitive and disciplined use of the capital-*M Maybe* eventually shuts down the spirals and what-ifs almost completely and I can live my new life with one of the shiny happy normal-people brains. I give it another shot.

Is the whole world going to find out I've been hoarding a dead body for nearly a month? Maybe.

Am I going to jail for this? Maybe.

If Ava found out, would she hate me? Maybe.

I force myself to stop thinking about it; I fail, so I bury the old thoughts in new thoughts. The new thoughts fight with the old thoughts. The new thoughts tell me I need to stop thinking about the old thoughts, because if I keep thinking about the old thoughts I'm going to get stuck in the old thoughts, and if I get stuck in the old thoughts in front of Hils, she's going to see the distress in my eyes and ask me about it, and if she asks me about it, maybe—see! I did it!—I'll feel bad enough to confess and if I confess she might call the police and if she calls the police I might go to jail or maybe they'll think I'm too crazy for jail and I'll have to go back to the psych ward and if I have to go back to the psych ward or to jail Ava will definitely find out and she will hate me and I'll lose my only friend and also get canceled online and then I might as well stay in jail or the psych ward forever because my life is ruined anyway.

I'm busy swapping out all my *maybe*s for *probably*s when Hils asks if I'm still hearing many of my intrusive thoughts through Michelle, and if I still feel the need to talk back to her. My palms get clammy. I worry my palm sweat smells bad and that Hils can smell it, but then I remind the OCD that we haven't invented smell-o-vision yet, and it can't really argue with that.

The Michelle thing always feels illegal to talk about. It's admitting to what I'm most ashamed of: that I'm crazy. Certifiable. I am one of those people screaming at subway station support beams. Hils says it won't last forever, that I can learn to manage it in time with regular therapy and medication when I need it. I hope she's right, but it feels pretty hopeless for now and for all of recently, and I'm tired, so tired I wish I would get hit by a bus and end up in a brief coma just for some rest. If someone offered me a lobotomy right now, I'd take it. I was already in a bad place before the OCD suddenly got so much worse. On the days that it's bad, it's so painful that all I can do is lie there and beg for death. I can't breathe I can't eat I can't drink I've thought myself into kidney infections before from the dehydration and told all my friends I just jacked off too much and gave myself a UTI that spread so they would think I was more funny than I was fragile.

I took the loss of Michelle badly and it all got really grim, and I already had this untreated, undiagnosed insanity in me waiting for something to take me down about. It grew big and strong feasting on all of the loss, and I was so sad and hurt I couldn't eat at all. And too weak to hide it anymore. I lost all my friends and something broke, and then to replace my real friends I had Michelle living inside me, only my Michelle isn't exactly like real Michelle. My Michelle doesn't have any of the shimmering charisma the real Michelle had, can't give all the love real Michelle once at least pretended to give. All she ever does is tell me the worst of my thoughts with her perfect mouth full of too-sharp teeth.

It's hard to answer the questions. For one, answering means I have to acknowledge that I'm crazy, which I don't love. But also, I see a world in which this is a test. There's a right answer here, and there's a wrong one. If I admit I'm still seeing Michelle, maybe Hils will just think I'm not working hard enough or that nothing is working, or worse, that I need more support and have to be put under some sort of supervision. If I'm put under some sort of supervision, I lose Ava. How am I even supposed to tell them about Ava if I'm put under supervision? Scream out, "Oh, by the way, I found this body a while back, she's over there!" as they strap me onto the stretcher and wheel me into the ambulance? Then again, she might go easy on me and I'll just have to keep a journal of every time I see Michelle for a week, or some light penance like that. Also, I don't know if I am seeing Michelle anymore. I don't usually see her when Ava is with me, ghost or body, and I'm with some version of Ava most of the time, so maybe it's fine. Maybe Michelle is gone and I can say no and not even be lying.

But if I say no, then maybe Hils will think I'm too cured and I'll end up getting evicted from therapy and then I'm down to only one for-sure-real adult that I can talk to about anything, and I don't want to have to talk to my mom about all of this.

"Not really" is what I settle on. "I still hear her sometimes, but not as much." It's the truth, at least.

I hold my breath waiting for Hils to tell me if it was the right or wrong answer, if she believes me, what she thinks it *means*, but she just says, "Okay, good! Well, we're out of time for today, but keep track of any Michelle reappearances and we can talk about them next week. I'll email you a list of times."

"Okay," I say. Good, I passed. And the journal's not so bad. I've had to do the journal before. "That sounds good."

Hils smiles. "Great! Take care, Savannah!"

"Thanks," I say. "You, too!" I feel stupid for saying "you, too" even though I do genuinely hope she takes care. It feels like when the barista says "Enjoy your coffee!" and you say "You, too!" even though the barista doesn't have any coffee.

She hangs up. I close the laptop.

Liar, says Michelle.

SAVANNAH

MICHELLE HAS HAD her teeth in my neck for hours, but she won't bite hard enough to kill. She loves to have me like this, paralyzed and hers to maim. I am so inside my head it feels like the copy of the world behind my eyes is more real than anything else. It's so real I can feel the blood dripping from Michelle's mouth. I swear that when I look down, my shirt will be stained red. It's the same thought as usual, or at least it started that way.

What if Ava's ghost isn't even real?

I list the evidence I've been gathering for myself. I can touch her. I can smell her. She knows things about herself that I wouldn't know. She speaks like she does in the *Decomposition Book*. She remembers what it was like to die. She remembers her time in the woods. She remembers that Megan is dead. The fact that her hair moves in the wind, that squeeze of my thigh . . .

But what if she's not real? What if you don't have any sort of relationship with her at all? What if you've bonded with someone who only exists in your imagination? What if you're just like those losers who propose to their AI chatbots? What if she's not real?

She is. I've touched her. I've seen her sleep. I've seen her eat. She's not a living person and some of the stuff she does is not what a tangible and alive person would do or be able to do, but she's still real. Even Hollywood ghosts are allowed to be a little bit transparent.

And if not? And what if by the time anyone finds out that you held a dead body hostage for weeks just so you could pretend to have a friend, you're too far gone and you've fully convinced yourself that she's real so you tell people about the ghost, too, about how Ava's ghost was totally fine with this all along and that's why everything you did was fine, too? If you do that, you're going to look so batshit, it'll almost be worse than the way millions of people will think you're a corpse fingerer—you'll look so crazy that people will pity you.

Michelle bites harder and thrashes her head so the wound tears and I struggle to breathe. I curl up tighter into a little ball on my bed. I never even made it down the stairs after therapy, never even made it to the stairs. I may never make it to the stairs again. It's okay. I don't deserve to. I deserve to lie back with my chin up and offer Michelle my windpipe to twirl around her fork.

Well, maybe they won't pity you so much after they find out you're a corpse fingerer. But you will get another vacation. They'll lock you in a little room with white walls and only let you write with crayons because you're not even sane enough to handle a pen.

I swallow a mouthful of sand I made up inside my head. Maybe. Maybe no one will find out about this at all. Maybe it will all be fine.

Maybe it won't. And, for the record, it's not like Ava knows everything, either. What do you think she'd think if she knew you were monopolizing her grave? You do realize that you are actively, every minute of your life, denying her friends and family answers?

The itch is back. I pull one leg up to my chest by the knee and start to scratch off the scabs on my feet and ankles. I scrape at the edges of the skin until the wounds are bigger. I don't deserve to have skin on my feet.

Can't you imagine what that would be like? Missing a loved one? You hate uncertainty SO MUCH; look at you now, Savannah. You're so tormented by it that you can't even stand up, Savannah. Too weak to carry around your own brain, Savannah.

She gets on the bed and straddles me. She's heavier than she should be.

Get up, she says.

I can't.

I said get up!

I'm trying. I'm really trying. I know I deserve this. I know I deserve worse than this. I know it's pathetic. I know that I'm weak. I try to move my wrist, just my wrist. She crushes it with her knee.

She laughs, and it bounces off the walls of my skull, which feels way too small all of a sudden. *Do you know what it will be like when everyone finds out what you've done? Do you know what it will be like? It'll be like when all of your friends walked out of your life one by one, except this time it'll be everyone in the whole world all at once. Ava's family is going to file restraining orders against you. You're going to be* People *magazine's brand-new necrophiliac. Because why else would you keep her? No one would believe the real story, but wouldn't it be just as sad for you if they did?*

Maybe. I try not to see images of everything she's referring to, of all the horrible things that people will go to all the horrible corners of the internet to say that I did. I fail. I see them all. I see them all in detail. She moves her straddle up to my chest and sits with all her stone weight. I wheeze trying to acquire air. She laughs at me when I can't breathe.

You won't be able to come back from this. No one will ever love you after this. Well, there's always me. I'll always be here to love you.

She bends and dips her tongue into one of the wounds on my neck, then drags it up my jaw to my ear, blood and all.

Is this what you want her to do to you, Savannah? Is that what it's all for? Because you can't get a real woman to love you? Because after this you know you never will?

"Maybe. Maybe." I say my *maybe*s out loud, an incantation, but it's no use. She's like the hydra. Cut off one head and she'll grow so many more.

Even if no one ever found out, how bad would it be living your whole life knowing that you not only kept someone's corpse—a stranger's, whose funeral you won't even be invited to—and kept answers from her family, from Megan's, from Chad's, but you also invented a whole personality for her? You invented a person who doesn't exist and pasted her on top of her memory. That's fucked-up, Savannah. That's the most fucked-up thing you've ever done. Yet. I don't know, keep going. Maybe you'll set a world record. See? I used your new favorite word—maybe.

I don't fight after that. I give up and lie down for her, limp-willed and crying, biting down on the back of my hand for some sort of lesser pain. I choke trying to get a breath past all of the regret in the center of my throat. I regret everything I've ever done. I regret being born. There's nothing I can do. I can't fight it. When it's this bad, it's like standing on the deck of the *Titanic* as it's sinking, holding a bucket and trying to keep it afloat by scooping water out.

No one would love you ever again if they knew what you did, not even your mom, and even if you called her from the loony bin to ask her if she did still love you and she said yes, you would know she was lying, because you know what you did makes you, once again—say it with me—unlovable. You don't even love yourself, you just have to live with yourself. But if you didn't have to, you couldn't. And after this, you won't be able to. You won't be able to handle the sheer volume of guilt. You will die from it. Slow and painful. And the world will cheer when your heart stops beating.

"Savannah?"

I feel a hand on my back, more solid than Michelle's, and the paralysis breaks. When I convince my eyes to open back up, Ava's there, lowering herself down onto the bed, eyes soft with concern. She's looking at me like I'm a scruffy kitten in the shelter and for a second I feel cared for, before I remember she might not even be real, before I remember I don't deserve to be cared for. My hand goes to my neck on reflex to check for wounds, but the only blood anywhere is on my palms and under my fingernails. And both of my feet drip onto my sheets from the wounds I scratched open and wide. I remember to feel embarrassed, taking myself in—it's always so embarrassing when people see me like this. I scrub the tears off with my hand, smearing my cheeks with foot blood.

"What's wrong?"

"Nothing." I shudder, trying to squirm out from under it. It helps so much that Ava's here, looking at me like she loves me in spite of my inability to win a fake war. "It's nothing."

"It doesn't look like nothing. You didn't come back down from therapy, and you're bleeding."

"It is nothing." I wipe my hands off onto my shirt, then bring the fabric to my face to scrub off the combo of snot, blood, and tears. At least I'll never be a necrophiliac. She'd never want me after seeing me like this. "I just scratched myself."

She walks my body with her eyes, taking in the sweat on the sheets, the exposed flesh on the top of my right foot, the bags under my eyes, the mascara smeared across my cheeks. I sniffle and wipe my nose on my wet pillowcase. It doesn't matter what Ava sees anymore. I'm ruined for everyone after their first glimpse of this. "This doesn't look like nothing," she repeats, quiet, like she's worried I'm too delicate to withstand real sound. And maybe she's right.

"I'm sorry." My face is still half in the pillow, so it comes out muffled.

"For what?" she asks.

"For letting you see me like this. It's pathetic. I know."

"It's not pathetic," she says. She puts one hand on my back and starts to rub in little circles. "What's wrong? What did this to you?"

"I can't decide whether or not you're real, and I can't deal with how crazy it means I am if you're not real."

My brain will scream at me later for being so honest, but I'm too exhausted to give her anything but the truth.

"Is that all?"

She asks like it's some small thing, like I haven't just asked her the most important question in the whole world.

"I can't live with my . . . self if you're not." My voice breaks in the middle of the word *myself* and she sees me trip over yet another crack in the pavement.

She has a face that makes me feel safe to tell her everything, that makes me feel like I'm being held. I'm scared she's just faking it—I'm scared I can't tell. "Are you real?" I ask, panicking about how unwilling she seems to tell me, about how long she's chosen to wait.

She laughs. "As real as a ghost can be."

"You're real?"

"I am real, yes. For now at least, if that helps."

"You're real," I tell myself more than I tell her. She's already seeing me like this, so I don't hide my need to convince myself for sure, my need to double down. I say it in front of her, over and over, giving her so many chances to take it back before I let myself have the safety of believing. "You're real, you're real, you're real. You are you and you are real."

"I am me and I am real." She brushes a tear off my cheek to show me how real she is, how tangible she can be.

You are you and you are real. You are you and you are real.

You are you.

And you are real.

My need to believe it throbs within me like a pulse.

AVA

It's strange to say, but after that night with the bear, despite everything, I think Megan and I were actually happy for a bit. Everything was fucked and we were hungry and dirty and hopeless, but it was nice. There was nothing to answer to except each other. No work. No rules. It was just us, living a cottagecore fantasy set to hard mode. We'd been in such an insane situation for all this time that my crush on her had faded into an irrelevant side plot. It was too good, actually, so good I was suspicious. There was no way it could last, not after this. If we got rescued, Megan would have other options. She wouldn't have to settle for me. I still hadn't even officially confirmed she was gay. I watched her as she slept during the nights following the bear, searching for some kind of sign, afraid to ask. She seemed pretty gay when we had sex, but it wouldn't be the first time a straight woman simply took what she could get. That's like a quarter of the plot of Orange Is the New Black.

One morning as we were sitting outside the cave, building our fire for the day, I finally mustered the courage to bring it up. I'd stayed up all night the night before, drafting different ways to open the conversation in my mind, preparing myself for news of a long-lost ex-boyfriend she planned to reconcile with on the other side. I watched her, head dipped low over the firewood, Chad's flintstone in her hand, and I took mental pictures of this time while she was mine just in case the conversation ruined it.

"So are you, like, canonically gay or just prison gay?"

She snorted and looked at me, her lips turned up at the corners, eyes absolutely dazzling. "I'm sorry, prison gay?"

"You know, like women who participate in lesbian activities in prison because it's their only choice, and then when they get out they go back to men. Prison gay."

She laughed again, with her head thrown back this time, just about kicking her feet in delight at my awkwardness. I fidgeted with the frayed hem of my T-shirt and watched, waiting for her answer with a dry throat.

"Are you trying to hit me with the what-are-we conversation?" Her smile was full because she loved to mess with me and she knew I was absolutely squirming inside.

I looked away because I couldn't help it. I was suddenly too exposed. It felt like locking myself out of a hotel room naked in the middle of the night and having to call some smug girl at the front desk to bring me a key. I marveled at how effortless this was for Megan, how my vulnerability thrilled her, and how comfortable she was to sit in it with me.

Sensing that I was close to retreating back to my comfort zone and saying never mind to the whole thing, she scooted up next to me so our thighs touched. She put a few fingers to my chin so I'd look at her. I did, begrudgingly. Still, I found her difficult to look directly at—she was like the sun. She still looked smug as hell, but her eyes had softened.

"Canonically, I'm bi, but I lean toward women."

"Really?"

"Don't sound so surprised! I wasn't that bad, was I?"

I laughed. "No, not at all, I just didn't think . . . I mean, didn't you come out here planning to sleep with Chad?"

She burst out laughing so hard that she started coughing and had to catch her breath before she could answer. "With Chad?!"

I blushed. "Not for love! Just for a promotion. Not judging, by the way. Do what you gotta do."

She laughed again, for a long time with her mouth wide open, wiping tears from her face. "No, oh my god, ew! No. No job is worth sleeping with Chad for." She turned her face to the sky and shouted "No offense" to Chad.

"But . . . the nightgown?"

She blinked at me, leaning forward, examining my face. "The nightgown?"

"Yeah. The sexy one with the lace that you brought out here but said we couldn't talk about. Why else would you bring lingerie on a camping trip?"

She opened her mouth, then closed it, stunned to silence.

"What?"

"Ava, what the fuck are you talking about?"

I gestured wildly back at the cave where all our stuff was, frustrated. Why was she gaslighting me about the nightgown? "The nightgown! The one you literally brought fucking camping!"

"Mmm-hmm," she said, nodding rapidly. "Yes, the nightgown. The one I brought out here for you."

"What?" I know she was actively sleeping with me, but I still couldn't comprehend it. Like, I'm sorry, I'm supposed to believe she found me desirable before *this??? I thought the trope we were in was forced proximity, not friends-to-lovers.*

"I brought the nightgown out here for you," she repeated.

I just stared at her, flabbers all the way gasted.

"I figured it would be girls in one tent, Chad in another. He said he'd bring all the supplies. I always assumed two tents was the obvious move, but Chad was, you know, Chad." She sighed. "I was going to get you in the tent with me and seduce you. That's the whole reason I even agreed to go, because you said you'd come, and I was going to shoot my shot! But then fucking Chad only brought one tent and cockblocked me. How heteronormative of you to assume it was for Chad though."

I shook my head. "It's not that! It's just that you're so far out of my league, there was no way."

She scoffed. "That's so not true."

"It is!!"

"It's not. You're beautiful and really nice and you sing actual opera, which is an insane flex. But sure, I'm the one out of your league. I'll let you believe that."

It shocked me that she seemed so sincere about it. I always thought she saw me as a couple notches beneath her, that hanging out with me at work was an act of pity that got her free coffee on Mondays.

"You're—" I just waved my hands at her a bunch because I couldn't even find the words to describe how overwhelmed I was by her all the time, how grateful I was that she'd even deign to look at me.

"Obsessed with you? Yes, yes, I am. I didn't really see an appropriate time to bring it up before. And then after the poison ivy . . ." She shook her head, like the poison ivy was her gravest mistake. "I just assumed you'd been permanently turned off by me, and I cut my losses until the bear scared me so much that I was like, fuck it. You turned out to be surprisingly easy to seduce, by the way."

I blushed, fidgeting with my hands. "That's because I came out here for you too."

She cackled. She squished her body into mine, wrapped an arm around me, and pulled me close. She planted a peck on my neck and rested her head on my shoulder. "So . . . Do you want to be my girlfriend, then?"

"If I say yes, do I get to see the nightgown?"

"I'd let you see the nightgown even if you said no."

I kissed the top of her head and nodded into her hair. "Facebook official?"

"Oh yeah, gotta be or it doesn't count."

We sat together like that for a second, basking in the unmatched joy of simply having each other. I felt relieved that she kept her head on my shoulder and couldn't see me, because I couldn't stop grinning like a psychopath.

Finally, Megan asked, "Do you think this is our punishment for being gay?"

I laughed. "What?"

"You know how religious people are always saying god punishes people for being gay? Maybe being stuck like this in the woods is our punishment. Maybe the woods are homophobic."

I snorted. "Oh yeah. The woods are definitely homophobic."

"Haters," she said, flipping off the endless trees.

And from then on we were official, and everything that went wrong in the woods was homophobic.

~AA Brown

SAVANNAH

WE HAVE A routine now. Every morning I get up way too early and slip into the woods before dawn to read your journal and keep your body company. I just got to the part in the journal where Chad dies. I didn't cry over him, but I stared at the paper for a long time. It's like reading the memoir of someone who survived a World War: terrible, but almost too distant to fully empathize with. I wonder how far away his body is from yours, from where we are right now. I wonder if he's bones by now. Probably.

You're not totally thawed yet. It's still acting like winter. I'm a summer girl by nature, but baby let it snow. I've really been worrying about what happens after I report your body to the police. I plan on sticking to my timeline. I'll tell them about you when we're down to your bones. Yikes, that last part makes me sound like a serial killer. I'm worried I'm getting too comfortable with visiting a corpse. I'm already part of the most desensitized generation ever to exist—I don't need to be any more desensitized. I'm supposed to be growing empathy.

But what if your ghost is only able to be here with me because your corpse is close by? I should probably answer that with "maybe," but I'm not even sure it's an OCD concern. It seems logical that when they remove your bones, your spirit will go with it. Right? I wish someone had done a scientific study on this. (I looked.) Good thing I set myself a strict decomposition deadline, because I don't think I'd ever be strong enough to give you up without that. I really like having you around. My visits to your body are shorter now, because I want to get back to my house to be with you as quickly as possible. I go to read your journal. I go to say hello, to ensure you are there and safe and your flesh knows that it's loved. (Not like that.) But the whole time I'm there, I just want to get back to the you that's beautiful and warm and responsive.

Usually, you're still asleep when I come back. You sleep with your door open a crack. I peek as I walk by, and I smile when I see your hand draped over your eyes, one foot dangling off the bed, out of the covers. Sometimes Zelda is there with you and I wish I could take a picture, but you don't show up on camera. We've tried. It doesn't matter. I keep a thousand pictures of you behind my eyes. I have a semi-photographic memory. It's why Michelle can haunt me as much as she does. It's okay now, though, because I'm not alone anymore and Michelle hasn't come around again since that last time. I'm wallpapering over the image of her with more of you. I don't want to wake you up, so I tiptoe past into my room. I take a shower. I brush my teeth. I put on some form of cozy loungewear I could have reasonably been wearing all morning just hanging around in my room. Today, it's a pair of black Lululemon leggings and a T-shirt I had overnighted that says Future Corpse on it—to show solidarity. It wasn't my idea. You like morbid jokes and when I saw an ad for the shirt on Instagram and tried to hide it from you, you snorted and demanded I buy it.

I do a fit check in the mirror and head downstairs to make coffee for myself and feed Zelda her wet food to go with her dry food just in case she forgets to drink water and dies like I read on Reddit can happen with some cats. Most mornings you wake up and come down around the time the coffee is finishing brewing. Today is your first time seeing the shirt. You almost die again laughing in my kitchen. Your coffee appears in front of you. We sit on my couch. We drink our coffee and we talk about anything. You're so smart and so kind. I've never felt so safe with anyone. And I've been so starved for *real* friendship. We're working through my little gay starter pack activities together. We just started watching *The L Word*. Jenny is my least favorite. And she's kind of a bad writer.

I'm learning about opera. You're showing me all your favorites, and it feels like my own personal backstage tour, seeing all of them with a real opera singer. Your voice in my ears. Commentary just for me. Today we're watching *Le Comte Ory*, which turns out to be gay and contains a short threesome. A few of the old ladies in the live audience gasp when the tenor sticks his whole head under the soprano's big pink skirt, and it makes us laugh.

We don't do anything too exciting; we just sit like this, all day every day, enjoying each other's company. In the late afternoons, I make another pot of coffee. I've been drinking a lot of coffee. I hardly sleep, because I know my hours with you are limited and I want to enjoy every minute while it lasts. We eat dinner together. I have wine. You have a Manhattan. I make one for myself after dinner because I've never tried one before and I have all the ingredients. I hate it. Every sip makes me shudder, but I drink the whole thing, because with every shudder, your Tinker Bell laugh rings around the room and bounces off the walls. I make popcorn. We watch scary movies under the same blanket. Only our legs touch. We go to sleep when you want to.

Separate beds, separate rooms, of course. I know we're just friends and I get that you've been through a lot. I'd never do anything you're not comfortable with. It's just nice to have a friend, is all. I love you, as a friend.

And I love our routine. Hils always says I should have a routine. Hils would like this.

SAVANNAH

I FINALLY HAVE one of my nightmares—the first one since you arrived. My brain isn't fun or creative with it. The dream is just that night with Michelle, exactly the way it was. I start at the beginning and wake up at the end, with a sob so big it's almost a scream. Usually when I wake up from these dreams, Michelle is standing over me or lying beside me in bed, asking "What's the matter?" with her shark grin of too many teeth. I try not to open my eyes now. I squeeze them shut tight, tears escaping from the tiny cracks in the corners like the world's saddest, saltiest juice press. I wait for her to bend over me so I can feel her breath on my face, lips brushing my ear while she calls me a coward for not looking at her—my own personal Medusa. But when the voice does come, it's not Michelle's; it's yours.

"Hey," you say, cupping my shoulder with your soft hand. "Hey, Savannah, I think you're having a nightmare."

I open one eye a crack, not entirely sure it's not a trick, but the body standing over me is too big to be Michelle's. For you, I open my eyes all the way.

"Ava?" I ask, my voice rougher than you've ever heard it, caked in the gravel of sleep.

"I'm here," you say, lowering yourself onto the edge of my bed like you did your first night.

I reach over and turn on my bedside lamp. You take my hand

and drag your thumb back and forth across my skin. Your hand is so soft.

"I'm sorry," I blubber. "I didn't mean to wake you."

"It's okay," you say. "Everyone has bad dreams. I just wanted to make sure you were all right."

I brush a few rogue tears off my face with the back of my hand and tell you I'm fine. We sit there for a minute. It's quiet except for the sound of my sniffling, which embarrasses me. I suppress the sniffling by not breathing, until you notice and tell me to breathe. The clock on my nightstand says 3:37. I make the executive decision not to visit your body in the woods today.

"Do you want to tell me what the dream was about?"

I'm already shaking my head before you finish the question. I'm too ashamed. Your corpse is one thing. But it's different when you're beautiful and breathing and there's eye contact to be made.

"It's fine. I just had a really shitty ex–best friend."

You exhale loudly so I'll know you can relate. "We've all been there. I get it. Nightmare about Michelle?"

I nod. You don't remember anything I told you before in the woods, but I've mentioned her a couple of times. Just like with my old friends before this, I can't seem to not talk about Michelle. She's everywhere in my vocabulary. Trying not to mention her is like this time in middle school where a group of us tried to remove the word *like* from our vocabulary thinking it wouldn't be that hard, only to learn that we habitually used it every other word every single sentence. We did not last long. It's like that.

Still, you only know of Michelle, not too much about her. Unlike everyone else, who couldn't wait for me to shut up, you're still looking at me for more words. I scramble for something to say about her that isn't the story of everything. Whenever I think about Michelle, a lump forms in my throat—I'm pretty sure it's the ball of words that come together to make up the explanation of what happened that night, but I've never spoken those words out loud, not to your body, not to anyone. I never even told Hils, not with my voice. I wrote it down for her in a letter. I want to tell you, but I'm not ready yet.

"Yeah. She, um . . . She was a lot" are the words I eventually manage to push past the lump.

"If you ever want to tell me about it—" you start, but I cut you off before you can finish.

"I know," I say. I force a tight smile. "Thank you."

"You should try to go back to sleep."

I should, but I don't want you to leave. I squeeze your hand a little tighter by accident, hoping you won't notice. You notice.

"Do you want me to stay? No pressure, I don't have to stay. I can leave you alone, too."

I want you to stay so bad, but I don't want to seem desperate, clingy, or childish, so I pretend to chew on the choice. Then I nod real slow and let the nod spread into a smile, like the idea of you staying here had never once dawned on me before, but now that I think of it . . .

"Yes. Please stay. Only if you don't mind."

"A bed's a bed," you say. "Scoot over."

I turn off the bedside lamp and scoot.

You slide in and wrap your arm around me. I tell myself not to get too excited about this. You're used to snuggling for warmth in the woods. That's all it is—a survival snuggle. And since you're used to it, while we're here, I let myself relax into you. I lay my head on your chest, which is warm and soft and squishy. Your boobs are like pillows, not that I'm thinking too much about your boobs.

I don't even remember falling asleep, but when we wake up together seven perfectly peaceful hours later, I'm still curled into you.

SAVANNAH

I HAVEN'T HAD any more nightmares in the last few days, but I find myself wishing for them. Before I go to sleep at night, I walk myself through all the memories of Michelle I've been avoiding and tell myself it's exposure therapy. I show myself her vicious smirk as she pushes me back onto the bed and tells me it'll be fine. I show myself her tipping that last shot into my open mouth. I feel it gurgle in my throat as I choke trying to swallow it. I even push myself to remember the parts I won't say out loud. Nothing. No nightmares. I wake up jealous of Megan. I wake up mad at Michelle for not being worse. The least she could have done was fuck me up enough that I could have you in my bed every night.

In the morning, you ask how I slept and if there were any more nightmares, and I tell you no and you laugh and point out that I seem disappointed and I stare into my coffee mug, letting my hair fall around my face, so you can't see the pink spread across my cheeks like teenage acne. I don't tell you that I'm barely sleeping, that every night I stare at my ceiling for hours and count the little white bumps in the plaster while I try to justify not telling you about my custody of your body. I don't tell you that I sometimes look at you and wish I had a different type of custody of your body.

At least I'm not tempted to sleep in, so I make it out to the woods every morning before you wake up. The weather is back up in the fifties and you've basically thawed out. You're not bloated anymore. You popped and started to ooze when the thaw started. The melted snow dripped off you, tinted smoky gray with broken-down bodily fluids, for a week. Now you look deflated and withered, a slimy grape en route to raisin.

The decomposition doesn't bother me anymore, but the rate of it as the season shifts from winter into spring scares me. I find myself spending fewer mornings reading your journal and more wearing my own minipath into the cold dirt between my tree and yours with all my pacing. I'll have to smooth it out again before the police come. I look at the you on the ground, gray and decayed, and think of the you in my house, beautiful and vibrant. The more I love you, the harder it gets. My stomach hurts so much from the guilt that I can barely eat. I can't look you in the eyes for too long without feeling the urge to confess. I stop pacing and kneel in front of your corpse; you're an altar that only I know to worship at.

I bow my head and whisper my daily apologies into the dirt between your boots as has become our ritual. "I know, I'm so sorry, I know," I say, over and over again, like you chastised me already, even though you didn't say anything at all. I watch my tears hit the ground and hate myself for crying. I shouldn't be crying. I'm the perpetrator. I shouldn't be allowed to cry over this, but it's impossible not to. The guilt presses itself into my ribs like a stamp and stews in my stomach and the more I love you the worse it gets. I'm trapped in the back-and-forth of it. I want to keep you with me, your beautiful soul. But I don't want to do it without your consent. If I tell you and you want me to report your corpse immediately, even if it means I'll lose your soul, I will. I'll have to. I can't claim to love you and also hold you against your will. But isn't that what I'm doing now? Telling a lie of omission? *If you love her, let her go.* The whisper comes from the back of my head somewhere. I bat it away like a fly.

"I can't," I say out loud. "I can't, I can't, I can't . . ."

You have to. This isn't what love is.

But I can't!

You're as bad as Michelle.

I know.

I can't handle the guilt much longer. Not that I'll have to; I'm sure there's not much longer until you're just bones and that'll be time's up. No matter how far I try to run from time, I'm still standing on a clock that's slowly counting down. I glance at my watch: 5:54 a.m., almost time to head back. The second hand ticks around the circle, dragging me by the ankles into the future. I look away and lock eyes with your corpse. Well, I lock eyes; your corpse locks eye sockets.

"I know," I say again. "And I'm sorry."

I reach one hand up and make the motion of cupping your cheek without touching your face. Then I stand to leave. I trudge back staring at my shoes. It starts to drizzle in that way where the droplets never seem to hit the ground—they just hang in the air like little bugs, creating a cold humidity. Instead of wrapping my arms around my chest and huddling against it, I let myself shiver all the way home. I don't deserve to feel warmth.

I hope you're asleep so I have time to take a long shower and talk myself back into being okay with what I've done, but of course you're not. I slump through the back door to find you already parked on my couch with your coffee. You know I take walks in the mornings—you just don't know why—so you aren't surprised to see I've been out.

"Welcome home!" you say with a big smile. You're comfortable now. You're healing from the woods. You feel safe with me. You shouldn't, though. I'm just as bad as Michelle. Worse.

I try to smile back, but the corners of my mouth stay stuck in a tight straight line. I turn away and start making coffee so you don't see that I'm holding back tears. I put the grounds in the filter and my stomach gurgles a warning that I shouldn't be trying to consume anything while feeling this guilty. I pour the water in, push the button, and back away before the smell makes me gag. I head for the cabinet with the mugs to give myself another excuse to keep my back to you.

"You know, I was thinking that since the weather is so shitty and gray today, we should have a Disney Pixar kind of day and just get cozy. Hear me out: we start with *Monsters, Inc.*, then maybe *Emperor's New Groove* and *Road to El Dorado* if we have time. You can veto whatever. I just really like those ones . . ." You continue on with various kids' movie suggestions, but I'm not really listening. My body is more full of guilt than blood. I can't take it. I brace myself against the counter, one arm pressed over my stomach. I try to breathe through it, but my throat feels thinner than usual, like I'm taking in air through one of those tiny red plastic straws used exclusively for stirring gas station coffee.

The machine beeps. I force myself through the motions. I get the creamer from the fridge. I pour a little into my mug, holding my breath against the sweet cream smell that I usually enjoy. Then the coffee. The steam travels up and fogs the glasses I wear occasionally. I take them off, leave them on the counter, and head to the couch, still trying desperately to act normal, but moving stiff and slow and feeling more and more like Pinocchio trying to insist that he's a real boy. I put my mug down on the coffee table and grab the remote, scrolling wordlessly through Disney Plus because I can't find it in me to actually respond to your suggestions. The plan is to get the movie on as fast as possible and distract you before you see that I'm acting weird and start asking questions. I race to find *Monsters, Inc.* in record time, but just as my finger hovers over the play button, it happens.

"Are you okay?" you ask. "You seem a little tense this morning."

Fuck. I close my eyes and take another two coffee-straw breaths before I open them. I put down the remote and turn my whole body toward you. I bow my head and stare at my hands for a moment before deciding that I do at least owe you eye contact. I look up into your shiny green eyes. My stomach twists in protest, but I have to do this. *Don't do it, bitch*, one side of my brain hisses at me. But I have to. I have to.

"I have something to tell you."

AVA

I told her I loved her for the first time the day we ran out of coffee. It was around 7 am and we'd been up the whole night before, just lying there and talking. I told her about my shitty childhood, raising my siblings against my will. She told me about her shitty childhood, a latchkey kid of a single mom who just didn't have the emotional or physical resources for a child. We talked about our exes. She told me that before me, she'd had such bad taste in men that eventually she had to swear off them altogether. I told her that before her, I'd dated four women, back-to-back, who were all also named Ava. They kept dumping me in lesbian bars. The fourth Ava broke up with me in Cubbyhole when another girl approached her and asked if she was with me. She said no.

"Wait, what?!" Megan said when I told her, interrupting the story. "So another girl came up to other Ava and was like 'Hey, are you here with anyone?' and she straight up said no with you right there next to her???"

"Yup."

"Fuck, that's brutal. You gotta stop dating Avas."

I grinned at her in the dark, running my thumb along the soft skin on the back of her hand under the covers. "I think I've dated my last Ava."

"We're going to have to redeem Cubbyhole for you when we get home."

"Oh, we will!" I pictured myself with Megan in the back corner of the tiny bar, squished on our little stools behind the ice machine and jukebox, cold draft beers in our hands, engagement rings on our fingers. I wished I could click my heels and take us there like Dorothy, but I settled for keeping my arms around her in the cave all night long, savoring the sound of her voice as she told me all her stories.

We still had to force ourselves up pretty early, since you can't do anything out here after the sun goes down, and we had a lot to do outside every day before it got dark. Megan kissed the tip of my nose, then crawled to our pile of firewood near the mouth of the cave to start a fire. I hauled myself down to the stream to get water.

"Devastating news," Megan said when I got back.

"What?" I asked, handing the pot over to her.

"We're out of coffee," she said, her mouth a flat grim line.

"No!!!"

"Yep." She tipped the open tin upside down and not a speck of coffee fell out.

"Fuck, and today of all days."

"I know, right? Homophobic," she said, shaking her head.

"Homophobic," I agreed.

We got through a few hours' work resetting snares and gathering firewood before the brutal caffeine headaches and leftover exhaustion from the all-nighter brought us both to our knees. We cut our losses for the rest of the day and slunk back into the darkness of the cave, passing a pot of weak tea back and forth.

"Ugh," Megan said, "the lack of coffee is somehow making me so nauseous, more than my usual hunger nausea, I mean. Are you getting that?"

"No, just the headache over here."

"Huh. Good thing I haven't eaten anything in two days, so I can't gross you out of loving me by puking everywhere. Although, you did *see the poison ivy rash, so maybe you'd be okay with it."*

"I would love you no matter what," I said, freezing in place as soon as I realized what I'd said.

"I know I kind of baited you into that, but . . . you love me?"

My chest tightened. I was so scared to say it again. I didn't want to fuck it up. "I do," I said in the end. "I love you."

She smiled the widest smile I've ever seen, all the way to her ears and everywhere in her eyes. "I love you too."

~AA Brown

SAVANNAH

YOU TAKE THE news better than I thought you would. You take it better than me, at least. I blabber and stutter the whole way through, tripping over my words like they're cracks in pavement. You deserve eye contact, so I stare hard ahead, barely blinking, through the welled-up tears ready to spill down my cheeks. I tip my head back a little in an effort to keep them in my eyes so it doesn't look like I'm trying to play the victim here. I'm not, I swear. I just feel really really *really* bad and I can't help it.

You, on the other hand, are stoic. You take in my breathless, frantic confession with an expression of shocked fascination that shifts minimally. I still don't tell you what happened with Michelle, because it's not important. I do remind you that she really fucked me up. I tell you that the way she went about leaving was really bad, that I had a breakdown and had to go to the psych ward for a while. I tell you that, at first, I'd been planning to go back to school. You're listening, but, mostly, you're watching me—you're not looking at me; you're looking into me—running my words through a sieve, trying to figure out how the hell me planning to go back to school leads to your body held hostage in the woods and played with like Slightly Rotten Barbie.

I grovel in advance of your anger. I plead with my hands out and open like they do in operas. I tell you I was really fucked-up and I tell you about the wine and the Ambien and about how

Michelle runs my brain when I'm alone or whenever the clock strikes midnight like I'm Schizophrenic Cinderella even though Hils assures me I don't have schizophrenia, just OCD, except OCD doesn't make you this crazy, not crazy enough to end up in the woods talking to a dead girl. Plenty of people have OCD and don't hoard bodies, I'm sure. The contamination OCD people probably actively avoid corpse hoarding.

I tell you that Hils doesn't know I'm hoarding a body or its ghost. I think she would have to report that. I tell you about the weird moment I had with your body when I first found you, when Michelle shoved me toward you and then she was gone, when I felt safe, when I felt like maybe you were my person, someone who could be trusted with a raggedy girl as broken as me.

And then when you—I mean ghost you—turned up, I didn't want to lose my only friend. It feels pathetic as I say it. Your mouth opens. This is pathetic. Your mouth closes. I am pathetic. "And if you want me to," I say, staring at my empty hands, pale cups in my lap, "I'll go to the police today and then we can see what happens next, and I am sorry. I'm really sorry."

My confession seems to have sucked the atmosphere out of the room. We soak in a silence that feels unbearably loud. I risk a glance at you, but you're still staring at me, disturbed and awed, like I'm a zoo animal giving birth.

"I'm sorry," I whisper again and then return my gaze to my hands, too ashamed for eye contact.

We sit like this for several minutes. I shiver trying to suck my tears back in. I do not deserve to cry. In the center of the carpet in front of the TV, Zelda pounces on a toy spring. It goes flying and bounces off the wall. You turn to look, and I flinch at your movement as if you'd hit me. You wouldn't hit me. But I know I deserve it. You see me flinch, and your soft hand goes to my knee. I hold my breath and try not to move, the way I would if a butterfly landed on me.

"Look at me," you say. Your voice is firmer than I've ever heard it. I try to swallow, but my mouth is too dry. I force my eyes up.

"I'm sorry," I tell you again.

"That's— It's—" You shake your head. Your mouth moves in search of a word, but nothing comes out for a minute and then, eventually, "Why?"

"I don't know," I say. I really don't. I know I tell myself it's because of giving her a good death, watching over her, and this, and that, and the third, but truthfully, I don't know. "I wish I had a good explanation, but I don't. I think a little bit of me genuinely wanted to give you space to rest in peace, but that's not even the biggest part of it. Really I'm just fucked-up, like I said. I'm just a sad nothing of a girl who's crippled by loneliness and needed a friend, but I drove all mine away by being weird, and I don't know how to get more. And you know how I read some of your journal? So, I knew you were gay, too, and you seemed nice and safe and older and wiser and I needed an adult—preferably a gay adult—and so, yeah, I hijacked your death. It was selfish, like I said, I know it was, but before I could think about why I was doing it, I was already too deep in. And for the first time in months I had something else to focus on besides just fucking drowning in Michelle. I don't know why you or why that—it just . . . happened."

You nod slowly. Your jaw moves a little and I imagine you chewing on my poor excuses like taffy.

"So you still have it? Her? Me."

"I do. That's where I go in the mornings."

You exhale for a long time. It makes me nervous, but all you say after is "I thought you were just one of those unhinged morning people."

I chuckle, but it sounds more like a sob. "No, no, not unhinged. Worse."

"Worse." The word drops from your lips and floats down, soft, like you're still making up your mind about what it means.

I hold my breath.

"Not permanently, though. You said you always planned to turn me in?"

I nod with vigor. "Yes, absolutely, yes! The plan has always been that when you're all the way bones, I'll call the police and pretend I just found you."

"I'm not all the way bones yet? Hasn't it been kind of a while?"

"Right? It takes a weirdly long time. I thought it would be a few days, maybe a week, but no, you're not bones yet."

"Huh."

I shrug. "It's still cold. You were frozen for a week. There aren't a lot of wild animals out here, or maybe they're hibernating. Anyway, it's taking a minute."

"Are my eyes, like, open and glassy?"

I shake my head. "You have no eyeballs."

"Yikes."

"Yeah, sorry."

"It's okay. Happens to the best of us."

"Yeah."

I think about how I still somehow can't fathom that it will ever be me even though I threaten to die all the time. It's quiet again.

"So, what do you think? It's your call. We can call the police right now. We can wait until you're bones. We can call in a week, a few days. Whatever you want to do. I'm—again—so sorry. I fucked up. I won't do it again, not that I'll have access to a random hiker's corpse in the woods again, I hope, but you know what I mean."

You provide me with a crumb of forgiveness in the form of a small laugh. I lick it off the plate, greedy.

"We can wait until I'm bones," you say.

"Wait, really?"

You stare at something past me for a minute before you snap back into focus. Your eyes are intense on me, but so much kinder than I deserve.

"Really." You sigh. "We don't know anything about what's happening now. Who knows? Maybe I'm just here until I'm bones anyway. Maybe it's that way *and* I'm stuck near my body. I'd rather be here for a while than in some morgue, staring at the closed door of my fridge. And if part of that is helping you get over whatever your friend did to you, then that's fine with me. I'll make myself useful. It's not like my family will be tripping over themselves trying to find me."

I bite my cheeks until there's blood as I remember your sister paying your rent, burning down her life to find you. But I don't say anything, because I am the worst. You'll be bones very soon. Soon, soon, soon. A month more of NYC rent, max. This is what I tell myself so I don't feel as bad. To your face, I paste on a hard little smile and say, "Mmm-hmm."

"How much longer?" you ask.

"A few weeks?"

"Huh. So a few weeks of this and then whatever's next?"

"If you want."

"Okay."

"Okay?"

"Sure."

You hold out your hand and we shake. The guilt rushes out of me like a long-held breath. It's okay. I'm okay. We're okay. I slouch back into the couch, relaxed for the first time in weeks, basking in your consent. I'm sleepy. I close my eyes for a second.

"Can I see it?"

And I'm awake.

"What?" I ask.

"Can I see my body?"

I straighten up. "Do you want to?" You don't look distressed or anything. And I'd be curious, too.

"I think so."

"Are you sure? It's pretty brutal compared to what you look like now."

You shrug. "I'm sure. Now that I know it's out there, I'm kind of itching to look. It's not every day you get to see yourself mostly decomposed."

"What, like, you wanna go now?"

"Why not?"

"I just assumed you'd need more time to prepare yourself."

You laugh. "I promise it won't be the worst thing I've ever seen. And after that, we can watch the movie!"

I know I haven't even gotten to the worst parts of your journal yet, so it's probably true that you've seen worse. And I'm not really in a position to judge.

"All right, yeah, sure. Do you want to go by yourself or do you want me to come with you?"

"I will probably need you to show me where it is, yes."

"Sorry! I didn't know if there was maybe ghost GPS that would point you there."

"If there was, I'd probably have known you had my body out here all along."

"Good point." I stand up and get my shoes from where I left them by the door, then head to the couch to put them on. When I get back, you've switched your outfit from cozy pajama pants and a loose gray T-shirt to a green cable-knit sweater, black leggings, and basic black Doc Martens. Unlike me, you don't have to gather all the stuff and physically put it on; you just think of what outfit you want and your clothes change themselves in an instant. You can get dressed the old-fashioned way if you want to and you say you do sometimes, when you want to feel normal, but usually you opt for the quick switch. Who wouldn't? I look forward to it.

"Do you have to break in the ghost shoes?" I ask as I slip into my coat.

You shuffle from foot to foot for a second. "I haven't thought about it, haven't been wearing shoes very often, but I guess we'll see! They feel fine so far."

I laugh. "I hope for your sake you don't. Docs are a bitch!"

You raise an eyebrow. "You own Docs and you're just now realizing you might be gay."

I blush. "I got them recently."

I watch your belly move as you laugh.

"Are you ready?" you ask, snapping me out of a daze.

"Are *you* ready?"

You take a deep breath and exhale in a fat gust. "Ready as I'll ever be. Let's go see my corpse. And that is *not* a sentence I ever thought I'd be saying!"

I open the door and tell Zelda we'll be right back. She could not possibly care less and doesn't even open her eyes. You take my arm and I lead us out. As we get closer to your body, I try to ease you into it. I'm going for the same vibe as the gynecologist explaining what she'll do in the exam while she lubes up the speculum. I tell you that the smell is bad, but not as bad as it was. I tell you it's a sweet-hot-trash-in-the-sun kind of smell. We've established that you can smell, so I want to prepare you for it, but I also reassure you that I'm not judging. It's just what bodies do! Very natural. I didn't even bring my mask, because I don't want to be rude and make a big deal out of it in front of you. I also explain that you're not exactly recognizable. You tell me you kind of figured that. You're amused by my nervousness, I can tell. I feel bad about being more nervous than you. I just feel like this is so personal and I shouldn't be here for it, but you seem at ease with my presence. I shut up, watching you out of the corner of my eye as we start to get close.

Just before we break into the clearing, you cover your nose and stop. "Oh God," you say. "That's bad!" You turn to me with your eyes watering. "It was worse than *this*?!"

I shrug. "Yeah, you get used to it, weirdly. Are you sure you want to go through with this? You're just beyond those trees, but we can go back."

You stare in the direction I'm pointing with an expression so mottled that I can't even begin to pick it apart. You don't answer; you just start walking. I follow wordlessly, pulled forward by the same force dragging you: curiosity. I still feel like I shouldn't be there for this, but I also don't want to miss a single second. It feels special. Intimate.

I step through the trees with you and stop to give you some space. You take a couple of steps forward, hand over your mouth and nose, and emit a small gasp like you've been poked in the back with a needle. You stop and gape. Your body stares up at you. Your face a leathery black skull dotted with matted tufts of hairy scalp. You take a shaky breath and kneel. Eye level to eye sockets, your torsos the same length. The clothes you wore when you died are still recognizable, if damp and discolored. Your gold bracelet's been eaten up by the swollen rot of your wrist.

You look up at me in shock, tears leaking down your cheeks.

"It's really me!" you say.

"Yeah." You. Undeniably you.

I stand and watch you cry at your own grave, fidgeting in my body, trying to take up less space.

You reach forward and run your fingers down your neck, not actually touching anything, just tracing the hollow where your throat used to be. Where your voice was. Your tears disappear when they hit the ground. I make myself choke trying not to cry with you. You reach back for me without looking, motioning for me to come sit with you. I do. Crisscross applesauce. A breeze rustles the brand-new spring leaves starting to grow around us. The birds chirp. You sniffle and reach for my hand. I offer it without hesitation. And there we sit. We three.

AVA

We had finally established a routine and a plan. We were mapping the area and foraging at the same time. Every morning I made tea out of pine needles instead of coffee and we drank it together, then we split from each other for most of the day. Megan went one way and I went the other. Usually she took the hunting knife, because she was the better hunter, and I took the Swiss Army and a spear we'd made ourselves. One of us checked fishing baskets, the other checked snares. If either of us found anything, our next task for the day would be to clean and smoke it. If not, we'd go exploring.

We both strove to find a new place every day, carving X's into trees as we went so we wouldn't get lost, drawing out our surroundings as best we could on scraps of paper from the smaller notebook. The idea was, at worst, one of us finds a hazard that she can tell the other to avoid. At best, we'd find new resources and maybe, just maybe, a campsite, or road, or even a damn 7-Eleven. Usually, we landed somewhere in the middle. Megan set new snares in new places. I got really into gathering acorns and trying to make acorn flour. Megan had taken to calling me Squirrel because of it. We found another couple katniss patches farther downstream. We caught a few fish, a small bird, and two more squirrels. Cannibalism, Megan said. At night, we each got our one small meal of the day, mostly katniss, which we were quickly running out of, as we still smoked and saved most of the meat.

It was getting colder fast as we eased into December, and we saw fewer signs of life every day. With our lack of good winter gear, we would be forced to hunker down soon too. Already we'd had to cut our third sleeping bag into a makeshift coat we tied on with strips of fabric we'd made while cutting it up. I miss zippers. Megan wore the coat every time she went outside. I have a much higher natural tolerance for the cold than she did. Chad and I are (were?) close enough in shoe size, so I wear his boots. The goal was one bigger meal a week. We had no idea what day of the week it was anymore—I wasn't willing to sacrifice the composition book to write out a calendar just so that we could know if it was Tuesday—but we had the date from Chad's watch, so instead of eating the big meal every Friday, Saturday, or Sunday, we counted the days 1–7 and ate well on 5, 6, or 7. It might seem silly, but keeping count of the days, giving special treatment to the weekend, helped us hold on to a shred of civilization.

One week Megan caught a squirrel on a 5—it was the best-case scenario. Fresh meat on the weekend?! Bliss! I started mentally preparing for date night the moment I saw her coming down the hill with the limp squirrel swinging at her side. I cheered for her, but she didn't seem excited. She looked grim and held the body out away from her.

"What's the matter?" I asked. "Did it die of disease?"

She shook her head. "No, I stabbed it. I'm just really nauseous today, that's all. Do you think you can clean it? I don't think I can handle all that right now."

"Oh no! I'm sorry, my love! Did you drink some bad water, or maybe something you ate?" I stepped forward and took the squirrel.

She shook her head again. "No, I'm fine. I'm sure it's just a stomachache. We've been out here for a while. It's just catching up to me. It'll be fine in the morning."

"Do you want to wait and eat the squirrel tomorrow instead?" I could feel the squirrel's body swinging at my side. It felt heavy. My stomach growled and I hoped she'd say we could still eat it tonight.

She smiled and said we could still eat the squirrel, so long as I cooked and cleaned it and made her some pine needle tea before dinner so she could lie down. I told her of course she could go lie down. She said she wanted to sit up and hang out instead of going to sleep, so I tucked her in, rolling up the coat sleeping bag for her to use as a pillow and prop herself up on. I went and cleaned the squirrel as fast as I could, and I gathered pine needles for her tea, and then I went and prepared both in the doorway of the cave while she lounged against the wall in the back. I pretended to be hosting a cooking show to make her laugh. She grimaced through the meal, barely managing to choke it down, but she reassured me over and over that it was just a stomachache. It was only supposed to be a stomachache.

~AA Brown

SAVANNAH

NOW THAT I have your consent to keep you, meaning the crushing guilt is out of the way, I'm back on my usual bullshit: trying not to think about Michelle, which your presence makes so much easier, and spiraling about whether or not I'm even actually gay. I spend my whole therapy appointment arguing with Hils about it.

"Well, have you ever liked men like that? Or genuinely enjoyed the experience of dating one?" she asks.

"Maybe? I don't know. I always saw dating men as a sport. Like, you meet a man and then it's about playing the game to get him obsessed with you enough to buy you dinner and things, and the more devoted he gets, the more you're winning. I think whenever I dated men, what I liked was the feeling of winning, but I also don't think that means anything."

"What do you mean about it not meaning anything? Do you mean that enjoying the feeling of winning doesn't necessarily mean you like the man?"

"No, I mean it doesn't necessarily mean I'm not straight."

One eyebrow shoots up before she catches it and rearranges her face into a completely neutral expression. I love when I shock Hils. It's like when I make her laugh; it's satisfying in a way that makes me feel like I'm doing a good job.

"Elaborate on that," she says.

"I'm not sure if straight women like men, either."

She laughs. "What?"

"Think about it! My parents have restraining orders against each other. I truly can't remember a time when my mom didn't seem genuinely disgusted by my dad. All the other moms in my neighborhood were like that, too. My mom used to throw these weirdly gendered dinner parties where all my parents' couple friends would come over to the house and immediately separate into two groups.

"The men would go into the living room and sit on the couch and drink beers and brown liquor and bitch about their wives. The women would always offer to help my mom in the kitchen, and they'd drink red wine and bitch about their husbands. I would sit on a barstool at the kitchen counter and watch until everyone got too drunk and my mom sent me upstairs. They were always talking about how their men didn't appreciate them, how they were messy, how they would do gross things like pee on the seat or, worse, near the seat, and not clean it up, how they forgot anniversaries and birthdays and referred to fathering their own kids as *babysitting.* I've never heard a straight woman talk about her man the way that lesbians talk about their women. It's never *he's so beautiful, he's so kind, he loves me, he appreciates me, I'd die for him.* It's never that. So how do I know that me being absolutely disgusted by men isn't just what most women experience anyway? Maybe I'm just normal and straight?"

Hils pauses for a moment to stare into space. I am victorious.

"Okay," she says. "I understand how if you've never seen a healthy heterosexual relationship up close you could think of it that way, so what about this: Do you like the idea of men? Male celebrity crushes, even?"

I think about it. Male celebrities blur together in my head like hard-bodied blobs. They all look the same to me. Their bodies don't seem inviting or soft. Penises are ugly, famous or not, so I don't ever try to imagine these celebrities undressed. None of it is impressive. Is it normal for women to fantasize about living with a man? Fucking a man? I guess so, but I never think about it. The men in my fantasies or in porn are only there to make the woman feel good so I can watch her face contort in pleasure. Still, it could be a fluke. It could be that I just haven't met the right man yet, which I know for a fact is what my mom thinks.

"I don't know."

"Fair enough," Hils says. "What about the women?"

I think of you. The soft inhale you take before every sip of coffee. The little peek of the soft skin of your hip I get when you lift your arms over your head to stretch and your shirt rides up. The ridge of your collarbone at the base of your neck that I kind of want to lick.

"Well, okay, so yes, there are at least six female celebrities that could get it, but I don't know if I could be in love with them."

Hils smiles. "Maybe you could and maybe not, but it's worth at least investigating the possibilities in real life. Set your dating apps to women for a bit, see what happens. If you don't like it, switch them back."

"But what if I'm not gay and I end up just using all these women?"

"All what women?"

Damn. Roasted.

"I'm just saying what if I'm that bitch with her boyfriend at the lesbian bar that none of the real lesbians want anything to do with because they don't want to be experimented on?"

She shrugs. "Maybe."

"Goddammit, Hils." The second I get hit with a *maybe* in therapy, I know I'm cut off of reassurances for the day, but she does laugh and I get the satisfaction of that, which softens the blow.

"We're out of time, but until we meet next, try to see if you can give yourself the space to open up to the possibility of it, even if it's just quietly on your own. I know you want an answer that feels certain, but there's no big rush to certainty on this, and it'll be good for you to practice accepting that uncertainty. Give yourself some grace, though, if it's hard to accept the uncertainty. It doesn't have to be perfect. Okay?"

"Okay."

I think about the phrasing of "quietly on your own'" and picture myself meditating on the concept of eating pussy. I hope I can meditate hard enough to know for sure. We make plans to email about a time for next week, then say goodbye. I shut the laptop and head down the stairs. Michelle doesn't come for me this time. You're on the couch with headphones over your ears, knitting something no one will ever be able to wear. I pour myself a glass of chardonnay with ice because I'm too lazy to put the bottle in the freezer for fifteen minutes. I stand at the counter with my glass and stare at the rise and fall of your chest as you breathe in and out. You notice I've come back down and wave at me. I sip my wine and pretend to look at my phone. You go back to your project and I put my phone down. My therapy appointment has me thinking about what it would be like to undress you, stitch by stitch, which I'm assuming is a problem only a lesbian could have. You look up again when I'm not expecting it and I can't look away fast enough, so you catch me watching you.

"What's up?" you ask.

"Nothing." I take another drink of my wine. Even full of liquid, my mouth feels dry.

"Then why are you staring holes through my skin?"

"I'm not."

"Sure, you're not."

I make my way over to the couch. You're watching me now out of the corner of your eye, one side of your lips curled up in what I think is amusement. I sit.

"How did you know you were gay? Like, *for sure*."

You take off your headphones. You put down your knitting.

"How did I know?"

"Yeah, like, did you feel that way your whole life, or did it creep up on you as an adult, or was there, like, one girl in middle school?"

"I kissed a girl at a party. I'm sure there were signs before then, but I was so deep in the church that I didn't really pay them any attention. I was more invested in following the rules and doing everything right. Then, one night—I think I was like twenty-five, twenty-six, maybe—my friend invited me to this party and I went and everyone was drinking and I was drinking, too, because I'm out of the church at this point, and there was this girl. We were dancing. She was radiant. Bouncy red hair almost down to her waist in a green dress, like Christmas. We left the dance floor and did some shots together, and then she backed me into the pantry of this guy's kitchen and kissed me and it was just different than anything else, better. And after that I only dated women and it felt right."

I try not to stare at your lips.

"I've never had a good kiss," I confess. "But I've also never kissed a girl."

I don't tell you about the one time I technically did kiss a girl, because I don't count that. Anyway, this is stupid. Shame drags its lips up my neck and turns my face red, the only lover I'm used to. I pick at a hangnail on my thumb, shaking my hair out around my face so you won't see me blush. It's too much even being in a room with you after exposing my inexperience. You must see me as a baby. I scan my brain for an excuse to leave and remember I left my wineglass on the counter. I form a plan to get the wine and make a run for it.

I'm about to get up when you say, "Do you want to? So you know?"

You look so calm, like you didn't just offer to pull the pin on a grenade, with your arm slung over the back of the couch, one leg on, one leg off. The little gold flecks in your eyes dance around your pupils, amused by my awkwardness. I am a scared cat with a puffed tail.

"What?"

"Kiss a girl, I mean. Sorry. Do you want to?"

"You?" I croak. So much for playing it cool.

"I'm volunteering. But again, only if that's what you want!" You weave a laugh into your words.

My eyes dart back and forth between your eyes, trying to assess whether or not you're playing with me, but everything in your expression stays warm and inviting, like a beach with clear blue water and soft white sand, pollution-less and expensive to visit. I'm so intimidated I can't even speak, but I also can't let this opportunity pass me by. It's an honor even to be asked. I should be giving a speech. But my mouth is so dry. I really can't speak, so I just nod and square up.

"Come here," you say.

I scoot forward. My heart throws itself against my rib cage over and over, trying to escape. I'm too stiff. Should I turn my head? Should I lean forward? I lean forward a little. Your face is getting closer. I can see your pores. God, what a privilege it is to be close enough to see your pores. Your eyes are closed. I wish I had time to count your eyelashes. I should close my eyes, too, though—it'll be weird if I keep them open. I close my eyes just as your lips touch mine. It's just a peck, but it stops my world. Your lips are so soft, like rose petals. I'm surprised by how comfortable I am. I squirmed through all my kisses with men, consumed with how gross their always-too-wet lips felt, how roughly they pressed into me. With you it's not like that. I'm enveloped in you. A kiss so perfect it could have been a hug. You were right—it's better. You pull back and I almost fall forward into your lap chasing more. You smile as I stare at you, doe-eyed and slack-jawed.

"Well?" you ask.

"Again?"

AVA

I told Megan about my journal project once. She never saw me work on it, because the whole time she was alive, especially when it became clear to both of us that she wasn't going to make it, I never wanted to do anything but be with her. The only other moments I left her side were to go do something essential to keep her alive for even a minute longer. So yeah, that was my Bridgerton*-level dramatic way of telling you she'll never get to read any of this, but I told her about my plans once in late fall, when we were happiest.*

I remember it being really nice out that day—not too hot, but sunny and gorgeous. It was one of those days that makes you understand why cats lie in sunbeams. Or, I don't know, maybe I just remember it being nice out because this is such a good memory and good memories in bad times turn into perfect memories in worse ones. I was sitting on a fallen tree we used as a bench outside the cave, making yet another fishing basket, when she stepped out looking so radiant and clean somehow in my T-shirt, her panties, socks, and nothing else.

"Whatcha doin'?" she asked.

I held up my half-finished basket in response.

"I have a confession to make," I told her.

"Oh?" She raised an amused eyebrow at me. "What, did you cheat on me with Bigfoot? So is it true what they say? Big feet, big . . ." She gestured at me to finish the sentence.

"I'm hoarding the composition book," I said instead.

"That's homophobic," she said and sat down next to me. I laughed. Then she said, "Okay, so why are you hoarding the composition book?"

"I want to start writing about this. Get our story on paper in case we die and hopefully someone finds it so everyone will know what happened to us, or if we live maybe I'll get a pity-Pulitzer or something?"

She laughed at my joke, which I appreciated because it wasn't that funny of a joke. She got up and stretched. I watched my shirt settle over her ribs. "So are you gonna write about me? Make sure you tell the readers good things!"

"What things do you want them to know about you?"

She paused, put her hand to her chin, and squinted at the sky so I knew she was thinking, then relaxed her arms to swing at her sides in that easy way she moved. "I want them to know I was hot until the end!"

I laughed. "I'll tell 'em!"

"So hot, in fact," she said, stepping closer, "that I was doing some superhot activities in the cave and came out to see if you wanted to join me."

"Really?"

She ran her hand across her hip and into her panties, and when her fingers came back out I could see them shimmering in the sun. She bent and ran that hand across my collarbone, then licked up the evidence, kissed my neck, and stood up straight again. Then she turned around, said, "More where that came from if you want it," and went back into the cave, leaving the makeshift door propped open behind her.

That fishing basket hit the ground so hard it ended up halfway to China. So yeah, just so you know, Megan was hot until the end!

~AA Brown

SAVANNAH

YOU'RE WALKING AROUND in a chemise the color of my favorite red lipstick. I'm trying not to look, but since our first kiss the other day I can't stop staring at you even when you're dressed in your typical lounging uniform of sweatpants and a big T-shirt. And this outfit is insane. I work very, very hard to keep my eyes on my phone. I click through nearly every app on my screen, trying to find something more interesting than what's walking around my living room, but I can't. My eyes keep sliding up off the screen to home in on the place right under your ass where the lacy fabric draws a line against your pale thighs. I catch myself squinting, like maybe if I put more effort into it, I can raise the hem just by looking and willing it to rise. You turn around so your back isn't to me anymore, and I look away out the window so fast I nearly pull a muscle in my neck. I stare at the trunk of a tree outside like it owes me money, but you enter my field of vision again, going to stand right next to my window.

"Whatcha' lookin' at?" you ask me.

You. God, of course I'm looking at you.

"I, uh, saw a squirrel, I think."

In the sunlight, your outfit is see-through. The pink of your nipples shows through the gaps in the lace. I can't breathe. I can't look away. I can't believe it. You're finally comfortable enough just to wear whatever around me and I'm no better than a man.

"Ah," you say. Your mouth curls up on one side. You look smug. "A squirrel?"

"A squirrel."

"You don't see a lot of squirrels out this time of year, do you? Most of them aren't even out of their winter hiding spots yet."

You start to move around the back of the couch.

"Guess this one was early."

I trace the curve of your hip with my eyes as you walk. I am made of shame.

"Mmm-hmm," you say, re the squirrel. It's somehow hot the way you say it.

You set yourself up on the other side of the couch and watch the TV while you chew the side of your thumb. It's then that I remember the TV has been on this whole time and I didn't even have to pretend to look at my phone or any specific trees. Fuck. I sneak another peek at you while you're not looking at me. You've got one leg straight and one bent. The bent one leans against the back of the couch. The position leaves your legs open. I can see the matching red crotch of your panties. For some reason, my mouth waters.

You're not really paying attention to me, still nibbling on the corner of a nail on your left hand, eyes on the screen. Your other hand rests on your bent knee. My mouth goes dry again and I reach for my drink. You start sliding one finger of your hand down your thigh and I forget to drink. The straw slides across my bottom lip, abandoned.

"Are you okay?"

"What?" It comes out in a squeak. I yank my gaze away from your hand, currently resting on your inner thigh. My face feels so hot. It's probably the color of your dress.

You laugh and gesture to the TV. "You hate this show. Usually you've changed it by now."

I turn to the TV. *Love It or List It* ended and now *Property*

Brothers is on. You're right; I do hate this show. I find their faces unsettling.

"Are you okay, though?" you ask again.

I'd be okay if I could figure out how to keep eye contact while your legs are open in front of me.

"I'm fine." I cannot look at you.

You put your leg down and scoot forward until you're sitting between my legs, which have at some point fallen open to you as well. You put your hand on the back of the couch, behind my head, to support yourself while you lean in. Your face is so close to mine I can almost taste you.

"Are you doing this on purpose?" I whisper.

"Doing what on purpose?" you ask. You won't let me drop the eye contact.

"I—I don't know how to ask without being disrespectful. I'm trying so hard to be respectful." I drop my head to stare at my lap, but you bring my face back up with a hand under my chin.

"Yes," you say.

"What?"

"Yes, I am doing it on purpose."

My mouth makes a little O of surprise. My heart raves against my ribs as I count the tiny lines in your lips. I can't speak. I start hyping myself up to grow a pair and kiss you now that I know you want it, but before I can get there, you stand and take a couple of steps back. I flinch, worried I did something wrong, but you still look happy. I relax a little, but not all the way. It doesn't feel safe to relax all the way. You see the confusion spread across my face and laugh.

"Come on," you say, nodding your head toward the stairs. "Your first time should be in a bed."

You turn and start walking. I follow you like a puppy that knows you have treats in your pocket. When we reach the bedroom door, you go in first and I hesitate. You leave the door open a few inches for me and I stare at the gap. I really talked this up to myself, but now all I can think about is what if I don't like it? What if I'm not good at it? I try to talk myself down quickly. I know how to get myself off; another woman shouldn't be too much different, right? God, what if I don't like it? What if I'm not even gay? Maybe. Maybe.

"You coming, or do I have to get started by myself?" your voice calls out through the crack in the door.

I picture you getting started by yourself and my stomach bottoms out. Everything goes all tingly and warm, like I'm drunk even though I'm not. I grab the handle of the door and pull. You're draped across my bed, propped up on my many pillows, looking perfectly relaxed. Meanwhile, I'm all but shitting myself. You pat the space on the bed next to you.

"Come here," you say.

I sit on the edge of the bed, staring at you with my heartbeat pounding in my ears. I'm hoping that you'll start things off, because right now all I can do is look at you. And looking at you is almost enough on its own. You're breathtaking in your lingerie. I fidget with the hem of my T-shirt, so oversized you can barely see my little cotton shorts poking out underneath. I feel underdressed.

"Are you up to this?" you ask, concerned with my inaction.

I nod. "Yeah, I'm fine. I mean, I want to! I promise I want to. You're really beautiful. I'm just nervous."

You smile. "It's normal to be nervous; I just want to be sure I'm not pressuring you."

"You're not! You're *really* not!" Wow, Savannah, way to sound like the desperate fucking virgin you are.

"Okay," you say. You place both hands behind you on the bed and push yourself up to a full sitting position. "So kiss me."

I give myself an internal pep talk, lean forward, and plant a small peck on your lips. You look absolutely bewildered when I pull back, but your face quickly shifts into amusement.

"All right," you say. "Sure. Or, we could . . ."

You place both hands on my waist and pull me down. I straddle you on instinct as you fall back against the pillows. You put your hands on either side of my face and drag me down. You start kissing me ravenously and I follow your lead. I open my mouth for your tongue. I let my hands run through your hair, leaving one to settle on the back of your neck while the other wanders, tracing its way down the bend of your chin, across your collarbone, down the side of your chest, up and down the curve of your hip.

You bite my lip and I moan against my will. You smile under my mouth at the sound. I try not to feel exposed. I grind my hips down against your pelvis. I hope you can't feel how wet I am through my shorts and your dress, but I fear you can. I'm dripping and ashamed. It happened so quickly. I kiss you deeper, trying to relax. I trail kisses down your neck, because it feels like that's what I'm supposed to do. You tilt your head back and release a breathy little sigh, which encourages me. Your hands go to my waist, both thumbs in the waistband of my shorts. Then you're lifting my shirt over my head and I'm letting you, helping you. You reach around and unhook my bra, then stop for a second to stare. I force myself to hold still while you examine me.

"You're so beautiful," you say, and I blush from my cheeks to my nipples.

"You," I say, bewildered. I can't even speak a whole sentence. I cannot believe you're calling me of all people beautiful when you live inside yourself.

You kiss your way down my chest until my nipple is in your mouth and I can barely stand it. I run my hands over every part of you I can reach over your dress until it's not enough. I make the executive decision that I need to develop bravery and lift my hips, tugging the hem of your chemise out from under me. You reach down to help me pull it over your head. I toss it to the floor and stare, speechless at the sight of you. Your boobs are so perfect, round and full, pink hard nipples at the center. Your fingers are back in the waistband of my shorts, but I barely even notice;

I'm too busy marveling at how your breasts feel in my hands—squishy, warm, and soft like the inside part of fresh bread. I wonder why it's so much better to grab boobs that aren't my own. You tug again at my shorts, harder this time. You lean forward and put your mouth to my neck, kissing and licking your way up to my ear. You take my earlobe lightly between your teeth and I shudder.

"I want to see the rest," you whisper, tugging my shorts down again for emphasis. Your breath tickles my ear.

I want you to see the rest. I need you to see the rest. I lift my hips and let you help me out of my shorts. I'm not wearing anything underneath. I lower myself back down wearing nothing, pussy to stomach, and to my surprise, you moan.

You put your lips back to my ear and whisper, "You're so fucking wet."

You flip me on my back, in one motion, before I can even get embarrassed. You pull off your panties to reveal the most gorgeous pussy I've ever seen. It looks like just about every other one I've ever seen, but it's attached to you and so I worship it. You put a knee on either side of my left thigh and sit. I kiss you desperately, panting into your mouth as I feel something slick and damp spread across my thigh.

"See?" you say between sloppy needy kisses. "I'm wet, too."

"Fuck," I moan back. I am so turned on it might kill me. I don't care if it does.

You reposition slightly so you're almost lying down on top of me, your knee grinding down between my legs, and I rock my hips, trying to get more of that sensation. I'm embarrassingly close already, but you pull your knee away at the last minute. I fall back against the pillows as you start to kiss your way down my belly. I watch you, trying to pay attention to what you're doing since I know I'll be doing the same to you soon. I want to be good, but it's so hard to focus on anything but the way your spine curves, the way your shoulder blades kiss together on your bare back as you arch it. I take a mental picture of this to place on the shrine I'm building to you in my mind. I think I love you.

You skip my hips when you get there and instead put your mouth to my knee and start working your way back up, too slowly. My hand goes to the back of your head, fingers in your hair, and you chuckle into my thigh before starting to go even slower. I groan, impatient. You brush the slit with the tip of your nose with barely any pressure, featherlight kisses on both lips while I writhe under you, bucking my hips for more. You look up at me, something devious shimmering in your eyes.

"What do you want?" you ask.

"You."

"Oh?" You smirk as you plant a few more little kisses in the space under my belly button.

"When do you want me?"

"Now." I try not to listen to myself speak, too breathy with want.

"Mmm . . ." You press one finger to my opening but don't put it inside. I can't even breathe. The want is becoming need.

"Please?"

"What was that?"

"Please, Ava. Please fuck me. Please." It feels like a stupid thing to say, but I am desperate.

Finally, you answer with your tongue, making little circles on my clit that feel perfect. The finger slips inside and starts to move.

"More," I beg, and you add a finger and speed up your motions. I grind against your face and grip the sheets, panting and moaning as I feel the orgasm start to build in my legs already. Like a teenage boy, less than a minute later my back arches on its own and I bury my face in a pillow to scream as you make me come harder than I ever have before. You leave your fingers inside me until the spasms stop and then you ease them out and lick them clean. When you crawl up and kiss me on the mouth,

I can taste myself on you. I kiss you deeper, tasting the memory of how good everything felt. And then I feel very responsible, determined to show you a good time.

"Your turn," I say, giving you a last little peck on the nose. "How do you want me?"

"Uhh, lying down, like I was. I want to try that first."

You lie back on the pillows and let your legs fall open, knees bent like a frog. Now that I'm not quite so blinded by my own horniness, I have time to get nervous again. I don't even know if I know where to start, so I try to mimic what you did to me. I kneel between your open legs and kiss you. I let my hands wander your body almost of their own accord. My right hand runs across the soft skin of your belly and down the outside of your thigh and then up the inside.

I cup your pussy, putting pressure from the heel of my palm against your clit, because that's what I like. You let out a surprised gasp and I pull back to look at you, scared I might have grabbed you too fast or too aggressively or maybe that I shouldn't have tried to touch you there so soon at all, but then you start rocking your hips back and forth against my palm. You moan into my mouth when I resume kissing you and, when I feel your wetness coating my hand, I moan back.

I'm addicted to giving you pleasure. Every satisfied sound from you emboldens me. I begin to make my way down like you did, kissing your neck, your collarbone, running my tongue down your breast and taking your nipple between my teeth before working my way down lower still. I kiss my way across your pubis, then stop and pull back. When I look up, you're watching me, patient, letting me figure it out. I pull your lips apart with my fingers to investigate and start mapping it out, tracing my way around with one finger.

Okay. The clit is there. The hole is there. I probe and find the ridges of your G-spot right at the front. I don't know what I expected, maybe that it would be scarier and more complicated on another woman, but from here it looks easy enough. Maybe once I'm down there with my face it'll be harder to navigate, but I think it might actually be fine. I wonder what men are doing that makes this so difficult for them. Now it's just a question of whether I'll like it. I sort of see eating someone out as the final frontier of gay. If I enjoy this, we can call it official. If I don't, I'm not sure I even know where to go from there. One way to find out.

I kiss my way up your thighs, one at a time, biting and licking on occasion, mimicking what you did to me. You sigh and relax back onto the cushions. I'm not 100 percent sure on what that means, but I choose to look at it as a good sign. I breathe deep as I get closer, taking in the smell of you. My mouth waters, like it did before when I was staring at your crotch on the couch. I can't wait to taste you. I shove my face right in, wrapping both arms around your thighs and pulling you down over my nose. You don't taste like much of anything—a little salty, a little sour, but it's neutral overall. I love it. New favorite food. I lap enthusiastic circles around your clit, small and fast with a little pressure, focusing like I'm threading a needle, trying to mimic the motion I make with my finger when I can't sleep. You get wetter and wetter, and your moans get louder, and then breathier. Encouraged, I push two fingers inside you and hook them against the ridges of your G-spot and you gasp. A reward.

"Fuck me," you moan over and over again. "Fuck me, fuck me, fuck me!"

I speed up and reach up with my other hand to massage the first titty I can find. I feel the muscles inside you start to squeeze and pulse around my fingers. You gush all over my palm and I groan into your clit. This is heaven. I'm so overwhelmed by how much I'm enjoying it that I don't see it coming when your body suddenly spasms under me. You tell me not to stop, so I don't. I marvel at the way your muscles close around my fingers. I bask in the sounds of your screams. They sound like the feeling of being applauded. I'm God now. I have been promoted.

Your hand comes down and pushes on my forehead, so I retreat, sitting back on my heels and licking my fingers as I watch you recover, blushing and breathless. I can't get enough. I can't wait until you'll let me taste you again. I think maybe I really am gay.

I crawl back up the bed and lie beside you, with my head on your chest, your heartbeat in my ears. You kiss me on the forehead. I smile and close my eyes and that's how we end Monday, with me asleep in your arms. I'm scared, in my last second of consciousness, that maybe this one time is all there is ever going to be, but it turns out this is how we start the single best week of my life. We spend all of it in bed, trying whatever I want; you say you want me to have the space to explore, and I do. I explore like I'm a cartographer getting paid to draw up a map of you. Every day we try something new.

I ask you to sit on my face and you do. You lean forward, bracing yourself against the headboard, while I help you rock your hips against my face with my arms around your thighs. At first, when I told you I wanted to try this, lying in bed after the first time, my head on your chest, you were worried, because I am smaller than you. But I said, "Baby, if I die I die," and now I love that the air is humid with the smell and taste of you. I untangle one arm so I can offer two fingers, and you bounce on them until there's a much bigger gush than I expected. I have to resist the urge to touch myself as your come drips down my chin.

I debate a strap-on next, but when I think about seeing it on you, the idea unsettles me. I'll try it someday, maybe. You kneel on the bed between my legs, one hand cupping the back of my head, two fingers of the other inside me. You put your face by my ear and tell me to touch myself and I reach down. You kiss me and I come into your open mouth.

We make a brief attempt at scissoring, but, as much as I like the bit of friction and the mix of wetnesses, we can't get the positioning quite right. Instead, we rock back and forth on a double-sided dildo, our juices mixing on the glass. Our moans fit together like we orchestrated them, a duet.

We set up a mirror at the foot of the bed. I watch you get wetter and wetter until you're dripping down your legs as you eat me out. You reach back to finger yourself, moaning into me so the sound pleasantly vibrates against my clit, and I sit enthralled by my in-person custom-made porn. I watch you finger-fuck yourself, trying to keep as quiet as I can so I don't drown out the delicious squishy sounds as your fingers slide in and out. I watch until I can't look anymore because my eyes are rolling back in my head.

We both feel lazy later, so we put on a scary movie and get set up on either side of the couch, facing each other. I watch you touch yourself and you watch me. The rules are: we can't touch each other, but we have to be touching ourselves in some way the whole time, edging. Whoever comes first loses. You win, of course, but the puddle you leave on my couch says I fought a good fight.

And Sunday is the Lord's day, so we rest. Kidding! Sunday I tie you to a chair and tease you until you beg. And as I take in your breathy open-mouthed moans, your face tilted back and contorted in beautiful ecstasy as you come, I can't believe that God would want it any other way.

AVA

Megan just kept getting worse. Everything kept getting worse. The nausea was back all day every day. It crippled her. She spent hours every morning curled into the tightest ball, rocking back and forth and crying. I gave her some of our ibuprofen stash every morning and evening for the first week. I had to force her to take it, begging, pleading, convincing her that I was perfectly healthy and wouldn't need it. She still fought me the first few times and tried to refuse to take it, but when the pain got to be too much, she finally did. She said it felt like her stomach was a gumball machine full of small sharp razors. We had to stop the ibuprofen after that week, because it only seemed to make her worse.

Any food, no matter how small, burned when it hit her stomach. She tried her best, but most days she couldn't keep anything down. And every time she threw up, she felt so guilty. I'd hold her while she sobbed apology after apology, sorry for wasting precious resources, sorry she ate food that could have gone to good use in my body. I didn't care. Even though I spent more and more time taking care of her than I did hunting and fishing, even though we were on the very edge of depleting our stockpiles because she'd always been the hunter, even though the weather kept getting colder and everything was dying and we were running out of time to gather resources, I didn't care. I just wanted her to get better. The rest, I told myself, we could figure out.

I repeatedly assured her we could get through this. I started lying to her, telling her we still had plenty of food and everything was fine. I'm sure she knew they were lies. Megan wasn't stupid. But I lied anyway. I worried any stress would make her worse. Food, I could fix. Warmth, I could fix. I couldn't lose her. All that mattered to me was getting her better. I'd give her every scrap of the food we had only for her to throw up most of it if it meant that she would keep down just a little. It didn't need to be perfect. It just needed to be enough.

My reassurances didn't help. The pain wouldn't stop. She started refusing to take even one bite of food. I went through the motions every day of tending the fire and boiling the water. Whenever I could find extra energy in myself, or if Megan seemed more stable or was napping, I'd spend some time checking and resetting the traps, but I didn't give those tasks the time we used to. I half-assed everything and ran home to her. I hadn't so much as caught a fish in weeks.

I gave up on mapping the area. I gave up on trying to find a way out. Finding a way out was time spent away from her, and I wasn't willing to leave her on her own. The helplessness was like nothing I've ever felt. I sat with our dead phones for hours, trying to see if there was anything I could do to get them to turn on. My brain was so far gone I wasn't even hoping for 911, just Google. I just wanted to get some information on what was wrong with her. Maybe then I could fix it. But of course there was nothing I could do. Nothing. All I could do was lie to her and say it would be okay while I rubbed her back and force-fed her more tea, because the taste of plain water made her gag. It was torture for both of us. My desperate need to save her chewed holes across my skin like the bugs in mid-July. I became obsessed with getting and keeping calories in her, but every day, in spite of my best efforts, I watched her get thinner and thinner. New parts of her skeleton revealed themselves like she was decomposing in front of me. And every night I wished I would somehow die first. I knew I wouldn't survive mourning her.

~AA Brown

SAVANNAH

WE SPEND OUR days doing whatever the fuck we want. It's incredible. Hils is always telling me I have no responsibilities right now and should try to enjoy my time off instead of wallowing around the house and rotting in my bed, and I finally know what she means. I just needed you to come along and rescue me from my mind. We can't really go anywhere. I don't have a car and we don't know how far you can travel away from your body anyway, but we manage to make the best of it.

We go on long walks around the property, skipping the woods on your request, which I understand. For most of the month you've been here with me, you haven't even wanted to go outside. Now that the weather's getting nice, you're opting for an exposure-therapy approach. We spend a little time outside every day when it's nice. I, of course, still go into the woods.

Yesterday, we walked along the tree line, holding hands. Then we went inside and I cooked dinner from a cookbook while you laughed at me for stressing over the instructions. (I'm still just learning how to cook and I take it very seriously.) After dinner we had sex on the couch while *South Park* played on TV in the background.

Today, the first really truly warm day we've had since spring started, I drag a couple of lounge chairs out of the garage and set them up in front of the lake. We put on our swimsuits even though it's still too cold to swim and honestly too cold to be in suits. Yours is a high-waisted two-piece, navy blue and covered in white polka dots. It reminds me of a pinup shoot from the '40s and I can't stop staring at you in it. I don't even try to hide my glances now that I don't have to look quite as respectfully.

I open a bottle of cold white wine and pour myself a glass. Your new party trick is that you can make yourself what we call a "ghost copy" of my physical things. Usually, we use it to play board games, but this afternoon we're using it for drinks and beach towels. When you grab my glass after it's poured, you pull away a copycat glass of wine for yourself. This way you, too, can drink your way through the impressive stash of bottles my mom insists on keeping here just in case she suddenly and violently needs to entertain a large group of people. It's only happened like once, maybe, but once was all she needed to stay prepared for the rest of time.

We lounge side by side in the sun, me wearing my towel as a blanket, our drinks on a little plastic table between us. I read and you lie back with your eyes closed. We don't speak much. You've been quiet all day. I try not to read too much into it, but the gnats in my brain wake up and scream at me to ask for reassurance that everything is fine and that you're not tired of me and ready to leave like everyone else. I desperately need to know you're still happy with me. I want you to tell me that you're just tired, that you're just enjoying the peace and quiet; I want you to tell me that you love me with your mouth to my ear so I can feel in the warmth of your breath how much you mean it. I want you to tell me in a way that makes me believe you, but I don't know if a way exists. You'd have to press it into my skin with something hot and metal, scorching enough to burn me and leave me with a scar shaped like your love, and even then I'd tell myself that the scar didn't mean what I wanted, didn't mean anything at all. I try not to think about it and instead focus on the pages in front of me, but that only makes me think about it more. I reread the same sentence over and over. I have no idea what it says. The paragraphs blur together into those black-and-white shapes psychiatrists ask people to interpret. In the shapes, I see you telling me it was all a big mistake and you want to leave.

"Are you okay?" I ask.

You take off your sunglasses and turn to squint at me. You look confused. I wonder if I shouldn't have asked, if I've ruined a good day by convincing myself it was a bad one.

"I'm okay," you say. "Why?"

I don't believe you, like I knew I wouldn't.

"You just seem quiet today."

Say something I will believe. Say you're thinking about a really good bowl of pasta you had once. Say you've got a song stuck in your head and it's gotten to the point where you're low-key writing an essay about all the different possible interpretations of the lyrics. Say you're deep in thought about the injustice of aquariums.

But instead you don't say anything at all. You just stare past me, at the trees. I wonder if you're thinking of her—of Megan. I sure am. I may be busy with you now, but I'm still reading. And the further I get into your journal, the more Megan is worming her way around my brain, munching holes in everything. I'm always thinking about Megan. She's the one thing I can't figure out. Your love for her in the journal is so visible, it's blinding, like staring at the sun. As I read about her getting sick, your desperation to keep her alive is heartbreaking. And we all know what happens next. Her death is going to be bad for you. Really bad. Really bad and really recent. In the journal, where I am, it's December and she's still alive. It's only April now. I don't mind being a rebound, but you loved her so much that I don't know how you can look at me at all. I don't know how you're okay. Are you okay? Even if you said you were, I wouldn't believe you.

AVA

Megan and I had three truly terrible conversations. The first was when Chad died. The second happened on December 19. This is how it went:

"You have to eat me," she said after an unusually long period of complete silence.

At first I laughed. I thought it was one of her morbid jokes, something witty about cannibalism and sex, but then I saw her face, grim and gaunt, her lower lip quivering, her eyes full of tears. I dropped whatever I was doing.

"I'm sorry, what? You aren't going to die, first of all. You're not. I won't let you."

"You don't know that," she said. "It doesn't look good. It really hurts. I can't eat. I need a doctor and we don't have one. We don't have medicine. We don't have food. We barely have clean water. Ava, listen to me. I need you to start trying to accept the reality of—"

"No!" I was shaking my head like a wet dog, crying already. She was always stronger than me. "I won't accept it, because you're going to be fine. Maybe it's nothing. We don't know. It's only been a couple weeks since it got really bad."

"It's getting worse fast."

It was. Horrifyingly fast. Plus, in that first couple weeks she'd been really sick, we'd run out of food completely. All the plants were dead. The animals had hidden themselves away for the winter. Neither of us had eaten anything in five days at this point. But I wouldn't even consider what she wanted me to do.

"Not fast enough for us to start thinking about your corpse."

"I'm just saying, if I were to die—"

"You won't." I stared hard at the ground.

She sat up with too much effort and held out her hands. I gave her mine and she ran her thumbs gently over my palms, her way of telling me to breathe. I choked air through my thin tube of a throat.

"Okay," she said finally. "I won't die for now, but hypothetically if I ever did, you have to eat me."

I opened my mouth to argue, but she shut me down.

"Think of it as my will, Ava—you can't contest it. I know we don't have a lawyer or paperwork, but this is it. This is what I want done with my body."

I couldn't speak. I just stared at her, shaking. I couldn't even imagine it. My brain didn't go that far.

"I don't think I can," I managed to whisper finally.

She squeezed my hands with what felt too much like her last shudder of strength. "You can. Think of it as an act of love."

"Why?" I'd never heard my voice so small.

"Because that's all I can do to help you live. And I have to know I did my best. I can't go to the grave knowing I'm leaving you with nothing and no one. I won't. You wouldn't survive it and we both know that. If I die, you won't get food for yourself, you'll just lie here and die too. This way you have to keep yourself alive. It's a task that'll take you a while and sustain you. It's me, doing my best."

She was right, and I hated it the absolute most I've ever hated anything. I promised myself I would not let her die under any circumstances, then said, "Okay."

She held out her hand. "Shake on it."

I shook.

She lay back against the wall, content. I tried to exit my body.

"I'm going to turn the smoker into a barbecue party for you," she said, smiling, trying to lighten things like she always did.

I must have paled or greened very fast, because she quickly asked, "Too soon?"

"Yeah," I said.

"Okay. I'm sorry."

"It's okay."

And it would be okay, I told myself, because she would. Not. Die.

~AA Brown

SAVANNAH

GOD, SEE WHAT I mean? "Eat my corpse when I die"? Jesus Christ, what the fuck kind of trauma even is that? I close the book and set it aside, sitting up on my knees. I stare into your eye sockets, trying to fathom how I would cope with you asking me for that.

"What is going on, Ava?" I ask your corpse, which looks more like a husk of you every day. A wet mummy. The decomposition has sped up with the weather. I try not to think about it, because when I think about it, I can't breathe.

When you don't answer, I let the silence settle between us and then ask an even worse question. "Did you do it? The cannibalism?"

Of course you don't answer that, either. I'm tempted to go home and ask you, but I stomp that thought out like a little fire, ashamed to even have thought it at all. I can't do that; it would be fucked-up. But I want to know. I guess that's natural, right? We'd all want to ask the question, right? Right? God, I hope that's a common curiosity and not just me being a little fucking freak again.

I grab your journal from the ground and dust it off, holding it to my chest. I guess I'll find out anyway if I keep reading, if Ava tells me. I hate how much I hope Ava will tell me. Feeling just the right amount of disgusted with myself, I sigh and stand up to head home.

"See you tomorrow!" I say to your body, tucking your journal into my own backpack and shouldering it.

I take my time going home, because I don't think I can talk to you yet without seeming suspicious. It's a beautiful day. The birds are chirping, and green is growing back on the branches of the trees; it's the type of beautiful that means our hourglass is running out of sand.

I decide halfway to the edge of the trees that I won't judge you if you did it. It makes sense as a survival move. I think we all would do it. I would. The possible cannibalism isn't what unsettles me; it's how fast you recovered from it—not so much from the eating part, but from everything else. In order to get to the point of cooking and consuming Megan, you would have first had to hang her upside down and bleed her out. You'd have had to lay her down, flay her open, and scoop out her organs. Then you would have had to cut her up into small, consumable chunks, and been sure to store them close to you at all times so the wolves wouldn't eat her first. All that while freshly grieving her?

Yikes would be an understatement.

I think of you smiling at me across the table the other night at dinner, digging your knife into a medium-rare steak, your teeth sinking down on the flesh as the empty fork exited your upturned lips. And yet you went the whole meal, unbothered. How, though? How are you okay?

The gnats in my brain swarm again, reminding me of the rapidly compiling evidence that all the LEGO bricks don't quite fit together. I push back, trying not to panic. Maybe this is just how you cope. Maybe you're in denial. Maybe something about the afterlife softens the blow of the worst things we experienced in our lives. Maybe you barely remember any of it. I lose myself in a spiral of *maybe*s of which Hils would not approve all the way back to the garage.

I try answering all the bad *maybe*s with good *maybe*s, but it all churns together until I have to brace myself against the garage door with my eyes shut and force myself to breathe. I'm okay. You're real. You're mine. At least for now. It's okay. I'm okay. Maybe you didn't even eat Megan in the first place. Maybe you chickened out. Maybe you . . . My eyes shoot open as I'm impaled with a memory. The memory of when I found the backpack, of going through it. One of the things inside, I remember holding it and then tossing it back into the bag, like it was nothing. My stomach turns.

I type the code into the panel at the side of the driveway and the door starts cranking upward. I walk into the garage and close the door behind me, nauseated. I turn on the lights and shiver as my eyes fall on the empty cooler where your backpack is stored, for safekeeping. I creep forward, tiptoeing, even though I know you never come in here. I undo the latches of the cooler slowly, a little at the time, like you're sleeping beside it and I'm trying to sneak a glance inside without waking you. I take the zipper between two fingers, my hands still gloved from holding your journal, and I peel it back slowly so it doesn't make a sound. Then I gently rifle through the items until I find it. My heart's loud. I try to swallow but my mouth is too dry. I take the faded Subway bag between two fingers and extract it like an arcade claw machine. I hold my breath as I open the bag and look inside, where I see the small handful of beef jerky inside at the bottom. Only on second glance, it looks less like beef jerky. The meat is lighter in color, not dark brown like red meat, more like pork.

And that's because it's not beef jerky, I realize as I struggle to shove my stomach back down my throat. It's Megan.

AVA

Remember how I said there were three truly horrible conversations? Well, this is the third. It was December 24, Christmas Eve, in the middle of the night.

"Cheers!" I said, raising my cup of tea that I worked extra hard gathering stuff to make—only the good *pine needles for Christmas. We clinked cups.*

"Merry Christmas!" she said.

"Merry Christmas!" I said back.

We kissed and then sipped on our teas, the fire crackling in front of us. She laid her head on my chest and sighed, relaxing into me. I was content.

"You know," she said, "I would have preferred us having some sort of a stew or something for my last Christmas, but as long as I have you, I'm good, baby!"

I tensed.

"It's not your last Christmas," I muttered, trying not to make a big deal out of it.

She turned around in my arms to face me. "Ava," she said, her expression soft with pity. "It is my last Christmas. I've accepted it. You should accept it too, so it'll be easier on you."

I shook my head in disbelief. "I don't have to accept anything."

She sighed and pulled back so we sat cross-legged, facing each other.

"I just think it'll be easier if you start preparing for this mentally as a very real possibility."

I wrapped my arms tight around my chest. "No, fuck you, why would you say that to me?"

"Because I'm dying."

"You're not fucking dying! Stop saying that!"

"Ava . . ."

"I won't let you!"

"Okay, well, that's just selfish, then."

My jaw dropped. "Selfish?? You're calling ME selfish when you're the one planning to leave me all alone here!"

She sniffled, tears rolling down her face. "I'm not being selfish. It's not like I'm choosing this."

"Well, you're not exactly trying to stop it when you're out here bragging about it being your last Christmas!"

"Oh come on, that's not fair!"

"How? How is it not fair, Megan?!"

"Because you know as well as I do that there's nothing we can do to fix this!"

"We could hold out some hope, maybe?"

But she was right. I knew she was right as I watched the distressed tears roll down her face as I kept laying into her. I couldn't stop. My own emotions around her death, my own unwillingness to face it, crashed over me like a giant wave I'd had my back to all this time. We went back and forth for the better part of an hour until I finally looked at her, really looked at her, really saw what the illness had done. I saw how the flesh clung to her bones and closed my eyes. I remembered how she used to look, sitting on my desk with a cup of coffee, healthy and radiant. I opened my eyes back up to see her, sniffling, slumped back against the wall with barely the strength to cry. She could no longer stand and walk on her own. Some days, she couldn't lift her own water cup to her lips. It was true. If I didn't get her to the hospital now, I would lose her. And even if I knew the path to take to walk out of here, she was too frail for the journey. I clamped one hand over my mouth and whimpered. Her face softened as she saw the denial slough off me for the first time.

"I'm sorry," I said finally, tears gushing down my face.

"It's okay," she said.

"It's just really hard. It's really scary. I couldn't fathom losing you in the real world, but out here, I don't know how I'll survive it."

She nodded. "You will. You're strong. It'll suck and I'm really sorry about that, but you can do it. I promise you can."

I shook my head. "I can't."

I really didn't think I could. I still don't think I can. She reached out and took my hand in hers.

"I know," she said. I drank in the freshwater blue of her eyes. "It's homophobic, isn't it?"

I gave her the dry laugh I knew she wanted as I scrubbed the tears off my face with the back of my free hand. "So homophobic."

We leaned forward and pressed our foreheads together, holding the backs of each other's heads, her fingers in my hair the way I liked. I listened to her breaths, trying not to count how many she had left.

That night, and every night that followed, I held her as tightly as I could without breaking her. My most precious one.

~A.A Brown

SAVANNAH

I WAKE UP sobbing for the first time since you started sleeping here with me. There was a window of time where everything felt okay. I wasn't seeing Michelle. I was living my best life loving you. I wasn't running—at least, I didn't think I was—and all my thoughts were just a little bit less, a vacation from myself.

I must be checking out of the resort soon, because I'm losing it again and you being here doesn't even help. I'm too distracted by the fact that you shouldn't be here. And if you *were* here, you wouldn't be laid out, next to me, naked and radiant; you'd be manically enlisting me in helping you get back to Megan, wherever she is. You'd be finding her, but instead you're fucking me. It's a plot hole. And whenever I think about it that way, I can't breathe. I keep trying to tell myself not to overthink it, that this is the OCD, that everyone grieves differently and maybe your way is fucking a doe-eyed crash-out nepo baby who's too young for you.

I sit up, fast and sweaty, clutching my chest, trying to self-regulate before I wake you. Zelda squints at me from the foot of the bed, her blue-gray eyes glowing in the dark.

"Do you see her, too?" I whisper-hiss at her.

Zelda just yawns.

"Bitch. You're no help."

Zelda lays her little kitten head down on her paws and falls asleep again, unbothered. You stir next to me and turn over. Your arm flops over to pull me close to you by the hip, but when you feel around, you find me sitting up. You open one eye and look at me. You clock the distress in my face even in the dark. The other eye opens. You move onto your side, facing me, stacking pillows for head support, and motion for me to turn on the light. I flip the switch on my bedside lamp.

"What's wrong?" you ask.

I shake my head, eyes pinched shut. I can't tell you what's wrong. I can't tell you that I don't know if you're real or not, that I was investigating, and then I gave up, and now I regret it. I'd sound crazy. I am crazy. And I'd lose you for sure. Even if I wanted to say it, I couldn't. My throat closes around the words like a Venus flytrap and digests them before I can start to speak.

"It's nothing," I say instead. "It's just the nightmares about Michelle are back."

You prop yourself up on your pillow pile with an elbow. "What happened with her?"

"What?" I ask, surprised by the question. You haven't ever asked directly. I've only ever written about it, in that letter for Hils, two bottles of prosecco deep at my dorm room desk just before I left school.

You give a half shrug. "You've never told me what happened. I know Michelle fucked you up pretty good, but I don't know what she did. You never talk about it. Maybe it would help if you could talk about it."

You wait, your eyes neutral and expectant. Everything about you is soft and safe, and still the thought of speaking it aloud makes my heart bounce. But I have to tell you something. And I can't tell you what's really wrong. And I trust you, so I will tell you. I turn away, because I worry I won't be able to talk about it if I can see you looking at me. I stare at the bare wall in front of us as I start to speak.

We started drinking in her dorm room. The plan was to pregame there and then we were supposed to go to this lingerie Christmas party Michelle was invited to. I was chugging White Claws, nervous about seeing so many mostly naked pretty girls in one place. And then there was Michelle, sitting in front of me in this two-piece set, baby blue, with a matching garter belt and little white thigh-high stockings with ruffles at the tops. She looked so beautiful she was bright; I had to look away. I drank more so I'd stop fidgeting next to her, in the Santa-red corset I'd bought for this, but it backfired. It made me feel safer with her than I should have.

Three cans in, I laid my head on her shoulder and told her I loved her. She just laughed and swatted me off like I was a fly.

"I love you, too, you drunk bitch," she said, and she stood up. "Now, put that down." I didn't want to go. I had a weird feeling. I wanted to stay there with her, where I felt safe and warm. But I was obedient. I followed her like a shadow, drifting through the streets as she dragged me along by one hand. The whole way, she kept talking about this guy, Derrick, who was going to be there. We had a Cultures and Context seminar together on Monday mornings, and Michelle kept trying to push me to date him. She said he liked me and he was a good guy and he was hot and blah blah blah. Drunkenly, I told her it was stupid that his name had two *r*'s and a *ck*. It looked weird on paper. Michelle giggled as she squeezed my arm and told me we'd probably be able to see his package through his boxers at the party, see what I'd be working with. I cringed down to my bones at the thought.

I turn to you and open my eyes, almost against my will. I don't think about it; I just want to look into your eyes, see the scrunch of your forehead as you react to the weirdness of his name. I almost turn away again, but you snatch my hand. You nod at me to show me that if I keep looking at you while I say it, I won't regret it. And then I'm doing it; I'm telling someone.

The party was at this international student's house. Her parents own a chain of hotels in Malaysia and are filthy rich, so she had a loft in SoHo to herself. When we got there, forty or fifty college kids were already inside, jumping up and down, screaming that song from One Direction where the girl's only hot because she doesn't know she's hot. Everything was decked out with decorations and red-and-green trash. Derrick was hanging out with a group of boys by the drink table.

"Let's get a drink!" Michelle yelled, then she dragged us over before I could answer. You could in fact see Derrick's package through his almost-see-through Grinch shorts. It looked like a loose worm. I kept my eyes on Michelle instead and made myself a Jack and Coke. We talked with the boys and danced for a little while. Well, Michelle talked and danced and I watched and drank, trying not to stare too hard at any of the girls in their underwear. I kept drinking, mixing liquors. Next I had a vodka cranberry. Then a glass of wine. Another. A red, then a white. A beer. A shot of tequila that Michelle made me do. She tipped it into my mouth.

I don't remember what happened in between, but at one point I stumbled over to her and put my arm around her, nuzzling my face into her glitter-covered neck. "I love you," I said.

She kissed my forehead. "I love you, too, dumbass," she said. "Like a sister."

"No, I really love you," I replied, my words slurred. "Not like a sister, like I lovvvvee you." The word *love* sounded stretched out, gross and wet, like it was made of snot.

Michelle laughed, but while she laughed, her eyes narrowed, like they did when she was deciding to do something mean. I remember feeling the dread cut through the drunkenness for a second, like the guillotine. "You're funny," she said, spinning me around, her hands on my bare hips. "Derrick, isn't she funny?"

Derrick grinned down at me stupidly, a Bud Light in one hand, blue eyes, sandy-brown hair, six foot two or something like that. I remember thinking other girls probably thought he was pretty, squirmy worm dick and all.

"I lost my corset!" I exclaimed, realizing it for the first time. I still had my bra on, but my stomach looked floppy and bloated. I wrapped my arms around myself, trying to cover up.

Michelle said something like, "We'll find it in the morning." And then when I squirmed, she told me I didn't need it. I told her I did, that it was her who didn't need hers, because she was pretty.

"Come on!" Michelle yelled over the bass. "Let's go somewhere private!" She laughed. "Savannah thinks we're pretty!"

Before I knew it, I was floating along behind her like a balloon on a string as she tugged me into a guest bedroom. Derrick followed almost as blindly as me, his head bobbing along to the beat.

Michelle closed the door and locked it. Derrick grinned again. He had something green in his teeth. Michelle sat me down on the bed. She looked like an angel, like she could save me.

"What are we doing?" I asked her.

My hands shake in yours and so you squeeze them tighter. When I try to look away, you hold my eyes in yours, tears and all.

You breathe big to remind me to breathe. We breathe together, twice. You nod me on.

> Michelle just laughed and *shhh*-ed me. She gave me a long kiss on the lips with no tongue and that stupefied me into silence. Then she stood up and kissed Derrick. When she let him go, he had a boner. She pushed him toward the bed. I moved away, but she came over and whispered in my ear that I should stop. She kissed my neck, pushed me back on the bed, grabbed my underwear, and pulled it down. He looked at me like I was a steak dinner she had cooked, extra bloody the way he liked it. She guided him on top of me and whispered something into his ear. He laughed and tore me open at the same time. When I looked around for her while he slammed into me with his sweaty hard body, his beer breath hot on my face, I realized she'd left me there.
>
> I don't remember anything else, but I woke up sore and alone in a stranger's house. And the next morning, this absolute linebacker of a woman in an MTA uniform, who smelled like coconuts and brown sugar, grabbed me by the waist as my feet left the platform for the Canal Street tracks, and she wouldn't let go. They had to tranquilize me in the end. I woke up in the hospital to a text from Michelle saying she'd heard about the accident and just couldn't deal with me anymore.

I stare at our hands on the bed between us until you realize I don't have any words left. I said it all. I don't know if I feel proud or ashamed. I wait for your opinion to decide.

"Jesus Christ," you say eventually. "No wonder you're out here in the woods to recover from that. I think woods are best-case scenario, to be honest. And I bet it wasn't good for the OCD!"

The first things to go are my shoulders, drooping halfway to my hips with relief. And then there are my lungs, exhaling everything I've been holding inside for months, everything I've been choking on in the middle of the night, the lump in my throat. I collapse into sobs, understood.

"No," I yell, surprising myself with the sound, "it wasn't good for the OCD. It was torture! I kept trying to figure out how she could love me and still do that to me. I went through every interaction we'd ever had all night long every night. I convinced myself I was the rapist all along, not her!"

You catch me as I fall forward into your chest and rock me back and forth. I use your body to shield me from the aftershock of what I've said. I anchor myself in your just-for-show heartbeat. It feels wrong to acknowledge it. It feels like I'm the guilty one. It feels like the police are going to knock any minute now and scoop me up for slander even though it's the truth. It's the first time I've ever admitted what Michelle was: a rapist by proxy, just as bad as him.

"I used to tie myself to the bed at night," I whisper into your chest, "because I knew if I could easily get up, I would kill myself. I asked my friends so many times whether I was unlovable that they all stopped loving me. And now all I'll ever be is this, this unlovable thing."

"I love you," you tell me. "I love you, I love you, I love you, I love you . . ."

Over and over and over, until I know for sure.

AVA

Megan died on New Year's Eve. I only realized the date after, when I pulled Chad's watch off her limp wrist. I've always hated New Year's Eve, and now I know I was right all along. They said I was crazy at the holiday parties where everyone else was drunk and having fun, full of hope. Nope. I was right to be suspicious. New Year's Eve was destined to be the worst day of my life.

I wasn't ready for what the day would do to me when I got up that morning. I woke up feeling bone-tired and starving, as per usual. I got the fire going. I boiled the water. Megan got up a couple hours after me, feeling shitty, but no more than usual. It just goes to show you, right? It could be any day that takes everything from you, any day at all.

I made her some tea. She told me everything hurt. I told her I knew, that I was sorry, that I would try to fix it, that I loved her. She told me she loved me too. Then she scooted back and relaxed against the wall. We went about our day. I ate a small piece of smoked fish for breakfast. She declined, saying she was really nauseous. I didn't think much of it. The sun was high in the sky, and my plan for the afternoon was to check the snares and fishing baskets. I set her up with some freshly boiled water and the little notebook, for something to do, and I turned to go, but as I was halfway out the door, she breathed in, once, very sharply.

"What are you doing?" she asked. When I turned to answer her, her eyes were giant, pupils all the way dilated, the blue of her eyes only

a sliver around the black. I actually laughed—the audacity of me. I thought she was just panicking because she worried about me being safe when I went out and she had to stay in.

"I'm just going to check the snares," I said.

"Ava," she said. She started shaking. It was violent.

I dropped my bag. "What's happening?"

"You have to stay," she said, her voice tense.

And then her body pitched forward, like she'd been electrocuted, and a gush of blood ran from her mouth.

I think I said something like "Jesus Christ!" or "Oh fuck!" I leaped to her side, and I wrapped my body around her back to support her weight. I remember crying, shaking just like she was, like I was going to die too. "Fuck," I said, looking around frantically for something that could help, for a bandage that would stop it, for anything I could do. I was rabid, feral, for a solution.

"Oh fuck," I said over and over as I grasped at her. "What do I do?!" I yelled at no one.

"Just stay with me," she said, her voice thinner than air. "Just stay." She shuddered and more blood dripped down her chin.

I shook my head. "What?"

"Stay," she said. "This is it. Just stay."

"What do you mean?" I sobbed. "No, I can't." I shook my head more and more. "I need to do something!"

She smiled, too calm as she shook in my arms like a brittle leaf. "Sing, then."

I offered a laugh, small and bitter. "What?" It was my only word.

"Play me out," she said. "Something fancy, one of your opera songs. I want to go out in style."

I started to tell her she couldn't go out at all, but then I remembered that I had promised, so I just nodded once, numb in every part of my body that wasn't touching her. "Okay."

I stared at her for a long minute, wishing we had longer, not quite knowing how to comprehend my own loss, trying to think of the last thing I wanted to say to her, trying to find the words that would be enough. "I love you," I managed at last, holding on to her for dear life.

"I love you too," she said, so soft I barely heard it. She looked up, tears streaming down her face. She nodded at me, eyes wet and so brave.

I started to sing the only thing I could think of that made sense, an art song by Mahler I'd learned recently called "Ich bin der Welt abhanden gekommen." It's about the feeling of being lost to the world when everyone believes you are already dead. I've always found it haunting.

It was the most poorly executed performance of my life, but also the one that meant the most. I choked out the words, my voice cracking with sobs, but I did my best to give Megan something beautiful. She deserved so much better. But I hope what I gave was okay. I hope it brought her something. I hope it was enough, that at least she knew I loved her more than my body could bear, more than music could.

By the time I finished the song, she was gone.

~AA Brown

SAVANNAH

YEP. I'M THE asshole.

PART FOUR

Skeletonization: The final stage of decomposition. The body is reduced to bone.

AVA

I know I've been in an acute state of need for months now, but I've never needed anything like I need Megan back with me. Fuck food, water, shelter. I need her more than all of it. Grief is exhausting. They don't tell you that it will hurt physically as well as mentally. My ribs are bruised from trying to hold my heart in my chest at night because it always feels like it's going to burst out. I constantly have a headache from my brain pressing against my skull as it tries to escape—it's holding as many memories of her as it can all at once, and feeding them to me on repeat in as much detail as possible. I can't lose a single second, and I don't have any pictures, only the ones I've drawn, which are so precious to me that I only look at them in emergencies. I don't want to ruin them with my tears. Less exposure, less risk. I keep them in the inside pocket of my jacket. Near my heart. For good luck. Always. My throat is rough and raw from screaming and wailing. I haven't had a voice for days to scream and wail with, but I scream louder every day. I hope my voice never comes back. I hope it dies with her. She's the only one who ever deserved to hear it.

The only reason I keep going at this point is because I promised her I would, but I keep wishing I would die. I don't believe in the afterlife and never have. I always hoped it would be a nice cozy void of nothingness. No work, no stress, no money, no problems. Lights out. But now I'm kind of hoping my parents are right so I can find her again. I'd do eternity anywhere if I could do it with her. The only thing keeping me going is if I get out of here, I can charge my phone and call her to hear her voice again on voicemail, look at pictures of her on Instagram.

Every day I survive without her, the less I see the point. None of it was unbearable until now, but the loneliness gnaws at my skin like a bad itch. I never used to value my life before this anyway, and I've been telling myself this whole time that I've been working so hard at staying alive because it's an extraordinary situation and it activated some weird instinct within me. The truth is, I think maybe I only lived this long in the first place because I wanted to be with her as long as I could. And maybe after this there would be a wedding and a honeymoon and a couple turkey baster kids and she'd cry enough tears to flood the parterre when I finally got Tosca *at the Met. But now I don't know. I can't bring myself to care about art. I can't imagine loving anyone or anything enough to hurt like this again. I'm looking at my dwindling pile of firewood and I don't know why I don't just let it run out. I don't know why I promised her I'd try to live when I knew there'd be nothing left to live for. I'll tell you what though: if I had a voice to sing with, my* Tosca *would be amazing right about now. I'm living it.*

Perché perché, Signore?

~AA Brown

SAVANNAH

LINES FROM YOUR journal keep pelting me like rocks to the front of the face, unwilling to let me forget the gravity of the situation I've inserted myself into. It's to the point where I'm starting to wish I'd worn safety goggles, just in case one of the specks of Megan's death nails me in the eye and scratches away my ability to see. Of course, I'd deserve it.

I cry the whole walk out, guilt dripping down my face and neck, pooling on my collar. It's pathetic. Here I am again, acting like the victim when it's just the consequences of my own actions, a serial killer sniffling on the bus to prison. I don't have your journal with me today. I don't have anything. I'm not going to read. I'm going to apologize.

Michelle falls into step next to me and I have to do a double take, because she's not inside my head this time—she's escaped somehow. She looks like she does in my head still, too perfect with too-sharp teeth, but she's solid now, like Ava. I guess practice really does make perfect.

"Congratulations, Savannah, you've really done it now, you stupid bitch. Fucking brava." She starts to clap and cheer, loud, obnoxious.

I ball my hands into tight fists at my sides and keep walking, trying not to whimper.

"Are you proud of yourself now, Savannah? You kidnapped a

corpse and went insane. Again. How does it feel?" She sticks her fist under my mouth like a microphone.

"Go away," I mutter at the ground.

"Aw, poor baby can dish it out all day but can't take it?"

I whirl to face her, angry tears on my cheeks. "Go away!!!" The screech comes from the middle of me. It's the loudest sound I've ever made.

She pouts and puts her hands on her hips. "Is that all you got?"

I square up and take a step forward until I'm right in her face. "You're not even real," I say.

Her perfect mouth stretches into a wide smirk. She leans in so her lips brush my ear as she whispers, "Neither is she."

She takes a step back and disappears and I stand shaking and alone again. I wrap my arms around myself and squeeze, tight like a corset, a straitjacket of flesh. I force myself to walk forward, taking my last couple of steps into your clearing. Your skull has rolled off your neck and now lies on its side in what used to be your lap. I get on the ground and curl up into a ball in the dirt, so I can look into your eye sockets. I owe you all the eye contact I can give. I reach out and run my gloved hand down the side of your skull. I hold the hinge of your jaw. I trace a broken-off piece of neck with one finger, where your voice was. I grip the sleeves of your wet shirt, caressing the bones of your arms, thinking of all the things they once held: Megan as she was dying. Not me, never once me.

"I'm sorry," I whisper over and over. "I'm so sorry."

I hold a bundle of skeletal fingers that used to be a hand. I don't know what to say. I don't know what I can do to make this better, so I just tell you what happened. I tell you I didn't mean it, that I just needed a break from being stuck in myself, that it was survival insanity.

"Ava, I'm so sorry. I didn't mean to hijack your death. I didn't mean to try and love you, or claim any part of you as mine. I didn't mean for it to go this far, to keep you this long, to love you like this. I didn't— I'm—I'm not sane. I've been hallucinating my ex–best friend, Michelle, too, since she left. I didn't think it would happen with anyone else."

I start to sob and squeeze my ribs harder to counteract the shudders.

"I don't know." I laugh even though nothing is funny. The sound is both wet and dry. "Maybe you are real, but it's— There's just too much that doesn't make sense. I guess we'll see. I'm gonna do that if-I-love-you-let-you-go bullshit and if you're still stuck moping around my house after that, then maybe I'll stay out of the asylum after all, but—" I swallow hard, and my throat feels swollen, like my body doesn't want me to admit the truth, either. I sigh to clear space for the words with my breath. I make myself stand up.

"I don't think you're real. There's too much that doesn't make sense. You're a fantasy, a beautiful, kind fantasy, but a fantasy nonetheless, way too okay for what you've been through, way too devoid of the huge grief I read in your words. You're perfect in a way real people aren't. I made you up inside my head, like that poem I wrote a paper on in high school. A mad girl's love song." I sniffle and release the anaconda grip I have on myself to wipe the tears off my cheeks with the back of my hand. I don't deserve them, but I hope you appreciate them. I hope you take my grief and my guilt as punishment enough for what I've done.

"I'm sorry," I say as my voice breaks. I try to think of anything else to say, anything better, but just like it always is looking for something to say when someone is dead, we've yet to come up with words that are adequate enough. And so, I just keep saying the one tried and true that we do have, over and over and over. "I'm sorry, I'm sorry, I'm sorry . . ."

I sink to my knees again in front of your bones, legs buckling beneath me as I beg your forgiveness. And that's when the second thing finally hits me.

Oh God. You're bones.

AVA

Okay. Fine, let's do it. We can talk about the cannibalism. I know you want to know. I get it, I do. If I were in your shoes I would want to know too. It's an important part of the story. God, I wish I could be drunk for this.

I tried really hard to treat it like a funeral. I'd been mentally preparing myself for it since I accepted the possibility that Megan was going to die. I thought a lot in the middle of the night, watching her sleep, sickening myself, about how I would do it. Treating it like the ritual of a funeral, honoring her life with it, was the only way I came up with that made me feel like I could maybe live with myself afterward. And in some ways, it was just like a funeral in the real world—uncomfortable and scary and horribly sad, meant to honor what Megan wanted done with her body in the first place.

I took her to the river. I remember being surprised but also not surprised at how easily I could carry her. She was so skinny, you couldn't even fathom it. She was like one of those dogs in the ASPCA commercials, with ribs you can count from a distance. I hitched the knife to my belt. I cradled her the whole way to the water, whispering "I love you" after "I love you." I removed her clothes and folded them off to the side. I washed her in the cold running water. Then I laid her down gently on the big rock, where she loved to lie in the sun and tell me her theories about what we'd missed in the world. What if Ben Shapiro got caught being gay? What if a single McDonald's hash brown is like eight dollars now? What if two billionaires crashed into each other while drag racing in space?

The rock slants down away from the river and anchors into the ground below. It's basically a triangle. I laid her on the sloped part—what was it in eighth-grade math, the hypotenuse?—face up, head tilted toward the dirt. It's not too steep, so I wasn't worried about her sliding off. I sharpened the knife on a nearby rock while sobbing hysterically, shivering because I wasn't wearing a coat.

I knelt in the dirt by her head. I kissed her lips, her forehead, her face. I laid my head on her chest for the last time. I whispered a thousand I love you*'s and promises of forever into her ears. Then I put my forehead to hers and held the blade to her throat.*

"Goodbye, my love," I whispered.

I squeezed my eyes shut tight and pressed. My body convulsed involuntarily as I heard the squelch of the slice. Her blood gushed, a red river running down both sides of the rock into the cold dirt. There she goes, *I thought as I watched it.* There goes everything I had. *While the blood ran, I made a fire to distract myself from thinking about what had to come next, which ended up being every bit as bad as I imagined. I cut her up mostly with my eyes closed and screaming at the top of my lungs.*

I ate her ribs first, roasted over the fire, violently dissociating the whole time. I tried to make myself feel better by thinking about how she would probably be taking this so much better than me; she'd probably be singing the song from the Chili's commercials in the early 2000s, about the baby back ribs. The only way I could eat them was with my eyes closed and not thinking about it at all. Instead, I locked myself inside my treasured memories of loving her. I thought about how her little nose would scrunch when she didn't want to do something. I thought about how she always laughed at my jokes, even though hers were funnier. I thought about how she called every minor inconvenience homophobic, how she cried every time she killed an animal, how her skin felt on mine in the night, like the only secure thing in the world.

I can't really tell you how it tastes. I don't know. I go to a place where

I don't taste at all. I did not eat her head or her heart. Sue me. I couldn't do it. Those parts were sacred. They were where her essence lived. I buried them in the soft earth where my fire had been. There were no flowers, so I covered her grave in a pyramid of rocks. She wasn't Jewish, but it's fine.

I put the rest of her in Chad's sleeping bag and went back to the cave, feeling empty.

~AA Brown

SAVANNAH

I FIND YOU lying on the couch in your blue cotton robe, reading one of my books. I stand on the last stair and watch you for a minute. My stomach hurts. My ribs push back on my lungs like tiny trash compactors, so I take miniature breaths that sit in my throat as I take you in. I stay on that last step forever, taking a million mental pictures of you like this. I capture the tiny fresh wrinkles around your eyes. I capture the way your hair shines, rainbows of light dancing against the black like an oil spill. Your mascara-less eyelashes. A sunspot on the base of your neck. The way your irises flick back and forth as you scan the page. The slight part of your lips. The way the soft fabric bunches in the curve of your waist. You're so breathtaking I almost turn around. Almost.

Instead I take one stiff step toward you, then another, forcing myself forward like an unoiled tin man. My hands are shaking so I dig my nails into my palms. This is it. In middle school when we learned about the French Revolution, my teacher showed us a YouTube video of how the guillotine worked. For months afterward, I had recurring nightmares about walking toward the guillotine and laying my head down on the block. This feels like that dream, except in the dream, I never wished the walk was longer. Now I do. I'd walk toward this guillotine forever to buy a little extra time before the blade.

I stop just shy of the couch and stand next to the coffee table, waiting for you to notice me, because I can't bring myself to start this on my own. I can hear my heartbeat and I feel like you must, too. In my head, it's pounding the same two words. *Don't look. Don't look. Don't look.* But of course you do. One look at my face and you put down the book. And now we're in this. You stand up and head over to me. I stare at your bare feet as you close the distance between us. You take one of my hands and try to work your thumb into my fist. I stare hard at the floor, avoiding eye contact at all costs like you're Medusa.

"Hey, what's wrong?" you ask. Your voice is a caress I don't deserve.

"Savannah? Honey, will you look at me?"

Hell no.

I feel two fingers of your free hand on my chin, applying the slightest pressure, encouraging me to raise my head.

"Savannah?" you ask again.

I savor the sound of my name in your mouth. Pretty soon, I won't be hearing it anymore. I remember that I won't be able to look at you like this anymore, either, up close and intimate. I look up. The hand on my chin shifts to cradle the side of my face.

"There you go," you say, the corners of your mouth pulling up into a soft smile. You trace my chin with your thumb and let your hand drop to scoop up my other hand. You hold my hands in the air between us, like we're at the altar. "So what's all this about?"

Your eyes are so gentle. I stare at the gold flecks gathered around your pupils. God help me. You wait for an answer as I cower in front of you, sniffling, trying to shove the words past the golf ball lodged at the top of my throat. It's like my tonsils grew back and swelled up as a last-ditch effort to stop me from ruining it all.

"You're not real," I manage after several long seconds. I am so tense when I say it that I swear at any second I will shatter in a burst like hot glass against ice water.

Something shifts in your eyes. You close them briefly. And

when they open up again, you're wearing a look of sympathetic understanding, but not shock. You knew this would happen one day. The realization is a punch to the heart.

"Okay. Elaborate on that a little."

Jesus, it was hard enough just to get that far and now you want more from me? I guess this is what I get for falling in love with an adult. I attempt a deep breath that ends up being more of a thick wheeze. Then the dam bursts and it all comes tumbling out.

"It's the little inconsistencies. You weren't mad enough at me when you found out I was keeping your body hostage. We don't fight enough. You didn't grieve long enough for Megan before you fell for me. You should be so beyond traumatized from your experiences out there—you should be catatonic. I know because I went through way way the fuck less and I was practically catatonic before I met you. But you're not. Instead, somehow you're perfectly upright and normal. Instead, you're taking care of me, helping me through my trauma and my pain, when in reality after what happened to you out there, the more I read, there's no way you'd be here like this, sculpted into a perfectly sexy wife–therapist combo platter that's just mine to feast on, always, with no real needs of her own, no real work to be done on my part. It's nice and you're so beautiful and I love our life together, but it's not real. You're too perfect to be human. And that's how I know you're not real."

You look at me for a minute, studying my eyes so intently I can feel you sifting through my brain, sizing me up, determining whether or not I'm ready to hear the answer.

"I know," you say finally.

Two little words that bring me to my knees. I thought I was doing well, staying strong and holding it together. Nope. We were wrong. I wasn't ready to hear it. I'm sobbing harder than I ever have in my life immediately after you say it.

"I'm sorry," I say. "I'm so sorry. I know that you were a real person the whole time and I just . . . I needed you. I'm so sorry." I apologize over and over, the guilt washing over me in big, crashing waves. I have to wrap my arms around your shoulders for support, because I can't bear the weight of it alone, and the fresh realization that I will have to from now on just makes me sob harder.

You wrap your arms around me and hold me to you, kissing the top of my head and repeating, "I know, I know, shhh, it's okay."

"We don't even know if you would actually say that. You're not real!" I despair into your neck. I'm crying so hard I can't breathe. I'm gasping for air in little gulps between avalanches of grief. I never even cried for Michelle like this. I wonder if all the pain I've ever stored in my body is coming out at once, exorcism style. It's violent. This was a bad idea. I take it back. I want to bitch-slap myself back into the before.

"Oh God, I can't do this. It hurts so much. Ava, it hurts so so fucking much, fuck, I can't. I can't. I shouldn't have. I— And without you? I'm supposed to— I can't. I can't I can't I can't I can't I can't . . ." I chant my new mantra as my knees buckle and I sink lower and lower until my forehead rests on your stomach. You don't even try to console me this time. You know I'm in too big a world of hurt for that. We just stand there while I tell you over and over how much I really, really can't, like that's going to make a difference at this point. I watch your robe get patchy with snot and tears. I try to take my breaths in twos but I can only gasp like a fish flopping on a deck.

"You can," you say eventually, lifting my wet face with both hands, making me stand. "You can and you will. I promise."

"You're wrong."

"I'm not."

"How do you know? I made you up inside my head."

"You're just going to have to trust me."

"How? I don't trust myself and you're not even you. You're just more me."

You smile and I melt a little. "I know, but I think it'll be easier for you to trust me than yourself, even knowing what you know now."

I snort. "Know what? That I'm fucking crazy?"

"No. Don't think of it like that. Right now you just need to put a little faith in yourself that you will survive this."

"I won't."

"You will. You're young and beautiful and you're going to call the police and turn in my journal and then you're going to go back to school and graduate and work and go out to drink at night with your friends and make all the usual mistakes that people make in their twenties. And somewhere in there you'll find someone else. Someone real. And she'll love you and you'll love her even more than me."

I shake my head. "I won't. I'll never love anyone like this again. It's not possible. I don't even know if I want to. Not if it hurts this much."

"It doesn't always hurt this much. It has the potential to hurt this much, but most of the time it won't."

"But what if I can't survive how much this hurts right now? I'm already weak from Michelle. I can't do this, too. You know what? Actually, this was a bad idea. I take it back. Let's just go back to doing what we were doing and we can pretend this conversation never happened."

"I'm sorry," you say. "I know. Believe me, I know."

I stand whimpering, weeping, holding on to you like you're the only solid thing I have to grab in a storm. Five stages of grief and I'm already at bargaining.

"Please," I blubber. "Please, I take it back. Please. I'm so sorry."

You shake your head, eyes full of pity.

"Please," I whisper again, leaning in. You catch the word in your mouth and swallow it before you kiss me on the cheek and pull back.

"We can't, my love. We will always end up here. You have a whole life to live, and for that, you have to let me go."

"I love you so much."

"I know."

"This is going to kill me."

"It won't. It will hurt a lot, but it won't kill you. You're going to be strong, remember?" You flash a shiny second of that perfect smile. "For me?"

I nod. I hold your face in my hands and bring it to mine for one last, deep, wet kiss. I cup the back of your head and pull you close so we're forehead to forehead, like we were all those weeks ago when you were still fresh in the woods. I close my eyes and see your skull, lying on its side in your clothes and in the dirt. This is a fight I have to lose and that's because I love you. You're right. I have to let you go.

"What now?" I ask.

"Come to bed with me," you say, taking a couple of steps toward the stairs. Extending a hand back to me.

I'm numb from top to bottom, but I let my hand float into yours and I follow you to the bedroom. You untie your robe and let it fall, motioning for me to do the same. I undress on autopilot. You pull back the covers and lie down, patting the space beside you.

"Come on," you say. "I don't bite."

"I wish you would," I grumble, crawling onto the mattress. "It would distract me from this."

You laugh. I curl up into a tight ball and you curl around me, wrapping me all the way up in your legs and your arms. I back into you like I'm trying to merge. Skin to skin. I start to cry again, silently, into my pillow and you press tiny kisses into my shoulder and hold me tighter.

"Hold me until you can't" is all I can choke out in the end. You don't say anything, just pull me in tighter. I squeeze my eyes shut as tight as they'll go and cherish the feeling of you breathing against my back.

When I wake up the next morning, you're gone.

AVA

I am a rag after one too many times at the washboard. All I am is bored or sad or both. There's nothing to watch. I've read everything there is to read a thousand times. In my other little notebook, I've been drawing and making lists of what I miss. Her name is written on every list at least three times. Above running water and toilet paper and toothpaste. Above music and french fries dipped into a cookies-and-cream milk shake. Above lights in the windows of skyscrapers and hugs from my friends. Above insulation and cold clean sheets and sour-coated candy on the Fourth of July. Above hotel slippers and the papery smell of bookstores and the sound of applause from the stage. All I really need is her. All I ever really needed was her.

It's okay. I'm lucky to have had her at all. At least I got one big love before I died, right? I'm coming to terms with that, with death. I think about it a lot. I wonder what will get me in the end. Will it be poison, like Chad? Or illness, like Megan? Maybe I'll take a wrong turn and fall off a cliff that was hidden by a bush. Maybe it'll get even colder than this and I'll freeze to death in the middle of the night. Maybe I'll starve. Maybe a bear will get me after all, now that I have nothing left in me to defend myself. Maybe it'll simply be exhaustion. Maybe one day I will just run out. Cease. Expire. Like spoiled milk . . .

Should I make a will? I guess so. Very well. Let's see. I don't really have much. For Jess, my jewelry collection, anything from the closet.

For Carli, my keyboard and the photography equipment and all the little knickknacks she likes in my house. For Lena, there are edibles in all the drawers, the artsy dead butterflies in jars, the board games, the yellow couch. For Paulina, the artwork. For Noelle, the books, the Jane Austen tea set from my 30th birthday. For Jenn, the Nintendo Switch game collection. For Alice, my vintage Star Wars figurines. I miss you all. I love you all.

Okay. You probably won't be seeing much more of me. We're just about at the end of the story and I'm running out of space in the notebook, but that's fine. I wanted her to take up most of it.

~AA Brown

AVA AND SAVANNAH

TODAY, OFFICIALLY, WILL be the day I found your body.

I can't stay here anymore. For one thing, there's not much out here for me in terms of resources. The animals are still hidden away for the winter. The plants are dead.

I put on my gloves and get your backpack from the garage first, so I can put everything back exactly as it was, so they have all the evidence of exactly what happened to you.

The name Adirondack, our guidebook says, came from the name Native American tribes of this region used to call European colonizers who were incapable of feeding themselves in such an unforgiving environment. The name means "bark eater," as the colonizers often had to resort to eating the bark off trees to survive the winters. I see what they mean. There's nothing here to support life anymore.

I let the bag dangle at my side instead of slinging it over my shoulder, so I don't accidentally contaminate it with any loose hairs.

The point is, I can't stay here much longer. I'm almost out of food. No one will find me if I stay. No one is out searching random small caves. And the truth is, I don't want to stay here. Too many memories.

I stumble through the trees, sniffling, bags under my eyes that could rival a cartoon supervillain's. I haven't really slept in days; all night, I just lie there, arms wrapped around myself like yours used to be, shivering, sobbing, holding my heart inside. I know you were never really mine, never really here, but I grieve you like we were married fifty years. My body yearns for yours, in bed next to mine. The worst part is, I'm all alone again. I can never tell anyone about this. I have to cope on my own. It's hard already and it's not like I went into this new round of grief particularly sane. I'm exhausted, wrung out. But I've read about everything you endured, and I know that if you can do that, then I can do this. I won't give up. I'm determined to survive, for you.

My plan is to pack up the bare minimum and hike out of here. I'll pick a straight line and follow it. Eventually, the woods have to end. Hopefully, walking straight in one direction will lead me to that end.

When I get to your bones, I put your backpack where I found it, covering it partially in dead leaves and dirt and things, like it's been there the whole time. I leave it open so I can deposit your journal last, when I'm done reading it. Then I sit down in front of you, in my usual place, crisscross applesauce. When your funeral comes, I know I won't be invited. All I can do is say goodbye to you like this.

I'm already packing light, leaving most of Chad's now-much-less-fancy camping supplies. And I'll keep shedding gear along the way as I get tired. We'll see. Maybe that'll backfire. Maybe I'll run out of everything before I reach something else. But maybe not.

I open your journal to the very last entry. Your handwriting in dark blue fades a little at the top of the page. Next to that is a scribble where you tried to get the pen to dredge up fresh ink. The words after the scribble are strong but then they fade in and out until the end, so I have to squint to make out some of it. You were running out of everything. Ink, space, time . . .

I'm pretty much ready to go, but I didn't want to leave you hanging. Just in case there is a you that exists, reading this. I had one full page left of the book anyway. How fucked would it have been if I didn't fill it?

As I'm reading, I notice you're right. There's really only a page and change left. Halfway through, I'm already crying. Looking closely at the paper, I can see there are some inky smudges there, from tears before mine. And now my teardrops are mixing with yours, our lives overlapping in a way that is real.

I haven't eaten all of her yet. The rest of the meat is packed up with me, but I don't plan on finishing it. I want there to be something left of her. Something for them to find, to know that I loved her, that I kept her, that I tried for her.

I hang on every last one of your last words. I can't read them slow enough. I read each sentence more than once. I trace the letters with my fingertips, imagining you in the cave, writing them. I'm stalling. I wonder if you were stalling, too, as you wrote this, if your pen dragged slower and slower, the ink crawling out, if you thought about your last line forever. Eventually, we both have to get to the end of the page.

And if I don't get out, it's okay, I think. I'll be dead and there's nothing afterward, or I'll be dead and be with her. Either way, it's alright. I'm used to it. The soprano always dies in the end. I just hope someone will be left who will cry for me the way I've cried for everyone else.

I will, Ava.

I will.

★ ★ ★ ★ ★

ACKNOWLEDGMENTS

Hi, guys! This is my first time in an acknowledgments and I'm nervous, but also so excited to be here to thank all the people who had a hand in making this book exist with me. First, thank you to my agent, Julie Flanagan, who knew exactly the writer I wanted to be as soon as she picked me up. You got me there *so fast* and with so much expertise, while being so nice to me the whole time. Thank you, Julie. I could not have asked for a better career partner in crime.

Thank you to my editor, Leah Mol, who saw every little thing I couldn't see that this book needed right away and guided me right there, over and over again, with extreme competence and patience, until we had the book of my dreams. I'm so proud of where we ended up and I absolutely would not have gotten there without you. And thank you to my copy editor and proofreader, Greg Stephenson and Lisa Basnett, as well as production editor Katie McHale, for catching all the little things that somehow slipped past the rest of us, but of course would have been caught by readers. May both sides of your respective pillows always be cold. And of course, thank you to art director Tara Scarcello for my beautiful cover; it's absolutely stunning! More broadly, thank you to everyone at Hanover Square Press whose names I don't know (yet), who have done so much work behind the scenes. It always thrills me to see all the changes you've made between rounds. It's what I imagine the world would be like if fairies were real. Speaking of fairies, thank you especially to whoever drew me that mushroom; I love my mushroom so much!

On the UK side, thank you to my agent, Rachel Mann, and her assistant, Daisy Arendell. You've both been so helpful in finding the best possible UK home for this one, which proved to be much more complicated than it was in the US. I could not be happier with where we ended up. Speaking of, thank you to Harriet Hirshman, for getting this book so completely as soon as you read it and working on it with me with so much enthusiasm. You, and everyone at Dead Ink, have been a blast. I'm so excited to share a shelf with all the rest of your perfectly weird little books. Thank you to my cover artist, Luke Bird, for a cover so fun, I'll be sure to stand out there. And thank you to my UK copy editor, Dan Coxon, for protecting my reputation overseas.

Okay, this is getting really Oscar-speechy really fast and I can sense they're about to start playing the music, so I'll wrap it up, but first I have to thank my family and the homies. Thank you first and foremost to my mama, who had me in a C-section with no pain meds like a legend (medical mistake, best believe my birth was free), and who always believed I would pull this off. I know you kidnapped my first-ever manuscript and took it to a trusted English teacher in my high school to find out if I was bad at writing—that way, at least you would know and could break it to me gently. But since then, you've been adamant that I was more than enough and have believed in me even at times that I didn't. Thank you to my little brother, Max, who won't read this, but that's for the best. Thank you to my dad, for all those trips to Barnes & Noble and Borders (RIP) and letting me talk about books forever over coffee and cake.

My wife gets her own paragraph, because she's my wife, and I love her so much that if she doesn't text me back in three minutes, my OCD tries to convince me she's dead. Elizabeth, none of this exists without you, because you taught me that perfect love doesn't only exist in fiction. You are everything to me and you are never allowed to die, but if you do, I promise to go insane and invent my own fake version of you and lock myself in our house with her.

To Stella and Gigi the cats, who also get their own paragraph, because of course they do. They're cats!!! Thank you, Gigi, for getting scooped up against your will so many times. And thank you to Stella for helping me edit by taking long naps on my keyboard.

And now for the homies. Thank you to my beta readers: Paulina, Lena, Rebecca, Tommie, Jenn, Jess, Emmery, Elizabeth. Special shout-out to Tommie Linen and Emmery Llewellyn here, who have been beta reading for me for fourteen straight years, since that first book in our freshman year of high school, which, yikes, but you suffered through it and encouraged me to write another one anyway. And special shout-out to Adelina Ceretto, my favorite poet. I love you guys.

Thank you to my English teachers! Ms. Filowitz, I think of you every time I use the passive voice. And, while not an English teacher, thank you to Alys for getting me through college. And thank you to my new writer friends, Sonya and Kerry, for reminding me that this year is not about sanity.

Thank you to my colleagues-turned-besties. Jeff and Andrea, thank you for enduring every back office crash-out I've ever had, and there have been many, and for bringing the whole party every time we go out. Dacia, thank you for yelling at me to keep going from across the lobby at four in the morning whenever you heard the typing stop. Thank you to the bar girlies, for the gossip. And the kitchen guys, for letting me hide and rant. Thank you to Alex for our Saturday-night therapy sessions by the wall. Thank you to Matt, for always telling me that it would all work out, even on that day when I found out my landlord was doubling the rent right before work and almost died of the capitalism of it all. Thank you to my favorite sky cunts: Amy, Rhys, and Anika. Work sucks, but the people that it gives you can be so special.

This is an OCD book, so thank you to my therapist, Hils (not her real name). Thank you for the diagnosis and for giving me the understanding of my own mind that made this book possible. Thank you to my psychiatrist, for the Ambien. Kidding! Thank you for helping me balance my brain so I didn't run off into the woods and befriend a corpse during my post-book-deal loss of my marbles. (But also thank you for the Ambien.) Guys, if you have OCD and don't have a therapist and/or a psychiatrist, or think you have OCD and don't have one, please employ the help of some mental health professionals. OCD is hard as fuck, but you aren't alone, and there are so many things that exist now to help us. No shame at all in that game.

And last but not least, thank you to you, for reading.